W9-AHF-951

Madonna of the Apes

Also by Nicholas Kilmer

Poetry (Verse Translation)
Poems of Pierre de Ronsard
Francis Petrarch: Songs and Sonnets from Laura's Lifetime
Dante's Comedy: The Inferno

Fiction (Art Mystery)
Harmony in Flesh and Black
Man With a Squirrel
O Sacred Head
Dirty Linen
Lazarus, Arise

Art (Biography/Art History)
Thomas Buford Meteyard
Frederick Carl Frieseke: The Evolution of an American Impressionist

Travel Memoir
A Place in Normandy

Madonna of the Apes

Nicholas Kilmer

Poisoned Pen Press

First Edition 2005

10 9 8 7 6 5 4 3 2 1

Library of Congress Catalog Card Number: 2005925398

ISBN: 1-59058-196-2 Hardcover

Poisoned Pen Press
6962 E. First Ave., Ste. 103
Scottsdale, AZ 85251
www.poisonedpenpress.com
info@poisonedpenpress.com

For Beverley J. D. Spong

Chapter One

The snake lay across his chest, brown and rotund. It had eaten. No, that was wrong. It was an arm. *Her* arm. A woman's arm. Fred could make it out in the fitful light coming in through the window, four floors up over Charles Street. He listened to the sounds of the advancing night, speculating on how much time might have passed. The arm was sinuous and graceful, yes, but that was not what had confused him. It was the snake tattooed around it, an expert and expensive job: the tail toward her wrist (her left arm), so that the beast's head could poise alert behind the woman's shoulder. Sally? Harriet? Something with that short "a" sound.

It was the snake that had wakened him, as they used to do in the narrow space underground he would not think of. And that explained his sweat—too much for this cool room—and the stealthy, trembling quiet that had come over him. They only wanted company. Once they had enjoyed it they would slither off again, passing through openings too narrow for him even to imagine escape.

The woman's arm was lovely, like the rest of her. Earlier, as the occasion warranted, they'd thrown her covers off to the warm breeze of Boston's late May evening. She lay on her front now, as naked as he was, and as naked as either of them had ever been, one arm, the one with the snake, across his chest, and her left leg cocked across his groin, its weight on his bladder. She breathed as placidly as any snake. Her face he could not see. Her black hair swirled away across the pillows. The window was on his side of the bed—Jackie?—no more than two feet from the bed. The smell of the river came in, cool and a little wild, given how tamed the river was. Tacita? Catherine? Katrina?

He wouldn't sleep again now, and the woman's living space contained nothing to read, not even a house or fashion magazine in the john. His watch, and his left arm, were imprisoned under the woman's body. The dusk of whatever time of night this was allowed him to see the room's spare furnishings. It was as if she lived here only occasionally. Besides the bed, barely big enough for the two of them, there were the bureau holding the small TV, and the big chair where he'd piled his clothes; a little table with two straight chairs next to the doorway leading into the kitchen alcove. Her clothes he couldn't see. They were in a bureau or in the closet he hadn't looked into. He hadn't seen her take them off. She'd taken care of that while he'd stepped into the john. They could be under the bed for all he knew.

Alison? She shifted slightly, becoming both more comfortable, herself, and heavier on his bladder. Live as she was, and large as she was, and heavy as she was on his bladder—her name should be somewhere. It happened still, scraps of things he cared about, disappearing.

The room was painted a dull yellow, somewhat leonine.

He'd never had anything to feed them, nothing they wanted at least, or nothing he could spare. Twice he tried saving wads of his meager portion of rice. But the snakes disregarded rice. The bits of fish or pork, when they came, he could not do without. No, if they wanted anything aside from company, it was the rats he was too slow and weak to catch. The rats against which he must protect his rice.

His trembling was subsiding. Some women it would have awakened, but this one slept on. She was not made uncomfortable by adjacent fear. Her bag was on the table. If he looked through it he would learn her name. But if she opened one glazed round eye and found him looking she would feel betrayed, thinking he meant to rob her. Fred was already easing out from beneath her before he realized his decision to be away. Their odors mingled with those of the river, imitating its murky depth. All life embraces its own decay. Find a French name for that scent, market it in a bottle, and eliminate the need for intercourse. For almost any human contact.

The gallant thing might be to cover her. But she seemed more comfortable nude. As Fred came out of the john again and started to collect his clothing she turned over and sprawled to take full possession of her bed. She was quite a spectacular animal, and she'd known enough to stop and let nature have a chance. Other than the snake tattoo there was no other interference, no other mark or piercing: nothing but woman. Janet? Was there a "j"? Luxuriant black hair curled at her groin and under her arms. The snake was coiled now, languidly, above her head.

Fred slid into his clothes, khakis and a blue Oxford shirt, and the loafers he had started wearing without socks once the season permitted. Had he been carrying anything? What did he have? The blue windbreaker on the chair's back must be his as well. Yes, it felt right.

"Fred?" the woman said as he opened the apartment's door. "Make sure you pull the street door closed until you hear it lock behind you, Honey, would you?"

"You bet."

"I don't want to wake up and worry."

Chapter Two

Fred pulled the street door to, firmly, behind him, and checked that the catch was set before he looked at his watch. Just shy of midnight on a mild night. Though the neighborhood's commerce had dwindled almost to a halt, enough people occupied the sidewalks that the place seemed inhabited, if not frolicsome. The pedestrians were mostly young, in couples or in groups. Taxis moved along the street, looking for late fares.

The air smelled of raw sex, because it was spring, and there was a river a block away. In spring a river turns, and its mud basin starts to think of the next generation. Charles was a funky, formerly seedy street running along the foot of Boston's Beacon Hill, separating it from the Charles River. The street was lined with restaurants behind whose locked doors the staffs were mopping up; and with closed shops that sold antiques, or soaps, or the many gift items that fall into the chasm between those two categories.

The woman he had just left—Bambi? No, he would remember that; it would come in time—lived three flights above an antique store whose windows were well lit, either to discourage, or to assist, marauders. The night's thin mist billowed against the lighted plate glass. Fred paused to look. Earlier, his need, or hers, or both, had been too pressing. The shop contained the usual disappointing jumble of pots and crocks and somebody's uncle's hand-done oil painting of a lighthouse or a waterfall: a sword, a Japanese kimono, bird prints back of dirty glass. But nothing sang, or lived; nothing betrayed an intimate connection between the maker's spirit and the shape or marking of the thing that had been made. A work of art should be as wild, and as alive, as was that snake tattoo, racing around the woman's arm before it froze time in its risky grip. You knew a work of art in the same way you recognized the killer's scent, because it made your hair stand up, and brought back the fear. It should be real, too real.

The night was mild enough. If he chose, he could sleep on the bank of the river. He would wake damp, no worse. Or, if he wanted cover, Fred could sack out in Bernie's place. He'd finished the job for Bernie, he and Bernie had hit it off; and Bernie had said, "I'll be in India for a month, maybe two. Use the place if you want to. Keep an eye on the Lagonda." Fred had the keys, and he'd drop in now and then anyway. If he felt like walking, he could walk back to his own place in Charlestown. Or he could exercise past skills and let himself back into the woman's place. But no, she'd feel betrayed. She'd believe, when his weight changed the balance of her mattress, that while he was gone he had left her and her building vulnerable, allowing the street door to remain unlocked.

He'd walk until he found himself doing the next thing. If he found himself stopping at Bernie's, he'd know that's what he was doing, when he did it.

He turned in the direction of Charlestown, walking more briskly than the other pedestrians, who had something to say to each other, or display windows to study; and against the vehicular traffic of the one-way street. If the next thing was to take a taxi somewhere, one was pulling into the curb two blocks ahead. It paused while a man got out and stood swaying, taking support from the taxi's roof while, inside, a second man managed the fare. When the second man reached the sidewalk, he undertook to substitute his own support for what had been offered by the taxi, and as the taxi rolled cautiously in Fred's direction, its two ex-passengers began to grapple clumsily as if they were fighting and neither had ever tried to fight before; or as if they were making love and, again, it was each one's maiden attempt. Neither, both being in business suits, was dressed correctly for either activity. Fred drew nearer to the struggling couple. At the same time, his fellow travelers on the street crossed to the opposite side.

The men were matched in height but not in age. Both were clumsy, the younger appearing to be clumsy with drink, and with the loutish self-confidence drink can exacerbate. The elder man, on the other hand, looked clumsy almost as a matter of policy, like a large flightless bird compelled by circumstance to try a turn in the air. His movements expressed a native diffidence that might have been embedded in the steps of an ancient, very formal dance the other man did not know. As Fred approached them, the younger man took a flobby swing at the older one, whose shock of thick white hair was flung back dramatically when the blow connected with his cheek. Still, at the same time, the elder man struggled to keep the younger from falling into the street or through the plate glass window of a store specializing in old maps.

Fred reached them on the run, propping up the younger man while keeping his flailing arms from making contact. "...into *my goddamned* britches," the young man was muttering. He fixed Fred with a glassy eye, then lost focus entirely and slumped as far as Fred would let him.

"His keys," the older man said, jingling a small set. "His place should be around the corner. He deserves it, but we can't leave him in the street. It's a great deal to ask. But he's too much, is he not? for one Samaritan."

His speech, though over-precise, did not suggest inebriation. The suit he wore, of a dove gray cut usually reserved for movies depicting the halcyon days of the 1930s, showed no sign of rough weather. The passersby, seeing that things were both apparently under control and potentially interesting, were starting to form small groups across the street, from which to observe events without getting wet.

"Where do we take him?" Fred asked. "What do we call him?"

The older man looked vague. "He did tell me his name," he started. "When we talked. And it turned out we were going in the same direction. Why not share a cab, he said."

"Fourteen Pekham, second floor," the younger man said. He gulped, retched and wobbled. "Love nest. Franklin. 'Preciate it. I answer to Franklin." The man's accent, when he spoke, was soft and rounded. From his accent he might well be from the south, having spent enough time in the north to have the southern excess beaten out of him. Or vice versa.

"We'll get him to bed. Do the keys," Fred told the older man. "I'll do the man. What the hell. When he pukes, keep your suit clear if you can." They got him around the corner and six doors uphill, skirting a row of elegant brownstones, until a polished brass plate at the top of a flight of stone steps told them they'd reached number fourteen. "Figure the keys out, then I'll bring him up," Fred suggested. "That way I'm not waltzing this joker at the top of the stairs. Come to that, I'd just as soon he doesn't puke on me."

Once the older man had found the key that opened the street door, Fred got Franklin up the inside stairs and held him on the landing outside the apartment's door while the other man selected and applied the key. Franklin wobbled and wavered, then stiffened abruptly and powerfully in Fred's grasp. "Alarm," Franklin gulped, lurching forward as the apartment's door opened inward. "You're sweet. The code. My birthday. Let me do it." He jerked away.

Fred's quick foot jabbed into the doorway kept the apartment's door from slamming closed with Franklin inside, leaving the two Samaritans gaping at each other on the landing. Fred followed his foot fast into the dark room.

"What's going on?" all three men said.

Chapter Three

"Alarm hell!" Fred said, making a grab that took Franklin by the belt. He held, fishing for a light switch. The older man hovered at loose ends on the landing. "Come in. Close the door," Fred ordered. "We don't need company."

"There's been some misapprehension," the older man demurred.

"We've been invited and then some," Fred said. He gave a jerk to Franklin's belt. "Somebody plays me for a sucker, plays you for a sucker—you don't know this guy? Right? That's on the up-and-up? Let's find out why."

"I have no wish, no interest, no desire," he began, but the place itself drew the older man inside, past whatever was left of his scruples. The light of the entrance hall allowed them to see a large room, almost without furniture, that gleamed with suppressed fire.

"The drunk's an act, Franklin," Fred said. "Drop it or I'll drop you." He slid his grip around to the back of Franklin's belt and held it tight enough to keep his captive from slipping his hold by unbuckling it. "His plan was to lure you in for a start, following his ass. That's your business. I don't care. It's a honey trap. Sprung too soon, because he didn't figure on the extra Samaritan. Close the door. There'll be a light switch next to it. Let's see who else is here."

"Remarkable," the older man said, peering around the dark room as he entered. When the entrance door closed with a click, Franklin said, "I'm alone."

The principal furnishing of the room was a lush oriental rug that covered almost the entire floor, hardwood, but it had been painted white. The carpet's colors—magenta, rose madder and viridian—burned in a dusky glow that leaped to flame when the older man located the switch, illuminating the room from wall sconces. Franklin flipped like a landed trout, hanging from Fred's right fist, while Fred and his fellow Samaritan stared at the walls, where paintings hung in profusion, a wilderness of styles and kinds and colors. For furniture the room held no more than a small gilded table bearing glasses and filled decanters, a carved and painted wooden chest, and a low bookcase filled, it appeared, with art books. The elder Samaritan revolved slowly in the center of the room, gaping frankly, and stroking a necktie on which paisleys, in modest riot, had been deeply shamed by the carpet's regimented orgy. It was too much information, much too fast.

"Nobody else here? We'll see. Meanwhile, let's get the scoop on our host," Fred said. He reached into the man's jacket pocket and, taking from it a leather wallet, flipped it open. But he could learn nothing from it without losing his grip on Franklin's belt. "I'm Fred," Fred told his fellow Samaritan. "What do I call you?"

"Reed. What do you mean, honey trap? What's a honey trap?" He raised a hand to stroke the reddening welt on his cheek, where he'd been hit.

"Oh, come on," Fred said. He lifted the belt enough to set his man swinging, then dropped him to the carpet. "Stay there," he said, and had the freedom of both hands. He said after a minute's study, "Our host carries a Georgia driver's license. Atlanta. Three credit cards in the name of Franklin Tilley. He's a Georgia boy. A Georgia peach. A peach with a sting in its tail. Who's in the back room, Franklin?"

The younger man had landed on his face on the carpet. He lay in a sullen crouch. "Twelve hundred dollars," Fred continued. "In cash. Another ten thousand in blank traveler's checks, in this other pocket."

Reed, continuing to revolve slowly, like a top in its last vertical play, observed, "Fred, there is more going on here than meets the eye. No matter. There is always more going on than meets the eye. Mr. Tilley, a question. As long as I am here. Albeit in grotesquely anomalous circumstances. The unsigned watercolor over your head. Tell me about it."

"Jeekers!" Fred said. "What is this? Business as usual?" He nudged their prostrate captive with his foot. "Sit up, Franklin. Make yourself at home. What the hell. Answer the man's question. I hold the wallet while we get acquainted." He put it into his back pocket.

Franklin sat and assembled the ingratiating smile used by the prep school's star athlete when he is discovered next to the headmaster's wife, in the headmaster's bed. "I'm alone here," he whined. "You've got me wrong. Let's fix this. Let me offer you gentlemen a drink," he said. "If it's my fault, I apologize. You've wrecked my suit, but that's fair. Rough trade, Fred. I love it." He tried a lopsided grin pregnant with innuendo, though it aborted quickly against Fred's impassive gaze. "It's—not a game exactly, more a sales technique. If I appear to be slightly incapacitated...."

"What do you sell?" Fred demanded. "Besides the obvious."

"Nothing for me," Reed said. "Maybe a small brandy. If you don't mind, Fred? While we explore."

"He drinks first," Fred said. His nod allowed Tilley to get up, step out of his shoes, and walk across the carpet to the table. He poured from a decanter into a snifter, breathed in, drank a half-ounce, smiled and spread his arms to illustrate the innocence of the brew.

"Okay?" he asked Fred. Fred nodded. Tilley poured for Reed and looked inquisitively toward Fred. Fred shook his head.

Reed, following his host's example, took his shoes off and sat cross-legged with his back against the wall, in a position from which he could watch the watercolor he had asked about, a faint and very tentative study that looked like a preparatory essay for one of Cézanne's *Bathers*.

Franklin, at the bar, poured amber into a snifter from a different decanter. Turning to catch Fred's eye, he explained, holding up the decanter, "This one's the 1812. Why waste my personal beverage on someone who might not understand it? Fred, I do ask my guests to remove their shoes."

Fred said, "Your guests. That leaves me out."

Franklin pouted and turned to Reed, twirling the liquid in his snifter while crossing to stand next to the watercolor, just one of thirty some paintings in the room, "You have an excellent eye. Unfortunately, you ask about the one thing in the room I am not in a position to sell. A client—*another client, perhaps I should say?*—has first refusal."

"Reed," Fred said, "you buy anything from this joker, you are on your own. I'm going to look around. Five minutes, then I'm on my way. You want to stay, that's up to you." He patted his back pocket, reminding their host that he carried the man's identity as well as a good deal of his money, and left the two men talking.

The bedroom was empty of additional players, and nondescript, but at least the man owned a bed—a queen-sized double with a spread bearing an Aztec motif. Lie there, my dear, and we'll cut out your heart. A writing table held reasonable papers, including bills addressed to Franklin Tilley here, at Fourteen Pekham Street. The closet held enough clothes to prove that Franklin was here for longer than overnight, but didn't live here. Nobody lived here. The scene was temporary: stage set for Act One, scene two. Next to the bed the top bureau drawer held a set of car keys, complete with a plastic penguin. And a serviceable Lublin .38, loaded.

Fred, passing the entrance to the main room, saw that Reed was now on his feet. The two men, like old friends, were examining the objects displayed on the walls.

"It's your funeral," Fred grumbled, shrugging. He held the gun where Franklin could see it and told him, "This goes into the toilet," moving toward the bathroom.

Franklin's petulant voice followed him down the hall. "Honest to God, Fred. That's not necessary."

Chapter Four

"Mostly Italian but some French," Tilley was explaining when Fred entered the room again. Reed, having apparently toured the room, was standing again in its geographical center, balancing the snifter but paying no attention to its contents. "So, as I say, the little Cézanne I have to reserve for the time being, " Franklin went on. "But this *Diana* from the School of Fontainebleau is worth a detour, no? The Greuze portrait is said to be of the Duke of—I forget—It's written down. I don't guarantee that's a Mantegna. It might be. We're waiting on the expertise. It's good, and it's fifteenth century."

The paintings around the room, too much to take in quickly, especially under the circumstances, projected an aura of authenticity more convincing than Franklin himself could manage. Even the Cézanne *Bathers*, which might be either fake or a thin effort on the great painter's part, sat uneasily on the wall, as if impatient of its cage. The picture Franklin described as a possible Mantegna represented Mary Magdalene. No artist in that time or place could exhibit that much nudity without either classical or religious cover. The woman, sitting in a desert landscape, was nude from the waist up, and contemplating a skull that lay in the dirt. The frame was excessive. Many of the frames were excessive, while a few pieces were not framed at all.

"Interesting collection overall," Reed said.

"I came into some money," Franklin confided. He shrugged. "I like nice things. The Mantegna. What *may* be a Mantegna...."

Reed walked over to the *Mary Magdalene* and took a slow and concentrated look. The work was on a wooden panel, two feet high by two wide. "I wouldn't have said Mantegna," he said, bringing his nose to within three inches of the painting's surface. "Since we're here, I might as well ask your price. It *is* for sale?"

"Three million," Franklin said smoothly.

"Indeed."

"Because it may be by Mantegna," Franklin said. "Why take the risk? I sell for less and it turns out to be Mantegna, I'm a fool. We're looking into it. Getting the expertise. Meanwhile, I like nice things. You yourself, being a collector—I see it in the way you study my walls, Reed—I'm dying to know what little treasures you might be prepared to de-accession, yourself. I'm always open to a trade."

Reed, disregarding this opening, continued to walk along the walls, studying other objects. He paused in front of a deep blue-green painting depicting a boar hunt and said, "Let's have a look at the back."

"Of the Mantegna?"

"Of course." Reed nodded.

The painting in its ornate gilded frame was heavy. Franklin struggled as he lifted it off the wall and put it on the floor, turning it so that its back faced into the room. The back was dark wood, well braced with a cradled trelliswork of wooden supports, and showing traces of old paper labels and splotches of crimson sealing wax. Reed fished into the breast pocket of his suit and drew out a magnifying glass through which he examined the back before he turned the painting around and began a minute raking examination of its face.

"I'm without protection now," Franklin complained to Fred in a hoarse whisper. "Honest to God, you didn't have to do that."

Reed held his hand up to command silence, and continued his survey. "I need daylight," he said. "Your price is ridiculous and exploratory, even if this were Mantegna. I shall return tomorrow afternoon with my conservator. I wish to consider the collection in the daylight, at my leisure. You will not need the firearm, I assure you. I am harmless." He stroked the livid welt on the side of his face. "No, tomorrow won't do. Tuesday is bad. Wednesday? Shall we say three o'clock?"

Franklin went through the motions of reflecting on his busy schedule before he agreed to the appointment. "Wednesday is good," he said. "By then I should have my prize to show you."

"Your prize," Reed said. "That is?"

Franklin shook his head, put a finger to his lips and grinned. "The keystone of my collection," he said. "I can't say more. Though I can tell you…."

"Yes?" Reed prompted.

"Actually, in fact, I can't say anything," Franklin said.

"I'll leave you then," Reed announced, moving toward the door, Fred following.

"My wallet," Franklin Tilley protested.

"Downstairs," Fred said.

"Then, when we get to know each other better, you will introduce me to your own collection," Franklin wheedled. "Treasures I can only imagine. You have a delicious eye."

"I shall look forward," Reed said. He sat on the painted box next to the door in order to put his shoes on again. The size of a child's toy chest, its sides were decorated with rather primitive flat angels, gilded arches, and lilies, and its top painted to pass for marble, on which a wreath of laurel leaves was resting. Reed's backside, in turn, now rested on the wreath of laurels.

"This box," Reed said. He smacked his palm next to his right buttock. "It might do for my silver."

"It's painted inside also," Franklin started.

"I saw that. It doesn't matter," Reed said. "I can line it. Have to line it anyway, to hold silver."

"It's old. I don't know how old," Franklin said. "I don't know what it is."

"In any case, it will hold my silver," Reed said. "It seems solid enough. I've been looking for something this size. Though, as you say, it is rather gaudy."

"I'll give you a price on Wednesday," Franklin said.

Reed stood and dusted his hands together. "Never mind. I'm looking at one tomorrow. I'm going...."

"Eight thousand dollars," Franklin tried.

"Six thousand would be exorbitant," Reed said. "But I'm willing to pay for the convenience. If you'll take six thousand, we can accomplish the transaction now."

"Cash," Franklin said.

Reed hesitated. "Cash is a different story. Five thousand I can manage."

Franklin's hesitation was palpable, almost entertaining. "It's highway robbery. But I need cash for another purchase. You'll have the chest picked up?"

"We take it now," Fred broke in.

Reed looked up at him with surprise. "As Fred observes, the weather is clement. Better that we complete the transaction now. I'll take it with me. If I may, I shall adjourn and avail myself of the requisite funds. Your washroom?"

Franklin jerked his head sideways toward the hallway, in the direction of the bathroom Fred had just come from, where the gun stared mutely out of the toilet bowl. "Money belt," Franklin told Fred, once Reed was out of sight. "You didn't have to do that. That's how they carry their cash, these Brahmins. Boston Brahmins. Maybe you'll come back too, some time." Fred shrugged, looking at the objects on the man's walls. It was a bewildering collection. It made no sense. Reed reappeared, his hand crackling with a wad of greenbacks. He handed them to Franklin and made an effort to raise the chest by the metal handles on its ends.

"Franklin and I will get it down the stairs," Fred said. "That keeps Franklin out of trouble while we exit the love nest. Take an end, Franklin. I go in front." He led the procession to the street, Franklin taking his end of the chest obediently, Reed in the rear. When he handed the wallet back he gave Franklin Tilley a final, careful look. The man was sallow and thin, but sufficiently robust not to worry his mother. He could well be the thirty-five years of age the Tilley license showed. His hair was dark and curly, too long for most white-collar professions that did not imply an artistic orientation.

"Wednesday, then, three o'clock," Franklin confirmed. "Be prepared to have your eyes knocked out. In case I get the other thing in time. When may I return the visit? I must see.... Sorry about the misunderstanding before. No hard feelings. And you'll bring your conservator? Wednesday afternoon. I've been looking for a conservator. Maybe...." He pocketed the wallet as he turned into the house, leaving the two men on the sidewalk next to Reed's painted chest.

Chapter Five

"Are you out of your flaming mind?" Fred demanded. "After the way the guy set you up, you leave him with a wad of cash? Even if you find a taxi at one-thirty in the morning, this damned toy chest won't fit, unless you find a wagon. What's the plan?" He broke off. Reed was trembling like a leaf in a high wind.

"I live on Mountjoy," Reed said.

"That's not far. You can walk it. No, obviously you can't. *We'll* walk it over," Fred said. "I've got nothing better to do."

The older man had stood undecided, watching as Fred hoisted the box onto his shoulder. It was a heavy, substantial object. "Be careful, for God's sake," Reed protested. He stood trembling under the streetlight. The color had left his face, but for the red welt on his cheek. "I'm faint," he said. "I'm going to faint." He sat suddenly on the bottom step of the brownstone they had just come from, breathing hard, and put his head with its mad tousle of white hair between his knees. Fred balanced the box.

"There was nothing wrong with the brandy. Anyway, you didn't drink it," Fred said. "What's wrong? Regrets? A fool and his money? I could, but I'm not going back for your money. You knew better. Hell, at your age you should know it's not safe to go cruising bars for young men. "

The older man shook his head and looked up vaguely, as if Fred were speaking from deep underground, and in Swahili. "The desecration! I sat on it! Sat on it! You saw me. As if I were at Brooks Brothers selecting shoes! Forgive me, I am moved." His voice was tremulous with shock and chagrin. But it was strong. He didn't require medical attention.

"Let's hump this thing to Mountjoy," Fred said. Reed, sitting up straight again, breathed a deep lungful from the cool dark air of springtime. "It is like sitting on the Ark of the Covenant. I shall never be forgiven. Lightning should strike. God help me, there was no other way."

"Let's move out, Reed," Fred said. "Your Ark of the Covenant weighs a fair piece."

Reed said, standing slowly, "You spotted that man's game. You saved my life."

"Maybe," Fred said. "I doubt it. The gun was next to the bed. Some people do that. Let him spend the rest of the night cleaning and drying it out."

"It's fortunate for me, your appearing when you did. I'm grateful to you, Sir. Fred. Clayton is fine, or Clay. My first name. We have become familiar, although we do not know each other. Thank you. I would appreciate your extending your courtesy as far as my home on Mountjoy Street. Truly, I am overcome. My heart is racing."

"Not my business. There may be a lesson here," Fred said.

Clayton smoothed the drape of his suit and the two men descended the hill and turned onto Charles Street again, heading left, in the direction of the Boston Garden. The night mist had grown heavier, but it was still warm for May, and the air was filled with the promise of spring blooming. They had the street to themselves.

Clay muttered, "He struck me! Then he has the gall to invite himself into my home? Mantegna indeed! What did he take me for? Magdalene was never a Mantegna subject. Show me a *Magdalene* by Mantegna. I defy you!"

Fred said, "Where did he pick you up?"

"I met him tonight at the M.F.A," Clay said. "Not 'cruising' in a bar. Perhaps you meant no insult. Still, one might take exception to your implication. The M.F.A. is Boston's Museum of Fine Arts. They were having a do ostensibly to show appreciation to their donors. Mr. Tilley was at my table. It was a dinner following which, as I should have expected, we were rewarded with instructions concerning methods we may use in order to entail our assets to the museum during our lifetimes, preempting later testamentary decisions."

"No need to wait till you are dead," Fred said.

"They were politely obvious about the whole thing. Next block we turn left. This is exceedingly generous of you. Uphill, I fear. I am an innocent. The sexual motive, if it was proffered at all by Tilley, I missed entirely. I should have seen it. We tend to see no more than what we are prepared for. From our conversation, I gathered only that Tilley owned paintings, and I am interested in paintings. Though there was no suggestion that I would see his collection. No suggestion! Why would I? I do not know the man.

"I lost track of him during the social mix-up after the program. Then, when everyone was preparing to leave, in the vicinity of the coat room, he materialized at my elbow. He had been friendly over dinner, and—I cannot understand that room or what was in it. He could only be so ignorant if he had inherited everything. Nowhere to sit? The Kashan rug would cost seventy thousand dollars in a shop if you could find it, and if you could bargain it down. At auction fifty thousand. I assure you, he didn't appear to be drinking or I would never have gotten into a taxi with the man. There was never any idea that I would go into his abode. The drink, fraudulent as it was, did not seem to come over him until after he'd given the driver his address."

Fred said, "He was playing the wounded bird until he could get you into his trap."

"Could he think I would do anything so dishonorable as to engage in a serious financial transaction with a man who is incapacitated?"

They'd passed the shop over which she was sleeping. What was her name? Patsy? Had she spread the sheet drowsily across herself? Caroline? They turned onto Mountjoy now. It was steep going.

"Maybe he only wanted to knock you on the head and feed you cooking brandy," Fred suggested, "then snatch your money belt."

"You are commendably alert. The brandy the man offered was, indeed, undrinkable. Following which he had the insufferable gall to regale himself, in front of me, with an old Napoleon. I could smell it. Exquisite. Which he downed as if it were drugstore coffee. He understands his liquor as well as he does the rest of his collection. He drank it because of its cost, and not its nose. In every way, a despicable fellow."

"We agree he's a bad host," Fred agreed.

Clay said, "May we go faster? I worry about moisture on the paint surface. We're almost there. I can't tell you how obliged I am to you, Fred. Never mind the man. We will put him out of our minds. Upsetting as the incident has been, it has been providential. Two blocks more. Let's see now, upstairs or down?" he asked himself, fumbling with his keys. "Downstairs is better, safer."

"I'm interested, especially since you left so much money in his hands, did you trust any of what was there?" Fred asked. "The Cézanne?"

"A ludicrous fake," Clay said. "Granted Cézanne drew badly, he didn't draw badly in that way. The imposture couldn't stand up to five minutes' conversation, not even with that ignorant youngster. The mixture of objects, events, and persons was outlandish, outrageous, and leaves me deeply, deeply uneasy. We are well out of it. "

They'd reached a handsome row of brick townhouses the first of which, on the corner, was set back by its own parking space, a rarity on Beacon Hill—large enough for two cars, although it was inhabited only by one. The chink of Clay's keys, and the readiness of one of them in his hand, proved they had reached their destination. Clay opened a low iron gate and led them through a brief plantation of dark ivy.

"One plays the hand as it is dealt. I had to pretend an interest in something," Clayton went on. "Therefore I chose the *Magdalene.* The supposed Mantegna. Here, down these steps. My study is on the ground floor. Let me go ahead of you. Never mind the sides, coming in. But treat the top as if it were the queen of Egypt."

"The fake marble," Fred said. "Right."

"I had to give him hope I'd come back," Clayton explained, fumbling with the door. "Let the villain believe I was toying with his bait. Meanwhile...." He'd gotten the door open and, turning on lights, led Fred and his burden into a wide hallway lined with filled bookshelves.

"Where to?" Fred asked.

"Give me an end. Let's get it into the study," Clay said. "Goodness, I'm all in a tremble and sweat."

Fred lowered the chest and allowed Clayton, taking one handle, to precede him down the hall and into a study the width of the building into which they had come. The room was both spacious and cluttered. A large worktable was heaped with books, papers, and magazines. The walls were lined with bookshelves, against which a few paintings rested, on the floor, their backs turned outward. One wall was taken up by the kind of old brown leather couch that no one can ever throw away.

Clay chortled, "So the villain, flailing at will-o'-the-wisps, reaches for three million? Let us now put him out of our minds forever. Meanwhile I slip out of his trap carrying with me a prize worth more than the gross domestic product of Bulgaria!"

They put the box down on a green throw rug, next to the worktable.

"Painted on the inside, you said?" Fred flipped open the chest's heavy lid.

"Jeekers," Fred said. "That's Leonardo!"

Chapter Six

Startled as he was, he'd let the top lie gently back to where it was supported by the legs of the worktable in the center of the room. The painting on the inside—that's all you could call it—had to be looked at sideways, since its foot was at the left side of the chest. Fred shivered. It was like looking at a ticking bomb. It was spectacular, an amazing thing. The room went still and Clayton Reed disappeared in favor of the work, the subject almost grotesque, the finish exquisite in its precision.

On the left a woman in blue—the Virgin, clearly, although she bore no halo—sat in a rocky landscape struggling to contain the exuberance of a naked boy child—Jesus, but again lacking a halo—who was twisting away in order to reach for a fruit, a fig, that a crouching ape on the right was offering. The ape was hairy and so lifelike as to appear not even malevolent, but, rather, its natural amoral self. It was an ape, no more, a creature native to this wilderness.

Aside from some sparse, meticulously rendered, heraldic vegetation, the landscape was barren, stretching toward ominous overhanging rocks. Beyond the rocks, and visible between them, were glimpses of sky and choppy water. Within that dangerous wilderness a half-dozen more apes were foraging or scratching for fleas or, even, grooming each other. The paint surface was smooth, vivid with cleanly modulated color, the browns and gold of the landscape set off by the rich blue of the Virgin's garment, the blue-green of the distant water, the ape's russet coat with meticulous gold highlights, and the chubby ochre pinkness of the child, whose skin reflected tints from the red cushion on which the Virgin was either sitting or kneeling. The woman's face was seductive in a way that offered not much hope. She was taken. Strap hinges, rusty with age, had been attached to the panel where, at the top, part of a toppling outcrop was obscured and, at the bottom, the spill of the Virgin's drapery, as well as an ornamental clump of grass, were partly covered. It was, on the whole, a piece of incredible workmanship and, given the circumstances, in astonishingly good condition.

Apparently Clayton Reed was speaking, and had been for some time. "…don't mean to impugn, I mean to say. And with you, Fred, I will not dissemble. *Cannot* dissemble, after the service you have performed, which is deeply appreciated. You may have saved my life. He struck me! He was armed. What further depredation did that man not intend? In my experience a man who is prepared to sell is equally ready to steal. Meanwhile—I don't know your last name."

"Taylor."

"It does, as you say, look like a Leonardo. That fact must never leave this room. Meanwhile I don't know you from Adam and, out of six billion people living on this sphere, the stranger who providentially appears to assist me in my hour of need, in the first second leaps to the same conclusion I did in that man's apartment. Can it be true that Tilley could live with such a thing and understand not even that it is a painting? Simply because it is at one and the same time pressed into service as the top of a wooden chest?"

Fred shrugged.

"The world is out of joint. Except through the malevolent interference of Providence, such things should not occur. I am an innocent. Why should you not deviously be in league with him?" Clay pressed on. "It is my nature to ask. And yet, how can I be such a churl as to doubt your *bona fides?* Why do you say Leonardo? Help set my mind to rest."

Clay had pulled out the chair that stood at the other side of the desk. He now sat there, twitching with impotent suspicion.

"I'll be off," Fred said. "On a hunch, yours is a mind that can't be put to rest. For an innocent, I'd say it was pretty slick the way you maneuvered this thing out of there. If you skunked the man, the man deserved it. For what it's worth, though it's much smaller, to me your box top has the look of da Vinci's *Madonna of the Rocks.* The one in the Louvre, obviously. The one in London is a copy, done much later, most of it, by a kindergarten class."

"I see," Clayton said, concentrating on the painting before them. "It's water in the foreground, all the way across, where the monkey is reflected. Also the thing he is holding in his, or is it her, paw? Hand?"

"The ape is male," Fred said. "He's discreet about it, but there's the edge of his testicles, there, under the tail. A male ape in this position almost conveys menace, but I don't see threat in the painting, do you? Seems pregnant with symbolism, doesn't it? Which people are always going to read wrong. How can anyone look at this and not remember Adam and Eve? Even though the fruit's a fig. See how it's split? And not an apple."

"It's what I was born for," Clay said, running a spotless handkerchief across his forehead. "To have such a thing in my possession. No one must know I have it. No one must know it's here. I'd never sleep again."

"So I'll forget it. But I can't make any promises for the other guy. Can Tilley find you again?" Fred asked.

"I don't want people knowing my business. With you, who may have saved my life, I am obliged to take a leap of faith. It is why I did not even consider writing him a check," Clay said. "I could have, and gladly, for the eight thousand dollars he asked, though to have given him what he wanted would have raised his suspicions. No, that would not have done. Had I been willing, he would have refused. In any case, even moved as I was, I knew more than to deliver my address to the man. Innocent I may be, but I am not hopelessly wet behind the ears. That man has no clue what he sold me. Because, palpably, he doesn't know what it is. To your question: I am not listed. My number, or address. Furthermore he believes, as did you, that Reed is my first name."

Fred yawned and turned for the door. "It was a treat to see it. Now I'll forget I did, and you can sleep in peace."

"Just like that?" Clay Reed said, rising to his feet and standing in almost pitiable indecision. "Overcome by events, I neglect my obligations as a host. At least the other villain offered cooking brandy. What will you take?"

"There's nothing I want," Fred said. "I barely want to be alive."

The silence around them echoed the truth and the surprise of the ungainly statement. It sat in the room as wild and mocking, as seductive and as demanding, as the ape who held the broken fig.

"Don't know where that came from," Fred said. "It's late. I didn't mean to be rude."

But the apology could not withdraw the statement. There it sat, like a turd on the carpet. You couldn't just walk around it. It had to be dealt with, especially if it was yours. Clayton was staring at him in alarm.

Fred said, "Forget I said that. When enough people have wanted you dead enough ways for a long enough time, you start thinking they have a point."

Clayton stepped toward him.

"It was rude. Forget I said it," Fred said. "Deal? And I'll forget your Leonardo."

Clay gestured toward the couch along the wall, where a few papers and magazines lay on a Kilim rug. "Where did you train?" he asked. The room was warmed by books, some of them on shelves and others piled on the floor. The paintings that leaned against the walls, their backs turned out—those paintings could be almost anything. They might be worth looking at. An open door allowed a glimpse of another room in which were racks holding more paintings, only whose outside edges could be seen. Back of the worktable a spiral metal staircase led upward into the house proper. "Where did you train?" Clay repeated. The suspicion had gone out of his voice, to be replaced by a sympathetic curiosity.

"Here and there," Fred told him. He shrugged. "Oh, you mean how do I happen to know a da Vinci when it bites me in the ass?"

"I'm Princeton," Clay explained. "Then Yale."

"And I pay attention to things I can't control," Fred said.

Chapter Seven

"A painting like that, you'd be a fool not to pay attention," Fred said. Clay's gesture toward the couch, inviting him to stay and reveal himself further, was ignored. "I'll be off." He turned, quickly enough that he could seem not to disregard the hand Clayton held out either in appeal, or in an effort to formalize their parting with a handshake.

Outside, the damp air blew in veils lit by the streetlamps. Fred walked down to the river and stood looking across black water. Cambridge, on the far bank, glittered with lights. The odd car moved on either side. No one was sleeping on the riverbank tonight, though it was warm. Either they'd been moved along, or they'd moved along on their own. It was a lot of real estate to be going so unused.

The ripples on the river carried light, and the river itself carried the reflections of lights. The river's darkness was either its own darkness, or the reflected darkness of the sky. The landscape could use an ape or two to jazz it up and make this civilization seem less of a wasteland. Or were the apes intended to represent the spirit of the place? What did they mean to Leonardo? Even though the notions of evolution were far off in the late fourteen hundreds, and you'd be burned at the stake for entertaining such a theory, still, any fool could see the similarity between ape and human. The similarity between ape and God—that would have been a stretch, even for Darwin.

Fred lay on the grass for a while, but sleep eluded him. His senses had been too enlivened by the pheromones of danger, intrigue, greed, and by the compact web of emotions that clung to and emanated from the painting Clayton Reed had, so improbably, discovered and carried off with his assistance. There would be no sleep now. The situation the painting had come from—Franklin Tilley, the subterfuge, the gun and all that stage set, so elaborately arranged—it was just wrong. It worked at the edge of his brain like a blade that is sharp, but pitted with rust.

Fred walked back to Pekham Street and looked at the dark building from which the chest had come, and at its dark windows. It would have one apartment on each floor, with the exception that the first floor, with its own separate entrance, seemed to be given over to dental surgery. If it became important, or if it mattered, there would be people to ask about the tenant of the second floor. Or tenants, plural. That was a double bed.

Pekham Street rose at the same steep incline as did the rest of Beacon Hill. It was a hill too steep for comfortable grazing back in the days when it was farmed. It was also too steep for corn or wheat. But maybe an apple orchard?

Fred crossed the street and found a shadowed alley where he could stand looking over the building and consider the neighborhood. From old habit he made note of the vehicles parked in the area, and of their license plates. He made note of the time—3:47—when a light appeared on the second floor, burned for three minutes, and went out again. An answering impulse took him deeper into the alley for a similar amount of time.

"We apes," he said, "why wouldn't it be our instinct to offer the child a piece of fruit?" Or—here was potential fallacy. The action of the painting was frozen in time, and the human interpreter might well mistake in what direction the action had been tending. In so far as the picture had to be about a story, why would the narrative not be equally likely that the child had given his fig to the ape? And with success: the ape had taken the bait. What did the child want in return?

The painting was *about* the wilderness of divinity and, in turn, the wilderness of humanity. But what was the suggested narrative? It would fit a moment during the flight into Egypt. An angel having betrayed to Joseph Herod's plan to massacre all the local boy children in order to exterminate the future Messiah, Joseph and Mary had slipped out of town with their child, leaving the other children to his fate. "Might have been nice to warn the other members of the nursery co-op," Fred mused.

So, in the scene Leonardo had chosen to elaborate, Mary was either in an imagined Egypt, or on her way; the Messiah was taking entertainment where he could, and Joseph, off-camera stage left or right, was looking for more figs. The apes were not canonical. How many of them had there been? One either offered or accepted fruit. Two groomed each other. One scratched. Either two or three more climbed the rocks. Therefore five or six apes. The painting was not large enough to support more.

Suppose, under the Madonna's robe, on the otherwise virgin arm, a snake tattoo?

What was that woman's name? Candy? Angelica? Nobody is named Angelica. Paris? Maris? Ferriss? Nobody is named Ferriss either.

The Madonna in the painting might be expected to register alarm. But she would understand that the symbolic wilderness all around her conferred symbolic safety also. The child she held, all milky behind the ears, wasn't going to be killed for another thirty-two years yet, and the apes, with their neatly parallel highlights of golden furry curls, had no interest in pulling her hair, tearing off her clothes, biting her buttocks, or stealing her baby away to raise him up as their Messiah. The painting invited thoughts of blasphemy—almost demanded them. But meanwhile, at the time of its creation, such thoughts were not to be thought. Therefore not to be imagined.

Still, the painter, by placing these elements together in this context, had allowed such grim imaginings any one of which, if spoken aloud in company, might lead to the stake. The collaboration between this human son of God and the most manlike of the animal kingdom felt perverse—an arrangement so wrong that it might contain even sexual implications.

The rocks in the background, superimposed upon a blue of Mediterranean tranquility, recalled Capri, that playground of Tiberius, Caligula and their pals. It was even now a watering spot for persons without visible moral ties. Who were the moral equivalents of Tiberius and Caligula in Leonardo's day? Whoever they were, they certainly existed. They always exist.

Should he sleep at Bernie's? It would be soft, and dry, and not that far away.

No, there was cardboard stacked in the alley, only slightly damp. Fred made a mattress of it and slept. If something moved on Pekham Street, he'd wake and see it.

Chapter Eight

Dogs woke him early, an inquisitive pair who sniffed at him half-heartedly until, concluding that he was not dead, they lost interest. It was almost six o'clock. He'd been here longer than he intended. He must have found a place the police were unused to checking for sleeping strangers who did not belong here, and probably nowhere else.

"Nothing for you today," Fred told the dogs. Fourteen Pekham, almost opposite his alley, was still. It wasn't his business. He had no business. No, wrong. Fred had an urgent, almost pleasant desire for coffee.

The drugstore at the foot of Charles Street let him buy coffee in a paper cup to drink by the river while the advancing daylight slowly replaced sleep. The river in the early morning steamed in a frankly bucolic way. It served as the common reference point for gulls, cormorants, a pair of mallard ducks, and swallows. Nothing commercial had any business on this river. But by seven the first of the institutional sculls, rowed by students, streaked slowly past, followed by the odd kayak.

Wind, blowing upstream at the same rate as the current flowed against it, seemed to hold the ripples steady, keeping the odd bits of floating material, leaves, sticks, or crumpled paper, in such ambivalence that they could not decide whether to obey the force of the current, give up, and move toward the Atlantic, or to give in to the wind and use it as an excuse to sail upstream. Since it was May the grass, though it was kept cut short, was struggling to bloom along with the clover. A few wild yellow irises bloomed against the bank, in places the mower could not reach. In the same protected areas milkweed was sending up its spikes. Swallows, swooping in swags after insects too small for anyone else to see, were too busy to make a sound.

The city was fully awake, with traffic bustling along the parkway separating the riverbank from the city. The river continued running against the wind. The wind continued blowing against the river. Two sculls from rival universities, happening to find themselves in the same stretch of water at the same time, moving upstream, started an improvised race too suddenly serious for the women in one boat and the men in the other to shout things at each other.

"Though it's not my business," Fred went on, "what's Tilley doing this far from Atlanta, with a queen's ransom in paintings he can't understand?"

The coffee was sweet and black. It no longer held even the memory of heat. Fred took a sip and rolled it around his mouth. A thin man, wearing jeans and a Red Sox jacket and hat, wandered down the bank from the paved footpath, slapping a folded *Herald* against his thigh. He stood looking up and down the expanse of grass. The sun, burning out from the early mist, made a long shadow lurch away from the man's feet so suddenly, with such visual violence, that the shadow should have made noise: a ripping or tearing sound.

"The box he sold us, was it inherited or stolen?" Fred said.

The thin man glanced at him as if he'd spoken aloud. Maybe he had. Being alone so much, perhaps he'd gotten into the habit.

The thin man with the paper began the elaborate calculations by which a single male on an expanse of public green decides the right place to sit and read his paper, given that the space is already occupied by another single male holding a paper cup and occasionally drinking from it. If the newcomer sits too close, it is a challenge, suggesting hostile intent. If he sits too far away that also is a challenge, suggesting that he suspects hostile intent on the part of the already established tenant.

"Correction. Nobody sold *us* anything," Fred added, quietly this time.

The thin man moved three paces upstream and made his decision. He sorted through the paper, held out the Sports section to read, and used the news sections to keep the night damp from his skinny rump.

"Nice day," Fred observed, gesturing toward the river. "Nice day for almost anything."

"Nice day for being eaten alive by ants?" the man asked, not looking up from his paper. "Maybe. Nice day to drown in dung. Or lose your money then get home and find your house on fire. I see your point."

Fred sipped at his cold coffee. "Thinking more about the weather," he said. "Not globally."

The man looked up from his paper. A screech and a honk behind them signaled trouble, but not trouble enough to make them turn around. "Nice day I grant you," he said. "You said nice day for almost anything. That's where you lost me. For example, say a taxi jumps the curb and takes us out like that."

"That would be ironic," Fred agreed. "Especially while we're having this pleasant conversation."

"Or the shooting war starts and there's thirty-nine dead just in the next block, in the first hour."

"I didn't think of that," Fred admitted.

"You see how many dogs shit on this grass?" the man said. "Nice day for that, too. And the birds, the geese, the insects. I keep something between me and the grass, I'll tell you." He patted the paper he was sitting on.

Two joggers passed on the worn path next to the water, a man and a woman, wearing the outfits, talking in a jerky way.

"Not to mention the wolves," Fred said.

The skinny man was interested enough to put his paper down and give Fred his full attention. "What about the wolves? What wolves?"

"I don't think we should disregard them," Fred said. "Wolves hate that."

Chapter Nine

Once his companion had moved off, Fred read the day's news, which had been influenced by the damp impressions made by the man's bony backside pressing the newsprint into the night dew.

"Hey, Fred!" The woman's voice lifted his head. Anne? Janice? Annie? Fanny? Pamela? She'd dressed to run in red shorts and a white sleeveless top and she, with a female companion similarly dressed but with green shorts, halted and ran in place next to him, the river running behind them. Fred struggled to his feet. "Can't stop," she panted. Martha? Bertha? Paula? Marcelle? "Call me."

"Great to meet you, Fred," the other woman said and the two ran on, leaving behind the scents of soap and bed and effort. The snake moved with her arm, its swaying head poised on the back of her left shoulder, keeping track, like a bird riding an antelope. She turned and called back something else, but she was too far away to hear. Long hard legs she had; dark skin, dark hair. And she was funny, though she did not smile; at least in Fred's presence she had not smiled, not that he'd seen, not even when something pleased her, or when she said something funny.

"As if it's all work," Fred said.

Clear five hundred years away and put Leonardo here, with his monkeys, his model, and the chubby baby. Who was the model for that Virgin? Was it a person? A comely boy? A genuine red-blooded woman with moving parts who, come eleven o'clock, protested, "Lenny, if you don't let me get out from under this stuffed baby and take a leak, and maybe grab a cup of coffee…."

A woman tied into a whole world of worlds you couldn't guess at or predict. Not that it mattered, and it wasn't his business anyway. But, if there was a woman involved, who was she? It was still an interesting question. How much did Leonardo's images (if the painter *was* Leonardo. Since it wasn't Fred's painting, it wasn't Fred's problem), how much did Leonardo's images depend on being records of what he saw? With talent like his, could he not just up and draw whatever he wanted, measuring it against his memory of something he'd seen no matter how long ago?

The folds of the Virgin's robe had been so sculpted and precise, they might have been carved from wood. The composite landscape, whose foreground came from a different country than its background, read more like the dreams of two different people pasted together, than like any places actually experienced. Those toppling rocks—gravity would not permit them to poise like that even long enough for a man to draw them. The world behind the Madonna was collapsing.

Was the whole thing not invention?

The baby didn't look like anybody's kid. But it wouldn't. In those Renaissance pictures Jesus never looked like a real person, much less like a real baby. You'd be in trouble with the armed and dangerous forces of theology if you said, Looks just like his Mom. Even, Just like his Dad. But the apes, on the other hand, were observed. That painter had not only seen, he had studied apes. He knew how they spent their time, how similar they were to humans and, once you had acknowledged the similarity, how disquietingly different.

The fig, also, was observed. Its split, and the seeds exposed there, had been depicted with an almost pornographic care. Was the boy circumcised? Did anyone—woman, ape, or child—throw a readable shadow onto the rocky ground? The plants in the foreground were clearly enough differentiated to have names, but even so they were too perfect, their leaves and tendrils too symmetrical and parallel, to be found in nature.

This painter was pretending a world whose skin was perfect, though its elements were hostile. You wouldn't trust the apes more than you would the rocks. You would not trust the colors, or the fine sheen of the paint, so glossy—was it oil paint or tempera?

Fred pulled clover out of the greenery next to him and looked at its clumsy, homely, serviceable lines. Once drawn by a Leonardo, it would be subverted into elegance. You might say that he studied nature. If Fred recalled his drawings, he was informed by nature. But he wouldn't leave it alone. The curl of any stem he drew was guided by mathematical aesthetics rather than, as it was in natural fact, by the conflict between gravity and hydraulics or—maybe more accurately—by the conflict between life on one hand, and the combined forces of gravity and hydraulics on the other. Because gravity and hydraulics are on the same team. Would a da Vinci bother with as humble a flower as this little fist of white tassels?

"We're assuming it is a Leonardo, aren't we?" Fred said, standing again and folding the paper. He'd leave it on a bench, or somewhere where the next reader could find it.

Fred sauntered to the Boston Public Library's main branch in Copley Square and stood with the others on Boylston Street until the main revolving doors to the new wing were opened at nine o'clock. He gave a cordial nod to the guard at the desk, glanced briefly at the exhibition concerning Artists of the Book in Boston, laid out in glass cases where the books could not be read, and took the stairs to the basement facilities.

When he found himself on the street floor again, he said to himself, "It's not my business, but I'm interested," and spent the rest of the day in the Fine Art department until, at eight o'clock, he noticed both that he was hungry and that the building would close in an hour anyway.

Chapter Ten

Wherever his sympathies might lie, Fred could not claim to be on the street, not as long as he had the place in Charlestown. It had been a derelict house in what was a rather out-of-the-way corner of Boston that he had bought with some other veterans of this and that, which gradually, as they made it livable, he had come to control more or less, although the aim was to keep the use of it fairly democratic.

Coming back to the States and slowly, with reluctance, setting up shop as he had, Fred had made a pact with himself that was almost as simple as the one they'd developed for the house in Charlestown. It included a vow of almost poverty, and the expectation of a life that, if it must be lived, would remain simple.

The world he'd left had been filled with exotic turbulence, intrigue, betrayal, danger, opulence, frightful extended periods of mortal boredom, and agony, some prolonged, some mercifully quick; some experienced and some inflicted. He'd had enough of death but that didn't make him wish to live. It was a dreadful quandary, he'd realized, waking one morning in front of the Cambridge Public Library, where he'd spread out his bedroll in the company of some gentlemen of no fixed abode. If you've had enough of death, but have no appreciable desire to live, it makes you accident-prone. And if you are accident-prone, you are not dependable.

If you are not dependable, you are of no use to anyone and, being no use, have not much reason to be around.

He, and these other folks, were better than that, he'd guessed, or inferred, then argued. And in a year or two the Charlestown place was up and running. Then, once he had a place, he had begun seeing women again. But he couldn't get past the quandary that kept him from joining the civilization that surrounded him. He wanted nothing, not in a passive, but in an active way. If he could live naked on a crag, his food brought once a day in a bowl, by pilgrims, that might suit him, except that he would despise the pilgrims and get tired of watching the birds circling and waiting for the moment when his wary eyes would close.

When he needed a jolt he would step into a shop that sold paintings or, if he was reasonably clean, into a museum, though in a museum he was obliged to suppress the knowledge that these places were prisons made for the protection of money, and for the capture of spirits that by their natures should be free. Free, that is, as a bird or fish should be. Hell, artists should get their wages, like anyone else.

Free, not innocent. A work of art had no innocence, and nothing like it. It held within it as much coiled and potentially vicious energy as does a seed. Passion went into it, and passion resided in it. Or so Fred felt. But aside from the rubbish he'd handled occasionally in the low end antique stores he wandered into, whose proprietors tended to watch him warily, he'd never had his hands on a painting that sang, or shrieked.

The door was always open at the Charlestown house. Someone was always awake at the desk in the vestibule. It was necessary to keep this sense of security. Some of the tenants were nervous, and of those, some had good reason to be. Fred took his turn at the desk, as the rest of the men did, if they were up to it. Though they did what they could to discourage people with substance problems that were beyond control, some were too far gone with demons of one kind or another to be trusted with access to the firearms that went with the post back of the desk. Eddie told him when he came in, "Floyd's not doing so well. I guess he's asleep, though."

Fred nodded. Floyd was in the room next to his, and it was easy to tell when he was not doing well. He had a tendency to hallucinate, and the hallucinations were seldom of the peaceable kingdom.

"Did he look like he'd eaten?" Fred asked.

"I had a sub saved for him," Eddie said. When Fred came in he'd put down the comic he was reading. The cover suggested well-developed women exploring outer space, perhaps in search of the garments they had misplaced. He picked the comic up again saying, "I know he likes ham. I made him eat it down here so he wouldn't forget. I used operating funds, and left the receipt in the thing. He's bad enough we might have to do something."

Fred nodded. Floyd thought he was wanted, and in fact he might be wanted. If they took him to a public hospital, or to a veteran's hospital, next thing you knew, he'd become public property. Social workers, in all due mechanical sympathy looking into his history, might next discover that he'd taken a lam from some rougher institution in Montana or Bangkok.

"We might want to vote on it," Fred said. "But as long as he's not hurting anybody, or threatening anyone, I'd as soon let him be." Eddie shrugged. "It might work itself out," Fred said. "He's not carrying anything, is he?"

Eddie shook his head. "We checked his room while he was out. I looked through his pockets when he came in. It's like he doesn't mind. He's like a child, thinking about something else. You can do anything. Try to search me, you'd better think again."

The room Eddie sat in, the vestibule or whatever it might be called, was as bare of decoration as a robbed motel room. They'd painted the walls white but they looked gray. The kitchen, such as it was, was not visible from here; nor were the two other downstairs rooms, one in which Floyd could be locked down if that seemed to be what he needed, and another in which the men kept the TV, a pool table, some comfortable chairs from the street, and a bookshelf with enough to read if you wanted to read.

Behind Eddie a calendar picture hung, a glossy photo, representing *Springtime in the Rockies.* It was from July of a former year. It had been left here by a former tenant, Henry, who had said it represented a place he would rather be, and whose body had been taken from the river last fall.

It was Fred's shift at the desk tonight. They took it in eight-hour watches, with some men working more watches in lieu of contributing money to the operation. Fred owned the place, along with the bank; but he lived there and he did his shift like the others. So at ten he took over from Eddie, who went upstairs to sleep.

Eddie had left his comic book on the desk, and Fred read that until it was finished. He read it again, translating it into a Hmong dialect for practice, then once again, translating it into French. The fourth time through, struggling to recapture his acquaintance with a Tibetan tongue, he found the American concepts refusing to make the transition into the high clear regions, even though both cultures were equally comfortable with cruelty and unlikely gods.

The men came and went. It was a rule that everyone's business be kept private. The place was to be a staging ground, not a halfway house. If people began discussing each other's business, friendships and enmities might develop, as well as relationships that suggested mentoring, discipline, dominance and submission, or even love. It was not to be a prison, camp, or monastery, but a place where men whose training had molded them to do well by exercising anti-social skills, struggled to turn their inclinations and expectations to patterns more closely resembling those of Main Street. It was meant to be an alternative to living on the street. It was meant to be safer, if less interesting.

They got together once a week for an hour and talked through anything that needed considering. When a man didn't show up for a week or more, unless he had made prior arrangements his room was declared vacant. He'd moved on, or been jailed, or gone back to Cincinnati, or nosed under the surface of the black river.

No one would settle down here because no one *could* settle down here. The idea was that you had to want to get out and into something better. But Fred, who had invented the system, seemed to have settled down in the room upstairs, like the abbot of a Godless monastery that boasted only two rules: No women in the rooms, and Mind your own business. Whatever might happen if a couple of men wanted to sleep together, that issue hadn't come up. But any coupling threatened the balance in a democracy. Besides, it wasn't really a democracy, because Fred's name was on the mortgage, and everyone knew that. And it was Fred who must meet the payment every month, whether the guys could manage their rent or not.

Chapter Eleven

Lester wandered down at six in the morning, looking unkempt and distracted. He was too lean. The recruitment of new tenants was haphazard. Bart had brought Lester in one day after they got talking at the bus station. The guys had agreed Lester would stay while they took his measure.

Fred told him good morning. "I'm not crazy," Lester said. "Not bonkers, crackers, missing a wheel, half-baked, half-assed, off my rocker, one sandwich short of a wedding, three sheets to the wind, or nuts."

"Good," Fred said.

"The other thing," Lester said, "I am not missing a wheel. Or a two-wheeler or a three-wheeler or four wheels and I am not the fifth wheel nobody knows what it is except it's a good thing. It helps steer. On a carriage. It's like a gear. And I'm not three sheets short of a picnic."

"You with the IRS?" Fred asked. "You're working pretty hard."

"Peanuts," Lester said. He turned and walked out into a day that was beginning with rain. The trees outside the house had put on enough leaves to be dripping generously, letting the rain wash itself off onto the sidewalks. Lester was dressed for it, wearing a waterproof jacket from whose pocket he pulled a cap as he crossed the porch. If he was playing a part, he wasn't going to push it far enough to get too uncomfortable.

They'd had a spy a year ago, and this might be another one. Some government agency or another might have developed an interest in the operation. It wasn't a good part of town where you really had neighbors. Still, a neighbor might have developed curiosity about a house where single men came and went at all hours, some of whom looked like people you'd rather lived somewhere else.

Lester was a plant or a spy. Fred would bet money on it. But there was nothing to find. No secrets. Nothing interesting. Nothing to reward curiosity. Nothing to look forward to.

Nolan, ten minutes late, parked his big frame back of the desk, taking over for the day shift.

"I may sleep in town the next day or two," Fred told him.

Fred's room was on the second floor, over the front door, a small room called a "borning room" in these parts, large enough for the single mattress and the chair. His clothes he kept in three cardboard boxes, all the same size, so they could be stacked. One held clean clothes, one dirty, and the third clothes that did not qualify for either of those two categories. Hooks on the back of the door did for the parka, the windbreaker, and the blazer that came in handy for visits to the bank concerning mortgage questions. A small steel box downstairs held anything else he cared about keeping.

Fred showered, considered his mattress, and rejected it. It wasn't his business; still, his mind wouldn't rest. "It's tomorrow Reed said he'd go back," Fred said. "Three P.M. It was a date but Reed didn't mean to keep it. Did Tilley?"

It wasn't his business.

He had laundry to do, and he might as well do it. He'd noticed a Laundromat on Charles Street, not far from Bernie's, in the neighborhood where he'd spent the last couple of days. That would give him something to do, as well as a change of clothes if he decided to stay in the area, keep his eyes open.

The walk to Charles Street took forty minutes and was a good way to stretch the kinks out of his legs. Eight hours behind the desk was a punishing stretch. There'd been no mail but crap. The phone hadn't rung. He was ready for something else.

There was no activity at the place on Pekham Street. Someone had taken his cardboard from the alley. He walked on uphill to the corner of Bolt Street and turned right, covering the four blocks to the garage over which Bernie had established his small but ungainly apartment. The garage was the reason Bernie had chosen the space, a garage being at a premium in this part of town. Bernie's cars were important to him, and this garage would hold four of them, although only one was here now, and that under tarpaulins. The apartment proper, on the second floor, had to be entered through the garage, via a circular staircase in back, next to the crusty workbench that held tools from another era, designed for purposes that might or might not be related to the carriage trade.

The living space was the size of the garage below, barely large enough for the ugly couch, the single bed, the table, and a minimal kitchen. The only extravagance Bernie showed on this floor was in the elaborate sound equipment, which was too complex for Fred to worry about using, even if he had a yen to do so. Unless he had hidden them somewhere in the walls or under the floor—and he likely had—there were no signs of Bernie's occupation. He was an international courier whose interests, Fred believed, were legal, although he did not know what they were.

Fred dropped his kit and the bag of laundry, then found a place on Charles that would sell him a reasonably straightforward hamburger and fries, and bought an apple next door to eat on his way to Mountjoy. He paused at the doorway next to the antique store's window. Miranda? Sheila? But there were no names posted next to the bells.

It looked as if Clayton Reed must occupy his entire building. When you stood on the sidewalk the walkway, between pads of ivy, gave you a choice between mounting stairs to ring the bell at a formidable black front door that also offered a knocker, or to follow the path by which they'd carried the chest to the downstairs office space. "Tradesman's entrance," said Fred. He climbed the stairs to the entrance designed for the Prince of Wales, and rang.

A mockingbird sang somewhere, probably in the magnolias across the street. A shadow flickered back of the peephole set under the knocker. Fred rang again and the shadow remained, watchful. "Let's not play games," Fred said. Then, louder, "Clayton, it's Fred." He used the knocker. The door opened on a chain, allowing a view of Clay's wild tangle of white hair, and a face pinched with alarm.

"You could be anyone."

"That's debatable. But it is an interesting concept."

"Are you alone?" Clayton's voice was tight with pressure.

"Rhetorical question," Fred said. "You see I'm alone. I prefer a question that actually wants information. You don't have to open the door. Then again, here I am."

The man was struggling. His breeding wouldn't let him ask baldly, What do you want?

"The answer to your unspoken question is, That chest I have forgotten is bothering me. I've been thinking about it. I'd like to see it again."

Clay closed the door far enough to let him take it off the chain and get it open.

"I'm paralyzed," he said. "I have to trust someone."

"I don't," Fred said, strolling in. "But I won't argue with you."

"The chest is where we left it. I can't move it," Clay said. He walked down a hallway whose floor was softened with prayer rugs. Its walls were hung with Japanese paintings on unfurled scrolls: here an iris by moonlight; next to that an armored warrior unsheathing his saber; next to that a bold and extraordinarily graceful exercise in calligraphy alone. The place seemed neither a museum nor a home, and you wouldn't call it a temple either. Open doorways led into what seemed a library on one side, and on the other a living room—what would he call it, a parlor?—dominated by a huge Hopper painting of roofs and balconies and an ominous summer sky.

Clay led the way down the spiral staircase Fred had seen before, from the other end.

Chapter Twelve

"I can't have anyone in, and I don't dare touch it," Clayton said. "Even my conservator. A thing like that in the house, it allows me no peace."

The chest was still sitting on the floor where Fred had last seen it, its top opened against the worktable.

The ape still fondled the fig. The Virgin still struggled with her offspring, with a distracted smile that could be seen as showing fey benevolence. The child still reached. His little pecker was in shadow. The painter had fudged the issue of circumcision, like all the other painters of the Renaissance who thus strove to correct, retroactively, the outward and visible sign of the embarrassing fact that the Messiah, their Messiah, everyone's Messiah after all, was a Jew.

"What you want to do is get that top off," Fred concluded. "But at the same time you trust no one to do the work. Because you trust no one to see what you have. So you are at a really sublime disadvantage, like the swimmer with the Olympic gold anchor around his neck."

"I am not following," Clay claimed. Fred was looking at the hardware. The hinges were old and rusty and attached with what appeared to be nails.

"What you have to do is disregard issues of value and importance," Fred said.

"Don't touch it," Clay ordered, as Fred lowered the top to look at its other side, where the painter, or *a* painter, or his workshop, had painted the wood, the wreath of laurel resting on a surface that resembled marble. "Serpentine," Clay observed.

"Like the back of Leonardo's *Portrait of Ginevra de' Benci,*" Fred agreed. "Except there it's porphyry."

"How would you know a thing like that?" Clay exclaimed. "Of course you are right. Porphyry with a sprig of juniper, because of her name, juniper, *jinepro,* which is Ginevra. It's part of what alerted me, at that man's place, when I saw the *faux marbre*; and that caused me to lift the lid. My heart stopped, I can tell you. I thought for sure I had given the game away. I believe that I knew it for Leonardo's creation even before I opened the chest. The man, Tilley, watched my every expression. But I raised no suspicion. Never have I dissembled so well. To the subject you raised: the *faux* stone back of the *Portrait of Ginevra de' Benci* is hardly common knowledge."

"It's not a secret either," Fred said, studying the hardware. "Yes, I was afraid of that. It's nails. Look how they've come through the wood, been bent over and pounded down, and the holes filled with putty and painted in to match. Not a bad job. But it's going to be a bitch getting the hinges off. Meanwhile, you say you're paralyzed. So, what you need is a bull in your china shop. Where do you keep your tools?"

"Tools?" Clay asked vaguely. "You don't presume we will further violate.... Stop! I insist!"

"Never mind," Fred said, taking out his penknife. Clay had turned green. "I won't hurt anything. Just take these pins out. The metal plates stay where they are. I can separate them without touching either the sides or the top. Why get a crick in our necks looking at the damned thing sideways?" He fiddled with the hardware while Clayton fluttered nearby, as nervous as any human mother watching her first child trying to learn to fly.

Clay said, "Vandals sawed the painting down to fit the chest. You can see on two sides. Criminals. Granted, until not long ago there was no work of art that was not discounted as mere wallpaper, to be trimmed as the occasion warranted. But Leonardo? I've been studying the panel. It's walnut, I believe."

"Like the *Ginevra.*"

"There's a piece missing from the bottom, do you see? Also from the left side. For God's sake, now, be careful." Fred had removed the first pin from the knuckle where it served as pivot. It was a matter of bending the pin, which was shaped like a nail, so that its bent end straightened and it could be slipped free.

"Hold the panel steady while I work on the other hinge," Fred ordered.

"I continue to stand by my original identification of this work as being from Leonardo's hand. You'll accuse me of presumption," Clay fretted. He struggled to keep the panel in place. Nature, it seemed, had intended him to arrive in this world already clothed in the blue suit he was wearing. Neither it nor he had expected him to be called on to perform physical labor. "Considering that the *Ginevra*, now accepted by all scholars as an autograph work by da Vinci, was earlier dismissed as the work of Ghirlandaio, or Lorenzo di Credi, or Verrocchio, or even—and here words fail me—of Lucas Cranach! Leonardo had been Verrocchio's pupil, granted, in Florence, before he was indicted. And his earliest works are primitive, as they should be coming under Verrocchio's guidance. But the *Ginevra* is a mature work, nothing like…."

"Got it," Fred said. He let the freed pin fall to the floor and, taking the full weight of the panel from Clayton, gently gave it the forty-five degree turn it needed.

"We should be wearing gloves," Clay pleaded. "Both sides are precious now, remember. Be careful. Both sides are precious."

Fred stood, holding the panel, freed now, by its edges. "Where do you want it, Mac?"

"You are going too fast," Clay said. "From the outset. I am not accustomed to such haste. I…."

"You like anticipation," Fred interrupted. "Rather than get it done. You like anticipation. Therefore you prolong it."

"Perhaps. Without anticipation life is flat, pedestrian and sad. Language itself, if lacking the spice offered by anticipation, is monotone. Anticipation is a quality of hope, without which...."

"Let's get it done. Upstairs or down?"

"It's not my habit to bring a work into my living quarters until it has been cleaned and framed, " Clay said. "But in this case...."

"Upstairs, then," Fred concluded. "Let's get it where we can look at it." He led the way to the staircase they'd come down, the panel almost warm between his hands.

"Be careful. Be careful on the stairs. We'll wrap it first."

Clay disappeared upstairs and came back carrying a Kashmir shawl, which the two men wrapped around the panel before Fred carried it up the spiral staircase and into Clayton's parlor. The room was a maze of comfort and beauty and almost immediately as they entered it Clayton Reed made sense. It was a mixture of Oriental, Victorian, antique European, and solid American objects and influences. "Put it on the love seat," Clay said, leading Fred to a rosewood frame covered in pink plush. "It will be safe here. I'll take the shawl."

While Fred propped the painting against the love seat's upholstered back, Clay crossed to a baby grand piano and smoothed the shawl over it before he took from its bench a photograph framed in silver, and placed it on the shawl. It showed a young woman, tender and beautiful, standing in an evening gown before a hazy background.

"My wife," Clay said. "Prudence Stillton. She was called Lucy. This was her family's house." He paused and stroked the shawl. "She died of an awful illness. Very suddenly. And very young. We'd been married...." He did not finish.

The Hopper over the mantelpiece, with its roofs and impending storm, might once have dominated this room, but it was challenged now.

"I have made a decision," Clay announced. "The new painting shall be entitled *Madonna of the Apes.*"

Chapter Thirteen

Fred found a chair whose solid design seemed likely to accommodate his bulk, and moved it to where he could sit in front of the *Madonna.* "She's better right side up," he said. He stared at the painting for five minutes while Clayton hovered in silence. "It's a grand painting," Fred said at last. "I don't care who it's by."

Clayton said, "There'll be books written about it. Academic conferences. Ph.D. theses. Letters back and forth in academic journals. All that palaver. But not in my lifetime." He smiled with a seraphic smugness and clasped his hands at his waist. "Because I shall show it to no one."

Fred said, "You might have found the one person in the world who truly doesn't care. But what you say is true, I'm sure. There will be future debate. People like to take sides to prove their friends are dolts. Rembrandt has a committee, I've heard, to decide that everyone's Rembrandt is a dud. Does Leonardo have a committee?"

"I don't know. Some scholars' opinions are presently in vogue. I haven't looked into it, and I won't look into it, because it is of indifference to me what such a committee, if any, might say." One side of the room was lined with the little gilt chairs they used to bring out during dances to hold the wallflowers in Louisa May Alcott's day. Clay brought one over and set it next to Fred's chair. "Today's moral equivalent to Berenson," he sneered. "I don't care who they are because they will not see this painting."

"Given the way da Vinci worked," Fred said, "if the work is his you might find his fingerprints in the paint. Or not. He used his fingers sometimes to maneuver his paint."

"Indeed," Clay said. "How do you know so much about it?" he did not say—but it was in the suspicion in his voice.

The Madonna looked imperturbably at a point that lay between the two men. The child looked at the ape, and struggled to reach it. The ape looked—it was hard to decide. At the fig, at the child; perhaps the ape even had a weather eye cocked toward the mother who was after all, by comparison, a mammal of considerable size and potential ferocity.

"Let them make, or break, or lose their reputations on someone else's picture," Clayton continued. "They are not getting near mine. May I offer you refreshment?"

Fred shook his head. "I have to go. Being in the neighborhood, I thought I'd take another look."

"Talking of fingerprints," Clay continued, "how do you know about Leonardo's fingerprints? You're right, but how do you know? But in any case, that will never be an issue, not while I live. No, to register prints, one would be obliged to subject the object to the X-ray procedure, which I will not do. It alters cells."

"Thanks for letting me visit the lady. I'm glad to see her the right way around." Fred stood and started for the door. "You have a program in mind for tomorrow?"

"Tomorrow?" Clayton asked blankly.

"Yes. It's not my business, but I am worried about tomorrow. The fact you are scheduled to call on Tilley again. Three o'clock, you said. According to him, he might have something really good to offer tomorrow."

"The man is as ignorant as he may be dangerous. Naturally I *won't* see him tomorrow," Clay said.

"Suit yourself. It's not my business. Maybe you really don't care. But the question is—you have possession all right. Not to impugn your motives—you asked for a price, the guy gave you a price, you tussled, you agreed on a price, you paid him. So far so good. But was the thing his to sell? We now see the painting could have phenomenal importance. If it is ever going to take its place in the big parade, even if that's only after your death, somebody has to explain where it came from, and how it got to you. Also where it was for the last five hundred years, if they can. Isn't that how it works?"

"I know what provenance is," Clayton spluttered.

"Of course you do. And if this honey of a painting is worth the gross domestic product of Rumania, as you say…."

"Excitement leads to emphatic expression. I said 'Bulgaria.'"

"Okay. If that is true anyone, even you, needs to know that the man who sold it to you acted…."

"You think I am living in Cloud Cuckoo-Land?" Clay broke in. "We placed him under no duress. I acted in good faith. You are my witness."

"His ignorance makes me wonder if he had clear title," Fred repeated. "I don't care if he collected the Commonwealth's five percent sales tax…." Clayton blushed. "I'm talking about, Did the box belong to the man?" Fred persisted. "Can Tilley prove it? All that stuff in that place…. If not, if he had no right to sell it; if it was hot, for example. Stolen, that is to say…you might as well know it. Supposing I sell you the Brooklyn Bridge…."

Clayton had risen to walk with Fred as he moved toward the front door. He held up his hand impatiently.

"So that I could see how there might be an advantage to your going over there. At the same time, I wonder, where's all that stuff from, and where is it headed? It isn't here by accident, and to me it looks like it's here in a mighty quiet and, shall we say, informal way."

Clay interrupted, "He strongly implied that he had inherited the collection."

"And you believe it? Enough said," Fred said, "on that subject. As I say, it's your business."

"This will afford me years of study," Clay said, changing the subject abruptly.

Fred said, "The *Madonna* looks to me like Leonardo's woman with the weasel. The one in the portrait in Krakow."

"It's an ermine."

"An ermine is a weasel."

"Painted in Milan," Clay said. "In 1489, maybe 1490. After he had departed Florence. Under a cloud. And disappointed. Yes, I agree with you. Do you think I've been sitting on my hands the last two days? You think I am not studying the situation? Considering my painting from every possible angle? I must know everything. There are thirty-one paintings existing in the world that are known to be by Leonardo, or mostly by Leonardo. That's if you don't count the *Mona Lisa* in the Vernon collection, and I don't. The Vernon collection's *Mona Lisa* is a copy, and the copy is not by Leonardo."

"For what it's worth, Franklin Tilley will look for you tomorrow afternoon at three," Fred said. "He's convinced you're a patsy. He's got more to sell you, including the big thing that's coming, he said. The big mystery painting. Most of all, he wants to follow you home."

"Let him wait," Clay said with a dry chuckle.

"I think you should go. And you should have someone with you," Fred said, "as backup."

"Backup?" Clay said. "I am unfamiliar with the term. It sounds unpleasantly medical."

Chapter Fourteen

"If ever I've seen a blind eye," Fred grumbled, on Mountjoy Street again, "that man has it in spades. He's dazzled by his Leonardo, and he's dazzled by his own success, and he's dazzled by an intractable worldly ignorance. Like everyone else in the world, he won't see what he doesn't want to see."

He gazed around at the world and it did not please him. It was unfinished, damp, and dangerous.

"We've got hold of the loose end of a crime that did happen, or is happening, or is on its way," he said. "Peter Pan. Cloud Cuckoo-Land, did he say? The guy's in Never-Land."

Thinking of something else, he'd left his sack of laundry back at Bernie's, and his grumbling walk took him in that direction, to pick up the sack, hoist it over his shoulder, and walk it back downhill on Pekham Street, toward Charles.

Tilley was coming out of his building. Wardrobe had given him a blue suit to wear, a distant cousin to the one Clay Reed was wearing. The package he was carrying was the right size to be one of the smaller paintings from his walls. His eye fell on Fred, studied him, discounted the laundry bag, and he rushed down to the sidewalk to cut him off.

"You're the other guy," he said.

"Many have said so," Fred agreed.

"The other guy, who was here Sunday night. What was his name?"

"Search me," Fred said. "You mean the guy you set up to mug?"

"A sales technique, and it worked. Too well, maybe. Now I'm looking all over for him. Where did he go when he left?"

"Taxi is all I can tell you," Fred said.

"I've got to find him," Tilley said.

Fred swung his bag to the sidewalk and sat on a stair. "Maybe I'll see him," he said. "What's the problem? In case I see him."

Franklin Tilley studied Fred for thirty seconds before he said, "I want my chest back."

"You want the chest back," Fred said. "Just like that." He shook his head. "You took his money. He took the chest. The money's yours. The chest is his. Transaction complete. That's how it works."

"I have his money." Franklin reached into the suit jacket's right breast pocket and brought out a fat envelope, which he waved more or less under Fred's nose.

Fred gestured to the space on the stair next to him. "Make yourself comfortable," he said. "Tell me about it." That wouldn't do, of course. If Franklin adopted a posture of relaxation he'd lose the edge of his urgency, which he apparently hoped might give him an advantage.

"That sale isn't binding," Franklin said. "You threatened me. For another thing, I changed my mind. And for a third thing, I'll raise him five thousand. For ten thousand I'll take back the chest. That's fair." A woman wearing a red raincoat and walking a dog, uphill, on the far side of Mountjoy, stopped to watch. On Beacon Hill transactions of any consequence are seldom executed in such a public way, not even in the stores.

Fred held up a finger and said, "Your first point, you're wrong. The second, if it's a point, and if it's valid, you'd have to demonstrate in a court of law. Your third point I grant you. You changed your mind. I see that. The lady across the street can see that. Also her dog." The woman and her dog resumed their exercise. "But that third point, though true, doesn't necessarily lead to action. And it is trumped by my response to your next point. You offer ten thousand, but we don't want to sell."

Franklin shook his fist. The envelope clenched in the same fist waved. Under his other arm the small rectangular package, in its brown paper, crackled. "We?" Franklin exclaimed. "'Us' again. What do you mean, 'We'? It looked like, you turning up the other night, that was an accident," he said.

"You've been telling yourself that," Fred said. "Of course you have." He shook his head.

"I want the chest back."

Fred shook his head again. "You sold it to us and, so far, we like it."

"'Us' again. You hardly opened your goddamned mouth. How did I know you were in it? Unless, what did you do, horn in on the deal later? I'll do business with the other man, Reed something. Tell him I've got his money."

"Food for thought," Fred said. "If I get it for you, what's it worth?"

"I'll talk with Reed," Tilley said. "Fuck you. I'll find him. I'll find him."

"I don't think you will." Fred stood, dusting his hands. Franklin, below him, moved a couple of steps down the sidewalk.

"I can pay...." Franklin started. Fred shook his head. Up the hill, on this side of Pekham, a couple was approaching, a man and a woman, probably in their thirties, probably courting, probably recovering from lunch. They were both dressed for the rain that had long since gone.

"Our business is done," Fred said, "as far as the chest goes. I can explain as we walk." He took Franklin's left arm by the elbow and started him down the hill. Tilley, smaller and having no better plan of action, reluctantly went along. They fell in behind the courting couple.

"What's that, the Cézanne? Never mind. The thing is, about Reed," Fred explained, "he's unusual. And the kind of unusual he is, once he makes up his mind, he doesn't change it. You and I, being reasonable, understand how the world works. But he, being unusual, feels he can disregard...well, for example, would feel he can disregard your offer. There's nothing I can do."

"So you and this Reed are friends, now, are you? I'm not finished," Franklin Tilley said. He shoved the envelope into the left breast pocket of his blue suit.

Fred told him, "My advice is, when you see him tomorrow—you made an appointment with him, didn't you?—*If* you see him tomorrow, don't mention the chest. That's the best thing. All the paintings you have you might sell him, concentrate on those other things, is my advice. The big new thing you're going to get, that's going to knock his eyes out. Did that come in?"

"Fuck you," Franklin Tilley said.

Chapter Fifteen

Fred walked Franklin Tilley to the bottom of the stairs leading to the Charles Street subway, which at that stage of its run was above ground. The evening was getting chilly. Good weather for the trees to put on leaves and flowers. Good weather for tulips and daffodils to poke their buds out of the earth in the little spaces allowed, between pavements, for such activities. Folks on the street were prospecting for a drink before dinner.

"Laundry to do," Fred reminded himself.

He chose a machine in the Nite-Rite Wash-n-Dry and sat in one of the chairs provided. It was not a bad vantage point from which to observe his fellow citizens. They came in all colors, shapes, ages, and sizes. What they had in common was that they did not live in places that had washing machines. You'd say, you'd assume, that the odds were anyone in an all-night Laundromat on a late Tuesday afternoon was single; but across from the washing machines a young man at a dryer was folding tiny pajamas and laying them into a red plastic laundry basket.

"Damned thing broke," he told Fred, catching his speculative eye. "Tamara won't wait for Sears. She can't leave the kids. Doesn't want to—she's tried it—bringing Jenny with her—that's the youngest—but this is a hell of a place to nurse a kid, and it's a lot to carry. The kid, the basket. Besides, there's something on she likes to watch, hospital program, and this gets me out of the house. I don't mind. It's not like there's diapers to do. The man who invented Pampers, he's the guy that should get the Nobel

Medal of Freedom in my book. Or the woman. And you'll say the next Nobel Medal of Freedom goes to the guy that invents a way to dispose of the disposable diapers, which I don't disagree with you. Or the woman."

He folded a little yellow dress, manipulating it on the table as if it were a man's dress shirt. Was that how a woman would do it? The dress, now a neat square, went into the basket.

"How old's the oldest?" Fred asked.

"Three," the man told him, patting the dress. He untangled three brassieres and tried to fold them, gave up, and crammed them into the basket in a state of abandon. "I've got one three, one two, and then Jenny. Jenny's the youngest. She was born last New Year's day. We missed the exemption by twenty-three minutes. It's how I knew she'd be a girl."

He paused for Fred to say something he couldn't think of.

"She was twenty-three minutes late," the man said. "You have kids?"

"I guess not," Fred said. "Not that I know about."

The young man thought of an answer that he kept to himself.

She came in carrying a blue plastic laundry basket. Tabitha? Jasmine? Stella? "Hey," she said, putting it down beside him. "Fred. Here you are all of a sudden, all fuzzy and domestic!"

Daniella?

She was wearing her wet hair in dark curls. A large green sweater covered the snake tattoo. "I'm starving," she said, leaving a kiss in the vicinity of his face. "But more important, I'm going to be arrested if I don't get some laundry done."

Marie? Marianne? Mary Anne? Anne-Marie? Mary? Frances? Bertha? Annie? Ann?

"The truth is, I forgot your name," Fred said. "I've been beating my head to a pulp."

"That's Okay. It's not a symptom of anything, or anything. There's a lot of things I forget too," she reassured him. "I'll be Anonymous. It could be fun."

"Then when we've finished our laundry, we'll eat," Fred said.

"How about Charlie's?"

"That's your name? Charlise?"

"God no. To eat. Three blocks away. You know it? I'll show you. No, my name I'll keep under advisement."

Fred strung out his operation as long as he could, but still there was waiting time before her drying cycle was done. When it came time for her to fold the sheets, Fred gave her a hand.

"I like a fresh bed," she said, "don't you?"

Side by side they carried their laundry to the antique and whatnot shop over which she lived. She balanced the blue plastic basket while she fished for her keys in the pocket of her jeans. Leading the way up the stairs she suggested, "And if you want, before dinner—after, I'm busy—we can have anonymous sex. At least you can."

Her apartment was no bigger than it had been, and no more comfortable. The only way there was room in it for two people was if at least one of them was in the bed.

"I can't keep calling you Anon," Fred said.

"I like it. It's like being in New York. Everyone knows your business but nobody knows you." She put her basket down and Fred dropped his bag next to the door. "But I see what you mean. It doesn't sound like a girl's name. Call me Amnesia.

"First we'll have coffee," she said, taking off the big green sweater and throwing it onto one of the stuffed chairs. The snake tattoo had slid easily, head first, from under the sweater, though its head itself remained under the shoulder of the pink T-shirt she was wearing underneath, above jeans that had seen a better day. "When I get to this outfit, I know it's time to do laundry," she said. "You like yours black I hope. I'm out of milk."

"Black's fine." Fred sat in the available chair and watched her work.

"We'll have coffee. Then we'll take off our clothes and make my bed." She kicked off her shoes and, busy with mugs, without looking, shoved them backward under the chair Fred was sitting in. She curled onto the foot of the bed, a lanky woman, needing a lot of bed. The instant coffee steamed well, but it was not good. "From previous conversations, although our name has slipped our mind, we know that I teach Math," she said. "Maybe you told me, but I didn't listen: What do you do, Fred, while you're not picking girls up in the Nite-Rite Wash–n-Dry?"

"Security," Fred told her.

"What, like in a store?"

"In a store you sit there and wait for it to happen," Fred said. "You'd have to say I'm more active than that."

"So, private," she concluded. She sipped from her mug. "You carry a gun?"

Fred nodded. "Not now."

"You've killed someone?"

Fred took another drink of indifferent coffee. She looked at him speculatively and bit her lower lip, shaking her head. "Given your size," she said, "and given how hard you look, I guess when it comes to making people pay attention, you don't need the gun. In class I sometimes think I could use a gun. Some of the kids we get…."

Chapter Sixteen

She stood, put the mug onto the table, and slipped the T-shirt over her head. The action roiled her hair, which she shook consciously. Her generous breasts swung, but more slowly, less consciously, and in a narrower arc.

"You don't need a gun either," Fred said, standing to put his mug down next to hers.

"Wait." She held up her hands to keep his distance. "We do this in order. First we make the bed. And before we do that, we take our clothes off. In the light this time. It was dark last time. I haven't really seen you. You first, Fred."

She gasped as his shirt hit the floor. He'd forget, sometimes, the number and complexity of the scars visible on his body, until someone reminded him. Her consternation gave him cover while he went through the routine of stepping out of his loafers and, more clumsily, getting the sequence of pants both off his body and onto the floor, next to the shirt and shoes.

"Okay," Fred said. "So far so good. When do you tell me about the snake?"

She was looking him over with frank interest. If she heard his question, she didn't let on. "Look what I get," she said. "God, you've been through some rough country, haven't you?" She stepped out of her jeans and was left in a narrow pair of pink underpants decorated with strawberries. "A gift," she said. "Another signal that it's laundry time. I didn't know you were coming. No," she discouraged his reaching arms; stepped out of the underpants and left them in the heap of clothing Fred had thought of as his. "Let's make the bed, remember?"

She rooted in her basket until she found the white sheets she and Fred had folded not half an hour ago and, one on either side of the bed, they started to unfold the bottom one.

"See, the part I love most, Fred," she said, "and don't get me wrong, because the whole thing's a blast—you've got some protection, yes? For when it's time—the best part is the anticipation. Like buying stock."

"Buying stock," Fred repeated. It was a fitted sheet, the reason it had been hard to fold earlier. He got the elastic of the top corner on his side in place.

"Yes, like my uncle said, the best time to sell stock is right before the big event everyone is waiting for. People buy hope. They love anticipation."

"Like my guy and his box," Fred agreed. He moved to the bottom of the bed and tucked in his share of that end. Their heads came close. She smelled of instant coffee, or he did, or both of them did.

"I'm not following," she said.

"I was doing security for a guy," Fred told her.

"I'll turn off the phone," she said, brushing past him to get to the night table on what must be her side of the bed. "For him or for the box? The security," she asked.

"For him, I guess. But he has this box to look forward to."

"And I have you," she said. "Hold this pillow while I get the case around it."

They lay together on her bed after a while, Fred tracing the serpent's coil around her arm, beginning at the wrist, and finishing at the flat head behind her shoulder. She was obliged to shift position somewhat, in order to accommodate his exploration. "It might be a good name for the snake," Fred said. "Amnesia."

"I'm liking the name," she said. "I'm enjoying how close we are, and me not having to be anybody."

"I'm not forgetting on purpose," Fred said. "It's like a hole I fall into, maybe, well, when, if I care about someone. It's not. . . ."

"I said, don't worry about it. Things come to pass. Like me. Waiting for my big break. You know? If you push it nothing happens, nothing comes."

"Your big break."

"I'm not teaching math in Quincy Community College forever."

"If we stretched it out, uncurled it, how long would it be? Is it male or female?" Fred asked.

"Like I loved making love with you. But next thing you know, it's done. There has to be the next thing to keep us going. Anticipation, like my uncle says."

"Like dinner at Charlie's?" Fred said.

"I guess you could anticipate that," she said. "Though maybe not as much if you've ever been there before. More like that man's box." She sat up and swung her legs over the side of the bed.

"Box?"

"You said some man was looking forward to a box. We were talking about anticipation. Tell me about the man's box."

"Oh, I don't know," Fred said. "I was watching out for the man. I never saw it."

"See, and that makes it stick in your head. Anticipation. Like stock. People buy what they hope is going to happen. It's human nature. It's *la condition humaine.* You remember the box because you never saw it, whereas if you saw it—well, who'd remember a box?

"Let's go eat. Bring your stuff with you, because I'm not coming back after."

"My worldly goods," Fred said.

Chapter Seventeen

She strode along the sidewalk, the big black cloth bag she carried swaying lethally from her left shoulder, making it advisable for Fred to keep to her right.

Charlie's, six steps down from the sidewalk, on Charles Street, was dressed like an Italian nightclub on a highway outside of town. The music was, or might be, Bulgarian folk rock, and the menu Franco-Lebanese. Once they'd fought successfully for a table, she studied the menu. "You sneaked off the other night. Man of mystery. You left me a ballpoint pen. Touching gesture. I've been treasuring it. It said *Bic* on it. I'll have the vegetable plate and the fat beans they do here. Fava beans. I could kill for their fava beans. And get me any beer they have on draught."

Fred took their order to the counter, paid, and accepted a woman's promise to deliver the order to their table.

"Given you know my name and, even after all this, yours has temporarily slipped my mind," Fred said, "I'm grappling with the question who has the advantage." He sat across from her with his iced tea. They wouldn't trust him to carry her beer.

"Knowledge is power," she said.

"Whereas, on the other hand, ignorance is bliss. Also a little knowledge is a dangerous thing," Fred said.

"I'm going to Cleveland," she countered.

"Just when I was getting to know you."

"A wedding. Leaving Friday morning, back Sunday. I'm maid of honor. You should see the commotion we went through to get half-decent looking matching dresses with long sleeves."

"It's a Muslim wedding?"

"Carla, my friend, the bride—you met her."

"I did?"

Her food arrived, and the beer, in a slopping mug. "Running. Yesterday morning. Along the river."

"That was Carla," Fred said.

The woman put a broad brown bean into Fred's mouth. It was the size of the first joint of his thumb, and spicy. "Anyway, Carla said either we cover our arms, or five bridesmaids get tattoos like mine. There's six of us. That would have been a bonanza for Big Sid in Hanover, and it would also have knocked their eyes out in Cleveland, from what I hear. But a couple of the girls weren't really that interested. A tattoo like mine, you have to want it a lot. You have to want it until you die, or at least lose your arm. So we went with long-sleeved dresses."

"All the same color," Fred said.

"A bridesmaid's first duty is to make the bride look good," she said. "By contrast. And the color she chose is going to accomplish that end. I won't even tell you what the color is, or what they call the color. After the wedding I'll dye it, and if that doesn't work I'll burn it. So, Sunday night, after you left, where did you go?"

"I told you, I do security."

She poked with her fork among her colorful array of vegetables, found a suitable victim, and held it in front of her mouth. "Tell me more."

Fred said, "Since it's security, I can't really tell you. Beyond I was doing security for a guy. Private operation."

"You have a beeper or something? I didn't hear it go off."

She bent a roasted carrot into her mouth and chewed it.

Fred, having drunk his iced tea to the dregs, rattled his ice and fished with her spoon for the lemon slice. He'd ordered something that turned out to be mostly ground lamb. "So she's going to live in Cleveland? The guy works in Cleveland?"

"Who?"

"Your friend. Carla. In the green shorts."

"Not only do you remember Carla's name, you remember her shorts," the woman said. "There's hope for you."

Fred ate some ice. The lower legs of people lined up to get inside were visible on the sidewalk, standing patiently, their owners facing each other, presumably in conversation, the women's legs for the most part bare, the men's in pants.

"No," Fred's companion was saying, "it's where the church is, and the family, the bride's family. He's from Richmond. Virginia. They met here. School. Her family's Cleveland, they do the whole Cleveland thing there, people send Cleveland-sized wedding presents like they're going to live in a big house with silver soup tureens, then they come back to their apartment here and there's nothing to do with the stuff. Except give it away one by one when their friends get married, which is where most of it came from anyway."

"Marriage," Fred said.

"You got that right. Candlesticks. Soup tureens. What is this, 1760? Thank you notes. Is this a parsnip? And they have to rent a storage locker to keep it in. It's the quandary of our age. Do they rent a locker in Cleveland, where it's cheap, or do they pay to ship it here and rent here for three times the money?"

"Imagine this," Fred said. "You're in your dress with the sleeves, whatever the color is. You all march in throwing the roses, whatever it is you throw. And there, over the altar, is one of those old holy pictures. This one shows the Blessed Virgin, sitting on a rock, with the baby on her lap, but he's reaching out for a fig a monkey is giving him. Or an ape. Or maybe the ape took it from him. You get the idea."

"What's your question?"

"Not so much a question," Fred said. "More along the lines of, Imagine that!"

The woman pushed her plate aside, still with a third of its original burden. "Have to tell you, Fred," she said. "I'm not much of a believer. Is it a Garden of Eden idea?"

"Hadn't considered that," Fred admitted.

"But then there'd have to be two apes. Two of every animal, remember?"

Fred said, "Something like that. You going to finish your beer?" She pushed it across the table to him. He'd chosen a dark draught for her that had gone warm and still. He polished it off.

"Those people would kill for our table," she said. "Let's have dessert."

Half an hour later, after she had damaged and dispersed a bowl of rice pudding, they reached the street again. The sidewalks were thronged with people, none of whom were the woman's friends to spread out their arms, calling, "Hi, Manuella!"

"I'll walk you home," Fred offered.

"Subway," she corrected him. "Will it rain again, do you think?"

They both looked at the sky, studying the question, as they walked.

"Bound to, sometime," Fred concluded.

"Back from Cleveland Sunday night."

"With a new dress with long sleeves," Fred remembered. "Can't you take off the sleeves, when you're done with the wedding?"

"Goddamned right. I'll tear off the sleeves and shorten the skirt by about a yard and a half."

"If the dye job works, it could come out looking like your shorts. Red, I remember."

"Good for you. Maybe I'll take the whole top off. I hate the top. It makes my breasts look like I keep them in a box under the bed."

They got her to her stop; she placed a kiss in the vicinity of Fred's face, and rummaged in her bag for a token.

Chapter Eighteen

It was almost ten by the time Fred reached the alley from which he could overlook the entrance to the Pekham Street building. There was a smell of spring in the air, from the river, stronger even than the smell of the alley. It was raining again or, more exactly, a fine mist hung in the streets, collecting the city's lights and diffusing them. If he stayed in the alley all night he was going to be wet by morning.

"The man was out of his depth," Fred muttered. "Even so, he was too docile. He wants the chest back but he's not desperate for it. If he knew what it was, he'd be desperate. Ten thousand bucks isn't much to offer for something that's worth the gross domestic product of Tasmania."

The windows were lighted on Franklin Tilley's floor. Cracks of light showed around the closed blinds on the Pekham Street side. Fred rang the bell for number 2. No name there. Persons living in Boston were apparently as skittish about revealing their surnames as the city fathers were about committing the names of streets to signs.

The street door opened on Franklin's anxious face, floating above that same blue suit. "I was passing by," Fred said.

"Fuck you. I'm expecting...."

"Yes?"

"I have guests," Franklin said, shoving at the door.

Fred reassured him, "I love meeting new people." He was moving Franklin backward into the hallway while he spoke. "Let's go up and talk about that chest you want."

Tilley hesitated and a confusion of expressions writhed across his face. "Not really a good time," he protested.

"Why waste the opportunity?" Fred asked reasonably. "As long as I'm here. This time tomorrow we could all be dead."

"Jesus!" Franklin seemed to make his decision while they climbed the stairs. "Don't mention the chest. I'll get rid of my guest." The door to his apartment was ajar and as it opened a young woman looked up from her spot on the rug.

"Wrong guy," Franklin told her.

The little black dress she wore had not been designed to handle the proprieties of sitting on the floor, but she was doing her best, arranged in that way women have that begins in a kneeling position but allows gravity to settle the buttocks on one side or the other of the bent thighs and calves. There was a lot of thigh, and a lot of calf, all in black net stockings—and there was a lot of blonde hair also, in a cloud around a charming, inquiring face. She'd taken her shoes off—house rules—and they sat, black with extravagantly high heels, next to the door, their toes pointing at an angle toward each other.

"Fred," Fred said, striding across the rug in his loafers and sticking out a big right hand like a man at a Rotary convention. She held a snifter in both hands, in which amber liquid slopped light. She had to put it down to accept Fred's hand.

"Delighted," she said, lighting the room with a dazzling smile.

"And you are? Beyond delighted...?" He kept the hand, looking frankly into her large blue eyes.

"Sorry. Suzette Shaughnessy."

"Please, your shoes," Franklin Tilley tried.

Fred gestured him to silence, sat next to Suzette Shaughnessy and looked at the walls. Was there less here than there'd been? More? Was it all the same stuff? The not-Cézanne *Bathers* was in the same place it had been. That had not been the package under Franklin Tilley's arm earlier. Or if it had been, he'd brought it back. The three million dollar not-Mantegna was also where it belonged.

"And Frank's letting you dip your beak into some of his famous brandy," Fred said. "Good boy, Franklin."

Franklin explained, crossing to the sideboard in his stocking feet. "The famous brandy's gone. There's Armagnac, Drambuie...."

Fred gestured the offer away and settled back, stretching his legs and looking at the walls he wasn't leaning on. Seen for the second time, the mixture was if anything more baffling. With a few odd additions, it was like what you might find in a museum in a large French city in the provinces. For the most part the good stuff was in Paris, where the good people were: the stuff Napoleon stole, or that had been left to the sudden new Republic by a headless count.

"Don't let me interrupt," Fred told Suzette Shaughnessy. "You staying in town?"

Chapter Nineteen

"At the Ritz," she said. So she wasn't local. Fred, without changing his expression, registered his lucky guess. She palmed her hair back from her face and took a sip from her snifter. Franklin stood with his, looking down at the seated couple.

"It's delicious," Suzette told Franklin. "The Armagnac. But it goes to my head. In a minute I'll start telling secrets."

"We're all friends," Franklin said. He tried for the laugh that went with Fred's Rotarian handshake. "Seriously, though, the offer's good until Sunday. If you can produce. After Sunday I can't promise anything."

"He'll be here Friday, we'll likely come by Saturday," Suzette said. Her dazzling smile promised half of everything that had ever existed in the world. In a remarkable feat of gymnastics she rose from the floor in a single fluid movement that managed both to preserve her modesty and to promise the other half. "Mitchell is obviously not coming tonight," Suzette said. "I can't wait. Fred, lovely to meet you," she said, taking his hand again as she swung her bag over her bare shoulder. "My coat," she commanded.

"Give me a half hour," Tilley pleaded. "He gets distracted. He'll be here."

"In that case call me," Suzette said. "I'm out of here. Get my coat."

Franklin disappeared into the bedroom and Suzette repeated to Fred, "At the Ritz. Room 503." She gave him a moment's searching glance that went vapid as Franklin came back into the room with a black raincoat, which he helped her get into. "Without it, I don't think he'll be interested, but I'll call you," she told Franklin. She stepped into her angled shoes without moving them, which made a sort of dance step that kept both men's eyes firmly on her body until the door had closed behind it.

The men were left staring as if the sun had suddenly been replaced by some unpleasant damp alternative. He'd stood to see Suzette off. Now Fred sat again in this chairless conceit of a room. He reached for the glass she'd left on the floor and took a sniff before he drank.

"I expect people to lie to me," Fred began. "It's what people do. It's easy, it's obvious, it's normal. So I don't mind." Tilley found a spot on the wall perpendicular to Fred's and sat where he could lean against that. Above him a portrait of a man in a red waistcoat looked Dutch or English, maybe seventeenth century. The man, whoever he was, had money enough to have his portrait done. Or he was dead and his wife wanted to remember him in his red waistcoat.

"What did she say?" Franklin protested.

"I'm not talking about the woman," Fred said. "What she said isn't my business. No, what bothers me is not understanding a person's motives. There aren't many motives to choose from, after all. There's envy, greed, hunger. There's always sex. This whole thing...." he gestured around the room, "I just don't understand it."

Franklin fiddled with his snifter. He unbuttoned his suit jacket. He stroked the fish on his necktie.

"If it's a stage set, what's the play?" Fred pushed on. "I don't understand. If you have all this money, why not be comfortable? If you want to have people over, nice people, like that lady, who have coats and shoes, and matching socks, why not be able to offer them a chair? Is it about sex or is that a side issue, maybe an avocation? You pretend the stuff is yours and you don't want to sell, but everything here has a price tag on it. If you're just fronting for all these paintings...."

Franklin said, "I didn't ask you to come. You came. You want to talk about the chest. Talk. Can you get it? I have to tell you, I'm—I more or less have to have it back."

"For example, talking of motives—my motive, coming here alone, is—I'm curious," Fred said.

Franklin stroked his fish. "It took me two hours to clean that gun," he said. "You didn't have to do that. Grandstanding for the other guy. What did you do next, go back to his place and let him suck you off?"

"I'm curious about your motives," Fred continued evenly. "Someone make a better offer? You sell it to one man for five, buy it back for ten, sell it again for twenty? Am I warm?"

Franklin stroked his fish, then he adjusted the knot, allowing his neck more room. "You have a suggestion?" he asked.

"Other motives," Fred mused. "Thinking of you still. Fear is a good motive. People will do a lot when they are inspired by fear. But they don't necessarily do it well. Fear closes the mind. Whereas curiosity, which opens the mind, might win the prize as the predominating human motive. Curiosity begins before sex, lasts longer, and when you come right down to it, a lot of the sexual instinct is curiosity anyway. Some of the sexual instinct involves issues of domination, true. As well as the internal itch. But curiosity is, of its nature, innocent, don't you think? It makes us human. Hunger comes and goes, and even plants experience hunger and thirst. After we get so old and sick that hunger and thirst are long lost memories, and even in the face of that last mortal fear, we have to be curious about what's coming next."

"What comes next is nothing," Tilley said. "The fact you are curious doesn't mean there's anything to be curious *about.* A person's hungry, the hunger has an object, like a ham sandwich, that will answer it. But hunger doesn't make the ham sandwich happen. It's a lucky accident. Your curiosity wants to know what it's like after you die? Sorry, there's no ham sandwich waiting. What happens, you turn off."

"Another thing I've noticed," Fred said. "When you ask a person a question, you put yourself in his power. You ask, 'Did you go home with him and let him suck you off?' you reveal interests of your own. If I ask you, for example, 'Where's the bathroom?' I express vulnerability. Now we both know I've gotta go. And I have given you the power to mislead me. You point to the left and I stumble into the bedroom. No ham sandwich, do you see? My curiosity is disappointed."

"Your curiosity let you down," Franklin said. He swirled the contents of his snifter, took a drink, and eyed the bar.

"No," Fred said, "it wasn't my curiosity that let me down. The mistake was to express that curiosity in the form of a question. The question signals I'm interested, and especially when you are talking to an adversary, it's stupid to give away your interest. You notice I don't ask you 'Who's Mitchell?' even though I know you are expecting something; and now I also know you are also expecting someone. Mitchell might therefore be carrying what you are expecting.

"About you, I know you want the chest back. So you feel you made a mistake. I don't ask you why. Because then I put the ball in your court, do you see? When I babble philosophy with you, and raise the hypothetical question, Where's the bathroom? your face changes."

Franklin Tilley stroked his fish and, absently, began to twist them.

Chapter Twenty

"I understand the change," Fred said, "because I noticed a good deal of cash mixed in with your dirty shorts and socks, in that wicker hamper, last Sunday night." He finished his drink, stood, and crossed the room to place his snifter next to the bottles. "If I wanted to waste time asking questions, you can imagine what they might be. But a reason I don't ask the obvious questions is I don't care what the answers are. Other less obvious questions, I'd get lies too. It takes too long to figure out what the lies mean."

Franklin had risen when Fred did, his face pale. "You didn't touch the money. Bastard. I looked after you left. Crazy I didn't look before. I was upset. What you did with my gun. Threatening. Bastard. Who are you? What do you want? What do you want with me? You want to play games? I've got to have it back. Listen, it isn't my money," he said.

"That's an answer to one of the questions I don't ask, that fits into the category of I don't care what the answer is," Fred said. "So. Three tomorrow. If he comes. Incidentally, speaking as one human to another, you might want to think about whatever it is you're doing. There's a lot of fear in this room, and I didn't bring it with me."

He left Franklin standing in the doorway, in his socks.

Boston's Ritz Hotel had for generations striven to serve as a living answer to the question, How old and rich can you be and still not take a bath? But some months ago it had begun a general facelift, and that had involved extensive cleaning, inside and out. Scandalous vandalism, some protested. It was like scraping the patina off the Parthenon. The outside of the hotel bristled with scaffolding. Inside was a chaos of work in progress even though, this close to midnight, no work was actually being done.

Fred took the stairs to the fifth floor and knocked at the door to 503. The smile of Suzette Shaughnessy lit the corridor when she opened the door far enough on its chain to see that Fred stood outside. "You didn't call," she said, taking the chain off and letting him in.

"Any friend of Franklin's," Fred said. The room was decorated as Laura Ashley's mother would have done it, in a manner that explained, almost condoned, the excesses of the Laura Ashley rebellion. Stodgy didn't begin to cover it. Suzette, on the other hand, was decorated in a way neither Laura Ashley nor her mother could have imagined. She'd de-accessioned the basic black dress, and the net stockings, and the matching underwear (how could it not match?) and was now draped in a transparent fiction made of smoke and sequins. A cigarette burned in an ashtray next to the chair where she'd been sitting watching something in black and white on the TV. Something with Cary Grant.

"I had them bring up champagne, just in case," Suzette said, suppressing the TV with the remote while, with the other hand, putting the cigarette to her lips for a fleshy drag. "My only vice," she apologized, and put it out, smiling through smoke. "I was going to give up at midnight and drink it myself or, I don't know, just leave it in the bucket. Will you open?"

"Being the *MAN*," she did not say.

Fred obliged. The business let him look around the room. Her clothes were out of sight, as were her suitcases. So she was neat or she had really expected him. Or someone. If she was reading anything, a book or magazine, it was hidden, maybe under a pillow. The bed was slightly disarranged. Fred poured into the two glasses and offered her one. She crossed a leg and wriggled the toes of the raised bare foot in pleased anticipation. She lifted her glass, higher than her foot.

"Appropriate sentiments," Fred offered in toast, raising his glass to touch hers.

"Appropriate sentiments," she echoed, and drank, her breasts moving under the transparent garment, and eying Fred as if they were her mildly interested pets.

"So he'll be here Friday," Fred started.

Suzette nodded and held her glass to a level that let her test the fizzle of the bubbles with her nose. "He won't want anything there. He's looking for names."

"Mantegna's a name."

She shrugged. "Two million? Even if it is a Mantegna, which it isn't. It's one of the also-ran Italians nobody knows and nobody cares. De Predis? Who cares? He won't."

"Two million," Fred said. "Franklin offered it to me for three, but I wouldn't take off my shoes. So you get a discount. Five hundred thousand per shoe. But you have nice feet."

"There was one thing I wanted," she said. "After courting Franklin for two weeks. And it's gone."

"Gone," Fred repeated.

"So, Fred, tell me about yourself," she said. She settled into a more alluring slouch.

"No hidden depths," Fred said. "What you see is pretty much what you get."

"You're in the business?"

"I do this and that," Fred said. "These days more this than that." He took a drink and considered. "Though, to be honest, I still do enough of that to keep my hand in. I try to." She'd emptied her glass and held it up. A summons. "You've done well," Fred told her, and rose to fill it again.

"When you walked into Tilley's place, I wondered, Did he sell it to you?"

"What?"

She studied him over the fizzle before she decided to proceed. "He had a painted box. It had angels and flowers on it."

Fred shook his head.

"Franklin Tilley won't tell me anything," she complained. "Par for the course in the art world. Everyone lies. If they tell you anything, which mostly they don't, that's when you know it's a lie. If you're in the art world, Fred, which to me seems like a safe guess, even though you look like you drive a truck, you may take that as a personal insult." Again, her brilliant smile added new sparkle to the bubbles in her glass.

Fred said, "That's what your guy collects? Painted boxes? You said he wants names. Now I'm confused."

Suzette studied the conflicting themes and found no way to resolve them. Instead she stood and allowed the light from the hotel's table lamp to make a mockery of her covering. She stretched and yawned. "Champagne does something to me," she confessed. She crossed to stand next to Fred and put a hand on the hair he cropped short so he wouldn't have to think about it. "My principal," she said, "the man I work for, will pay good money for that chest. I know his taste."

"I guess I could look around."

She stroked the side of his face, bristling now at the day's end.

Chapter Twenty-one

She was more naked in this packaging than if one or the other of them peeled her out of it. Not that the garment presented any obstacle.

"You must know the locals," Suzette said. "Who's a likely candidate."

"Problem is, in the art world, everybody lies," Fred said. He put an arm around her hips. The hips were there, the arm was there. The hips swayed briefly toward him. He let them go again. "There's more bubbly." He reached for the bottle, which sat patiently in its bucket of ice; poured some into his glass. "Will you have some?" She shook her head. "Even when they're lying with each other, they're likely to lie," he said.

She laughed and went back to her chair.

"Not for publication," Fred said, "who's your principal, and how much money are we talking? In case I get lucky."

"I assumed Franklin Tilley told you. I'm curator, personal assistant, whatever you want to call it, for the Agnelli Collection. No relation to the car people. We're in Toledo. I'm the one you go through. Tony Agnelli." She held out her glass again. Fred poured.

"Yes?" he prompted. "On the 'How much?' issue."

"I have to see it again," she hedged, "and show it to a couple of people. But I'd say, if you can find it for me, you can ask pretty much what you want."

The poise of her body was as suggestive as her words.

"Some box," Fred said. "Describe it."

Suzette gave an accurate description of the outside of the chest, so brilliantly pedestrian that it would have earned her an A in any graduate program worth its salt. "Then you open it," she finished, "and on the inside is a weird holy picture, the Virgin and Child and some monkeys. The box looks Italian. My principal, Tony Agnelli, is Italian. Duh. Italian-American. You probably guessed that. The collection needs objects, not just pictures, I told him."

"You'll be here," Fred said. "In case I have information for you."

She nodded. "Tony makes all the money decisions. I can make promises but not commitments. That sounds wrong. You know what I'm saying. How do I reach you?"

"I move around a lot," Fred said. "You won't want me unless I have something for you, and in that case I'll get word to you here. Or should I leave a message with Franklin Tilley?"

She said, "Let's not get Franklin Tilley mixed up about who's working with whom. And by the way, Fred. Don't get ideas. Agnelli doesn't buy anything except through me. That's what he pays me for. Go after him yourself, either you spook him, or his people send him to me."

Fred said, "If I have anything to sell, I go through you."

Suzette shook her head. "About some people you have an instinct." She flicked from her breasts imaginary crumbs, or bees, or the pollen from imaginary exotic flowers. She looked across at Fred in a direct and unmistakable manner. "Next question. Unless you're one of them, but my instinct tells me I'm warm here, when do we move this expedition to the next plateau?"

"It would be a pleasure and an honor," Fred said. "But also not prudent, at least for me. I get confused when I can't make out the line between business and pleasure. Let's wait till we see where this is heading. Otherwise we both lose sight of the main objective."

"Hell, with her it's all business," he muttered five minutes later on the stairs, after he and Suzette had made their wary farewells. "The packaging, the time spent in the gym, the big grin. She's the personal assistant and curator for big money from Toledo named Agnelli, who puts her up at the Ritz, and I'm invited to dip my wick? Thank you. Weird holy picture, she says. She's spotted our Leonardo.

"Correction, Clay's Leonardo."

Though the rain was long over the night was damp. Fred took a taxi to Charlestown and slept in his solitary bed.

Wednesday morning he was on Mountjoy Street at around ten, carrying two cardboard cups of coffee in a paper sack, along with containers of cream and packets of sugar. A couple was just leaving the basement entrance, a man and a woman, in their late fifties. Clay, in the doorway, splendid in a blue satin robe, was telling them, "Next week, then," when he saw Fred on the sidewalk. Fred stood aside to let the couple pass, then held up his sack and called, "I brought coffee. I was in the neighborhood."

Clay said, suspiciously, but hesitantly making room in the doorway, "An unexpected pleasure."

"Franklin Tilley. I ran into him on the street and—well—the upshot of the matter is, he wants to buy it back. The chest. His offer is ten thousand."

"Inside," Clay ordered.

Fred carried his sack to the worktable in the office and began taking out its contents. "Actually," he said, "and it's not my business: there are other things you should know."

"You're stirring things up," Clayton said. He stood indecisively next to the desk that was being commandeered by this large visitor. The blue satin robe had been put on over gray suit pants, a white shirt and tie. The man's hair was in the same wild tousle of white strands. If this was his idea of dishabille, it was as conscious as Suzette's had been, in her appearance at the Ritz. The painted chest, stripped of its top, still sat there on the floor. Its top had taken so much of his attention up to now, Fred hadn't really looked at the rest of the object. The interior was dark wood, unpainted, pocked with worm holes. It gave off a musky smell, as if someone had been keeping his grandmother in there, clean, but dead. Outside, the decoration, carved, gilded, and painted, was not easy to place, mostly because Fred had never bothered to spend time looking at such things. If it was evidence of anything, he was too ignorant to read it. The angels were nicely painted, with large, flat, delicate wings. The angels reminded him of something. Maybe Fra Angelico? Except it was furniture.

"Stirring things up," Clay repeated.

"Maybe. But things were already stirred up. Heavy objects. We want to keep track of them if we can."

Clay hesitated a long minute before he sighed and shifted course. "My one desire is to be left alone, to study and to think about what I have purchased. Would that the present might be simple, so that I could indulge the complexities of the past. Yet the present is not simple. Here you are again. It is difficult to welcome you, since you bring bad news. Still, most kind." He sighed again. "The coffee. I regret—it is my single eccentricity—that I eschew stimulants. Forgive me. I appreciate the gesture." He sat in the chair at the worktable and motioned Fred to the couch. Fred, taking his coffee black, left the litter of condiments on the table next to the extra coffee, the sack, and a pile of books on whose covers and spines the word *Leonardo* seemed to predominate.

Fred began, "I'm told that in the art world people either say nothing about their business, or lie."

Chapter Twenty-two

Fred looked across at Clay and waited. The older man pursed his lips. "About me you are correct this far. I cannot bear for anyone to know my business. It is an instinct. Almost an obsession. And yet, apparently, perhaps heeding a deeper instinct, I take you into my confidence. At a time and in a circumstance when a great issue is at risk. With a prize such as my Leonardo at stake, why would I not lie, or stand mute, to protect it? If you infer, or aver, that I am in the art world, I will not argue, although I don't think of myself as belonging to any world at all. If I accept your premise, and wish to confirm it, my next move is either to lie, or to say nothing. We reach an impasse."

"In *my* world, on the other hand," Fred said.

"What *is* your world?" Clay interrupted.

"In my world, I hate to waste time."

"You keep coming back," Clay said. "Why?"

"There are things about the neighborhood," Fred said. "Moving on...."

"You told me you want nothing," Clayton reminded him. "I hold a vulnerable treasure, which indeed you helped me to procure. Unavoidably, through happenstance, your business and mine coincided, briefly, while you saved my life. I acknowledge it. I have thanked you. Forgive me if my instincts were at fault, but you seem a man of considerable pride, and I believed that to have offered anything in the nature of a financial reward—yes,

I see that I was right. You say that you want nothing. I must respect that statement. Yet you keep coming back."

"Moving on," Fred said. "There are things you don't understand. That makes me nervous. There's too much wrong. For one thing, Tilley keeps a large amount of cash in the house."

"As you know I had on me, on Sunday night, a notable amount of cash. It comes in handy sometimes, as the event developed. It would not surprise you to learn that I had more cash in the house."

"Not in the bathroom hamper with the dirty socks and skivvies," Fred said.

Clayton Reed blushed. "You were thorough," he said. "Still, people are free to do what they wish. I prefer a safe. Many persons prefer to effect their transactions in the form of cash. If their reasons are dishonorable, their dishonor is their business."

"Upward of fifty thousand cash," Fred pressed on. "That's a guess. That kind of cash in that kind of place means trouble. Normally it indicates traffic in contraband. When I called Franklin on it, he turned green."

Clay started, "I didn't hear…."

"Last night," Fred explained. "I was in the neighborhood. He had a woman there, representing the Agnelli Collection, she told me later. She also wants your chest. She didn't mention a figure."

Clay jumped to his feet, almost chattering in alarm. "This is an unforgivable intrusion."

"Without which," Fred said evenly, "you would be ignorant of the forces that are moving. Without my interference you wouldn't know that Franklin Tilley regrets making the sale. You wouldn't know he keeps a gun. You wouldn't know about this new player, Suzette Shaughnessy, or her principal…."

"You didn't…." Clayton started.

"I told her nothing."

"And now you want…."

"You thought you were home free. Now we know about two parties who are looking for what you bought."

"What do you want from me?" Clay demanded, smoothing his lapels with trembling hands.

"I can make allowances. You are worried. But understand this," Fred said, slowly, and with measured force. "You don't know me, but you've had a chance to take my measure. Do you really want to suggest that I will either betray or blackmail you, just because I could do both, so easily?"

He let the question hang. Clayton sat again, poised behind his desk, his eyes wary. The words from the large man in his office, with the square farmer's hands, and the face as craggy and alarming as the deliberation that had given force to the spoken words, had offered no threat. But threat hung in the air.

"Living in Boston so long," Clay said, "perhaps I forget my manners. I do apologize. I am overwrought. Give me a moment to collect myself." He began to pace nervously in a small area between his worktable and a bookcase against which three paintings leaned, unframed, their faces turned away. "In fairness, and in fellowship, I must accept your word," he said finally. "However, you say you want nothing, and that is impossible. Therefore I am confused. And with me, confusion and suspicion are indistinguishable."

"Moving on," Fred said. "Help me understand this new player, Suzette Shaughnessy. Let me ask you, do you know Tony—Anthony, I guess—Agnelli? Is he a known quantity? The Agnelli Collection."

"You mention heavy objects," Clayton said. "Agnelli is, to adopt your term of art, a truly heavy object. Agnelli is the only man living who can, and will, successfully challenge the Getty Museum." Clay perched nervously on the edge of the table and settled the satin robe over his knees. "The Agnelli money's plumbing. Three generations of plumbing that, under Anthony Agnelli's guidance, went from drains and faucets to encompass an empire of everything hydraulic. Hydroelectric dams throughout the world; the digging of new canals; the plans underway to restore the Saharan aquifer, and to save Venice both from the sea and from its own pollution. He's a major force in the world, a Bechtel or Halliburton in his own right, since he won't go public.

"Ten years or so ago he began to buy art. He buys only the work of Italians, or works done in Italy. He owns six of Corot's Italian landscapes. When he started buying, a person like myself might compete for a lesser name—a Baldovenetti, a Cosimo Rosselli—among the Florentine painters of the Renaissance, for example—the Renaissance is where he started. But because of his competition nothing slips by. As for the big names—I happen to know that he bought the Brierstone Bronzino at Christie's London sale last October. He arranged to bid not only against the Getty, but also, in order to ensure that the price might rise to a level the National Gallery of London could not match, by public subscription, to keep the work in England as a National Treasure—he arranged for a shill to bid against him."

"Bid against himself," Fred said.

"And brought the Brierstone Bronzino, the *Sebastian Transfixed,* back to Toledo. There was nothing for the United Kingdom to do but watch and wring its hands." Clay looked up sharply at Fred and paused, waiting.

"You've lost me," Fred said.

"The subject is life-sized. The martyr Sebastian pierced by arrows. Lord Brierstone had brought the painting to England, probably in 1730, following a tour of the continent. Then, four generations later, when the family and its fortune were both falling into disrepute...."

"No, the other thing," Fred interrupted. "The bidding and so on." He took the other coffee from the desk and began on it while Clay changed horses.

"The United Kingdom, England, like many countries in the Old World, has passed laws designed to keep within her borders all works of art that a committee of interested parties determines to be National Treasures."

"Go on."

Chapter Twenty-three

"The British spirit of fair play does not allow its citizens to lose their financial interests in their properties. Suppose the work is placed at auction. Let us extend the hypothesis to suggest that Lord Brierstone's descendants owned the *Venus de Milo*'s more presentable younger sister, Diana, who also has her arms. The smooth and pomaded elderly gentlemen from Christie's, accompanied by the ravishing titled young woman whom misfortune has forced into trade, also from Christie's, persuade the family to place the piece at a suitable London sale, and they so notify the world. The competition is strong and relatively unimpaired by collusion, and we'll assume that the Getty places the highest bid. Since you are indulging my hypothesis, let us say that the Getty's successful bid is for two hundred fifty million pounds, hammer price, which means that in addition they must pay a commission at whatever rate they have previously and privately negotiated with the auction house. At those figures nobody pays the published rates.

"At this juncture a great noise and commotion is heard in the land. The committee, egged on by the press, declares the *Diana* to be a National Treasure, meaning that the United Kingdom would suffer a severe loss if the *Diana* left its borders. That's all very well, but now Christie's, and the Getty, and the under bidders, have all demonstrated that the Diana is worth two hundred fifty million to its owners. The crown may not simply confiscate the property. They're going to get their share anyway, when the taxes are collected. The Brierstone family, as long as they get their money (two hundred fifty million less taxes and the commission they have previously negotiated with Christie's, which will be less than what you read on the printed page), agree to allow the *Diana* to be set up in a public place, such as the National Gallery, and the crown begins to organize a subscription to collect a fund to match the Getty's bid. School children are invited to contribute their lunch money. Lord this and Lady that, the fellow who owns Harrods (who's hoping one day to be knighted), and the rest of them, are importuned to make their tax-deductible contributions. And if the Getty's price is matched within a specified time—I forget what that time is, it doesn't matter—if, as I say, the bid is matched, the Brierstones get their money from the fund, the government takes back its share in taxes as expected (unless the government forgoes its taxes? After all, it is getting the work in question), Christie's, I presume, collects its commission as expected, the *Diana* remains in the National Gallery, and the Getty's people slink back to California emptyhanded."

"Ah," Fred said. He toyed with his cup. "The Brierstone heirs would be unusual, especially if their fortunes have fallen into disrepute, if they welcomed this worldwide attention to the sale of a family jewel."

"Indeed," Clayton said.

"Not to mention, the loving attention of the crown would ensure that they lose between a third and half her value in taxes, yes?"

"Indeed," Clay repeated. "Roughly speaking. Forty percent, I believe. On a sale of two hundred fifty million, the government would pocket a hundred million."

"Then what I'd suggest," Fred started.

"If you were unscrupulous," Clay said. "If I see where this is going...."

"Yes. Is put this *Diana de Milo* in a cast, let's say a fiberglass cast, make her look like a sculpture by Niki de Saint Phalle, one of those bulbous she-women painted up like a circus tent, then sell her. She's too big to be smuggled out in a suitcase. Sell her as a modern work that is imitating Saint Phalle, for whatever it costs—fifteen hundred pounds?—to a confederate, pay the tax on the fifteen hundred pounds, the confederate ships the thing to the U. S., for example, and then strips off the fiberglass cast, and sells the *Diana* quietly."

"Right," Clay agreed. "It's done all the time with paintings and antiquities. Since Egypt, a bit late in the game, has decided it doesn't want its ancient papyri to leave the country, the smugglers face them with modern tourist copies and they travel disguised as souvenir junk. Once arrived at their point of destination, the false front is removed and the originals are quietly placed on the clandestine market."

"Another thing you could do," Fred said. "Say, as a hypothetical, you had an important painting that happened to be on a wood panel. Why not arrange to have that painting seen not as a painting at all, but, for example, as the top of a kid's toy chest?"

"Indeed," Clay said. His response registered no surprise.

"Next question," Fred pushed on. "Were we smart, or were we lucky?"

"We?" Clay asked. The single syllable stretched languorously over a considerable space of time, and Clay twined his long fingers, unraveled them, and wove them together during the course of the question.

"This may not be news to you," Fred said. "This brilliant original idea of mine."

"Such a procedure demands trust between the confederates," Clay said. "The trust that is elsewhere called Honor among thieves."

"In the case of the Brierstone *Diana,*" Fred continued, "if the heir wants more than the sixty percent he'd get on the open market, it would pay both him and the buyer to arrange a quiet sale, say for two hundred million. The buyer saves fifty million. The seller gives a commission of maybe ten million (let's be generous. It's only money) to the confederate brokers, the heir takes in a hundred ninety instead of one fifty. There's a profit of forty million for the heir. Everyone's happy."

"With the exception of the government," Clay pointed out. "Which had also expected to pocket its fifteen percent VAT, or sales tax. Unless the buyer can claim an exemption."

"And within all this," Fred said, "The *Diana* has become just another commodity, like a crate of bananas."

Clay nodded.

The remainder of the chest, from which they had removed the top, was still sitting on the floor in front of Clayton Reed's worktable where Fred had left it, a body without a head. The interior dark with age, its painted sides were luxurious with pink and grass green angels, accentuated by vivid swirls of gold and ultramarine. The sides were as nicked and scratched as any such object might be if it had been used for many years.

"What do you make of the box?" Fred asked.

"It worries me."

Chapter Twenty-four

"The angels, the lilies, the arches, the curlicues," Clay said, "all of it worries me. It looks convincing for the fifteenth century, though earlier than my Leonardo. You can see that it is almost primitive. Although there is shading in the angels' draperies, nonetheless they are not presented with any illusion of volume. The arches are not architectural, but formulaic. Listen to me, I speak of it as if it were a painting, rather than a decorated object. I've sat on the floor and studied it. Whether as painting or as decorated object, I am troubled, albeit I know nothing about wooden furniture or joinery. It simply doesn't fit."

"We already knew the chest and its top didn't go together," Fred pointed out. "I look at it here, even without its top. What do I know? For what it is, it looks pretty good to me. Maybe the original top was damaged? Someone did their ironing on it or something."

"Horrible thought. But less so if the box is a fake," Clay said. "As I fear. If this is true, how recent a fake concerns me. I do not wish to think about it. But nevertheless, it is here. It is a part of the story, like it or not. If it is late nineteenth century, as I surmise, it raises the specter of a whole school of master forgers who worked out of Siena. They were skillful enough either to hoodwink, or to collaborate with, such expert aesthetes as Berenson. Among them, they filled American collections with frauds."

"We don't care about the chest," Fred said. "Do we? Why should we?"

"When the *Star of India* turns up in a plastic setting," Clay worried, "something is amiss."

"We already know something's wrong. Even if your Leonardo's a fake, you didn't pay enough for it."

Clay said blandly, "My practice is to separate issues of monetary value from aesthetic considerations."

"When you buy an egg for a penny," Fred said, "don't cry when it stinks in the pan."

"I am not doubting the egg. The painting. It will stand up to any scrutiny, though the only scrutiny it will enjoy is mine. No one...."

"The couple who were leaving when I got here," Fred interrupted.

"Have been with me for years. They clean. They are honest, reliable, and thorough. They do not notice or, God forbid, dust, the collection."

"And you won't have the straps of the hinges removed from the face of the painting?" Fred pressed. "Or when you do, you'll blindfold the conservator?"

"Since it appears that, contrary to my better judgment, I open my mind to you, here is one cause of my misgiving. You surprise it from me because of the violence of my emotions. Indeed, I can scarcely speak," Clay said. He paused, allowing room for Fred to cause an interruption that would let him off the hook; but Fred sat quiet.

"The cut edges," Clay said. "Not only are they the explanation for the fact that the wreath of laurel, on the marbled side, is now off center. More, I perceive through my horror, the cuts are recent. Must be. I can't believe they are more than twenty years old. When I examined them under a lens...."

"Should we go up and look?" Fred suggested.

"I have made the examination," Clay said mournfully. "It grieves my heart. The cut edges have been darkened with oiled pigment, so that they match the color of the other, older edges that have not been tampered with. Worse, before that, the villain abraded them, with fine sandpaper or something finer, perhaps an edge of broken glass, until they could pass for being worn enough to match their apparent age."

"The wood's not old?" Fred protested.

"Of course it's old. Five hundred years and then some. Only the wood exposed by the new cuts had never been subject to the deleterious effects of oxygen, and of pollution. Therefore they were not dark. Not aged. Until the forger tainted them."

"Forger," Fred said.

"A similar trick is used by many dealers. Suppose they must stretch an old canvas on a new wooden chassis? Often the new wood is stained so that it will not embarrass the painting it carries by its palpable youth. It is unnecessary, of course. Only the impossibly naïve are fooled, unnecessary as that is. Still, it is a kind of forgery. And the honest age of the wood of my Leonardo, on these two violated edges, has been forged to look, to the careless eye, as if the cut is as old as the painting is. If there was ever any doubt that such a work should be in such a place, and in such hands, that doubt has vanished. I have liberated a hostage."

Clay stood slowly. "Time is passing," he said. "I have enjoyed our visit. Our *visits* I should say, using the plural form of the noun."

Fred suggested, "Carry the rest of the chest to the Museum of Fine Arts, if it bothers you. Get someone in Furniture to look at the wood, the paint, the gilding, the joinery, what's left of the hinges. You kept the pins?"

"And ten minutes later anyone in the world who wants to, knows my business," Clay said. "They are all in league. No one in any museum is able to keep a secret. Or wishes to. If they are to be interesting to their friends, they must do commerce in other people's business. They have none of their own."

"Then it's a problem," Fred said. "Thanks for the coffee." He stood, grabbed his windbreaker and made for the door. On his way out of the room he hesitated, turned, and asked, "May I use the phone? Local call."

Clay, taken aback, gestured toward the telephone on his desk. Fred pushed three numbers and asked the noise on the other end, "Atlanta, Georgia. Franklin Tilley." He waited, listened, and affirmed, "Yes, Pearl Street," and jotted the number down. He looked a further question at Clay, who nodded and answered, "Why not?"

Fred punched the number and waited until it had rung long enough without a response. "No useful answer," he told Clay. "And no answering machine."

"That is to be applauded," Clay said. "When you have such a device, they are able to spy on you."

Fred tried the number again. After a dozen rings a male voice answered, "Yes?"

"Franklin Tilley?" Fred asked, and the phone went dead.

"I've pushed myself into your business, and I won't waste your time apologizing," Fred said. "I don't explain because, well, I can't, beyond I helped you get into something that feels wrong, and that might turn dangerous. I feel some responsibility. Also, I'm interested, and it's been a while…." He let that thought lapse.

"I *am* somewhat concerned about the meeting with Mr. Tilley this afternoon," Clay said. "I must know the Leonardo's provenance. As you pointed out so brutally, and as my own better angels advise me in tranquility, if the painting was not Tilley's to sell, it cannot be properly mine."

"My thought was, I'll go," Fred said. "If the conversation leads in that direction, I'll let him believe the chest now belongs to me. He'll figure that, knowing he was interested, I took advantage of you. In order to cheat you, I bought the chest off you for less than the ten thousand he offers. Why not? So I'll be the owner now. If you continue as the owner of record, you are a sitting duck. Let's shift the field away from you. It gives me more freedom to work."

"To work," Clayton echoed.

"So I shift their attention to me, find out what I can, and then disappear. I can do that, you can't. You're better off. The love nest, so called, is a temporary setup. Whatever their business is, these people will do it and go. They've got to. The

Commonwealth's revenue officers won't take forever. Franklin Tilley, and somebody else he mentioned, named Mitchell. Does that name ring a bell?

"I don't ask your permission, because I don't ask permission. But I am going to do what I can to find out what's going on. While I'm at it, why shouldn't I watch your back?"

"Do what you wish," Clay said. "As long as I am insulated from further contact with this matter. Much as I hate the fact, I see that circumstance has placed me in your hands. I cannot keep you from going back. I shall be occupied. I must understand my painting. I shall undertake to establish its provenance otherwise, working beneath the surface, starting when it was made. In any case, I won't keep the appointment. The man is insufferable. Take care. Since I do not expect to see you again, if you don't mind—on your way out—I'd like to thank you again, and shake your hand."

Fred took the offered hand and slipped out the basement door into a brilliant May morning, fragrant with the caresses of the spring breezes.

Chapter Twenty-five

Suzette, in her room, answered the house phone at whose other end, in the Ritz lobby, Fred was standing. "Fred?" The brilliant smile lit up the phone line and made it tingle. Ten minutes later she joined him in the lobby, wearing a beige suit, and balancing a handbag taken from the back cover of *Vogue.* "You found it," she said. The tone of her exclamation was impossible to read. It lay somewhere between "You good boy," and "Die, alien!"

"Let's go somewhere and talk," Fred suggested.

"You've seen it, at least?" Suzette demanded. "Come up to my room."

"There's a place on Newbury Street," Fred said. "I was just headed there for an early lunch, late breakfast. Join me? It's a nice morning. Flowers, wind; and the rain is over and gone."

The cloth of her tailored skirt was of a light enough material that the sun, shining through it, after traversing the plate glass of the lobby's street-side wall, made the morning even nicer.

"I'll take that lunch," she decided.

"I know a place," Fred had implied; but he didn't really know Newbury Street that well. He walked her along the sidewalk, therefore, until a likely looking window offered *GRAND OPENING! Sylvia's Kitchen,* promising "Meals like Grandma used to make." The concept was staggeringly out of place for Newbury Street's pretensions.

It was almost noon but, aside from a meager staff, they had the place to themselves. The hostess, struggling to use Suzette as bait, tried to make them sit in the window, but Suzette insisted on a table. "Out of the light. My eyes," she explained.

Grandma had specialized in macaroni and cheese, liver and onions, tuna casserole, and meatloaf with all the fixin's. "Grandma was from Toledo, I guess," Suzette said. "Yes, look, for dessert you can get Jell-O or apple pie or chocolate cake. No junket, but that may be too 1940s, even for Grandma."

"You're not from Toledo," Fred said.

The waitress hovered. Fred ordered a draught beer and she shook her head. "No license," she said. "They've applied." At this rate Grandma might last a week before she had to close out of sheer loneliness.

Suzette told the waitress, "I'll bet you could make me a salad? I don't see one on the menu, but there must be a salad that comes with some of these orders. That's what I'd like. With a diet Coke."

"Diet Pepsi," the waitress corrected her. They'd forced her to wear a dress of vertical pink and white stripes, along with an apron arrangement that Grandma's Grandma would have called a pinafore. "I'll ask them about the salad. You, sir?"

"Meatloaf," Fred decided. "And iced tea."

"Excellent choice," she approved. "I'll ask if we have iced tea."

"If the chef has ice, he'll figure it out," Fred reassured her.

"All right. Let's talk," Suzette said briskly, as the waitress disappeared into the kitchen. "You've found it. You've seen it. You've made a deal on your own. With Reed. Typical. Cutting me out."

The waitress reappeared. She'd put on a nametag that gave her name as Carol. "We *can* do iced tea," she crowed. "It'll just be a minute. About the salad. What we do is coleslaw. A side of coleslaw. Would that be all right?"

"Sure thing," Suzette told her.

"Excellent choice! I'll get your drinks."

Fred said, once the coast was clear, "You have Reed Gingrich's name from somewhere."

"The man's a fool," she remarked. Her eyes neither blinked not widened as she registered and salted away the prize she'd surprised out of him: Reed's last name, Gingrich.

"I won't argue," Fred said. "My hasty impression of Reed...."

"Not Reed. I don't know Gingrich. Franklin Tilley."

"I get the impression he's out of his depth," Fred agreed.

"Whatever you paid, we'll raise," she said. She paused, fooled with her fork, and added, "Then add a commission for you."

"We?" Fred asked. He could not make the syllable last as long as he wanted, but he did what he could.

"This morning we had a frank exchange, Franklin and I, and decided that we had a common interest," Suzette said. "We are working together, just on this one project."

"Common cause," Fred said, then looked up and left off as the waitress leaned toward them with beverages. Suzette's soda clinked with ice. Fred's tea, in its glass, was pale and thin, and warm, and carried a fingernail of ice in the thin film of scum on its surface.

"There was ice at first," Carol apologized. "It probably melted."

"Grandma's not from Toledo," Suzette remarked behind Carol's retreating back. "Toledo may not be Savannah, but in Toledo we do know how to make iced tea."

"Relax," Fred said. "You're not from Toledo yourself. Not anywhere near."

"Where you from, big boy?" she asked. She sipped from her drink, dark with its diet caramel coloring. "What is this, a truck stop?"

"So, you and Franklin Tilley and the Agnelli Collection all have the same interest? I can negotiate with any one of...."

"You talk to me," she said briskly. "Franklin's a fool. Tony's not here, and in any case I represent Tony's interests. Where appropriate."

Carol came back. She carried two shallow dishes of coleslaw and a plastic basket of rolls that Grandma would have recognized from the cover of a 1950's *Family Circle* magazine as able to emerge from a tube in order to imitate something served at the Parker House. The rolls she put in the center of the table. She put one dish of coleslaw in front of Fred, and the other in front of Suzette. She studied the arrangement, pouted, and shook her head.

"When you get a chance, would you bring me a glass with ice in it?" Fred asked.

Carol adjusted the dish of coleslaw in front of Suzette, putting it off to the side. "That way you have something to eat while the gentleman has his entrée," she explained.

"Something to look forward to," Fred said.

"Excellent choice," Suzette said. "Fred, are you with me?"

"With you and Franklin Tilley and the Agnelli Collection? I don't know. That's some party."

Chapter Twenty-six

"I reckon Franklin hasn't told you everything," Fred said. "People don't. Or they lie. Good. Here's the meatloaf. Thanks, Carol. Maybe some ice? I'll drop it in my tea and that will make it cooler."

"You're already working with Franklin," Suzette guessed.

"The main thing is, according to Reed, the chest is already out of circulation," Fred said. "Off the market. It's gone into a private collection and it's not coming out again."

Suzette teased her coleslaw with her fork before putting some into her mouth. "I don't know how far I can trust you," she said, after chewing deliberately and swallowing.

"I wouldn't," Fred said.

"Wouldn't what?"

"Wouldn't trust me. Why trust anyone? Do you trust Franklin Tilley? Did he tell you that he and I already reached an understanding? Tell you I'm working with Gingrich?"

"What?"

"So all in all it's a confusing business, in addition to which you can't believe what anyone says anyhow, according to you, since everyone lies."

Suzette eyed him over her next three forkfuls of slaw. Fred attacked the meatloaf plate, whose fixin's included canned cranberry sauce and mashed potatoes that had been powder until very recently.

"My offer is twenty thousand dollars," Suzette tried. "For yourself. Commission. Once we get the chest."

"We," Fred said. "We as in you and Franklin Tilley? You and Agnelli? Or We as in you, singular? If I can get hold of it, which I haven't said I can. Gingrich says it's in a private collection. Any offer you make me, I have to measure against something I heard last night. An extremely attractive woman in a see-through nightie told me, 'I can make promises but not commitments.'"

"That was our first meeting," she said. "This is our second. And it was late."

"Our second meeting, actually," Fred corrected her. "This is the third. It doesn't matter. What matters is, the chest is no longer in play. It's out of reach. The collection it went to—I won't say it's the Agnelli...."

"What?" she exclaimed.

"My lips are sealed," Fred said before he proved the opposite by inserting a chunk of meatloaf.

"Agnelli wouldn't.... Tony would never," she said. A real emotion showed itself in those lovely eyes. Panic, was it?

Fred swallowed. "Because my lips are sealed. So, as far as the ownership of the object is concerned, there may be no further play. I'll live longer if I skip dessert. Don't let me stop you."

Suzette Shaughnessy shook her head. She had not gotten to the bottom of her coleslaw. Grandma made it with iceberg lettuce instead of cabbage.

"However," Fred said, speculating as he put together a last bite of meatloaf, peas, mashed potatoes and cranberry sauce. He ate it deliberately while his partner watched and waited. "There's the question of provenance," he continued. "The initial purchase may have been hasty, and the subsequent sale hastier still."

"Agnelli screwed me," Suzette said. "I was right. Cut me right out."

"I haven't said who the end user is," Fred reminded her. "I note in passing that you aren't actually on Agnelli's payroll. That was just a little shorthand on your part, that suggestion?

In all fairness. Don't jump to conclusions. What I was going to say—where was I?"

"Starting with 'However,'" Suzette said.

"Right. Though I can't make either a promise or a commitment, I can make a suggestion. My take is that the collector would be happy to purchase the provenance to go along with the object. How much he or she might be willing to pay...."

"You want me to tell you where it came from," she said.

"The collector prides herself or himself on his or her research, according to what Reed Gingrich told me. He or she or (if it's a collection, *it*) would be pleased to have the item's history, and would likely pay a fee. Trying to be helpful here. Since Gingrich acted hastily and bought the thing without either description or history, just on impulse, as long as you and Franklin are working together, if you want, why don't you ask him and if you can, get a package together. Name of the seller, when the work came into the collection, exhibition history if any, customs declarations, all that."

Suzette Shaughnessy had gone an interesting shade of gray that went badly with the blonde hair and the beige suit. "Where has it gone?" she said.

"I've already told you more than I know," Fred said. "More than I even guess. In this business everyone lies anyway. Talk to Franklin. Maybe he'll have something. You know where to find me. Well, actually, you don't know where to find me. But you'll be at the Ritz, I guess. Or—where are you when you're not at the Ritz?"

"Customs declarations?" Suzette asked.

"Maybe I jumped to a conclusion," Fred said. "A chest that size, and that old, it had to be somewhere else before Franklin Tilley got hold of it. If Franklin wasn't the owner, and we think he wasn't, who was? So if you, or Franklin, or both of you, can get me that information, I'll take it to Gingrich and see what he'll pay for it, and we can split the fee. After he sees what his client will pay, which will depend on how good the information is, after he sees it."

"We have to know who the client is," Suzette decided. "If there's anything we can do. When you say 'Split the fee...'"

"Two ways," Fred said. "Half for me, half for your team. You're only asking Tilley what he already knows." He stood, took a twenty from his wallet and secured it under the warm glass of weak tea.

"Why don't *you* ask him, since you and he have an understanding?" Suzette demanded.

"My understanding with him doesn't match yours. I'll drop by tonight, maybe tomorrow; see what you've got. Give me your card."

Suzette stared at him for thirty seconds before she concluded, "In my other purse."

Chapter Twenty-seven

One fifteen. The street was crowded. Tourists, in town for Boston's spring, poked or jostled along the sidewalk looking into shop windows or selecting places to eat that were not Sylvia's Kitchen. Here and there the darling buds of May, most of them tulips and daffodils, found places to push forward in the small plots allotted to them. The leaves on the trees, flatter and wider each second, were also a deeper green each second. A damp breeze made them flutter. It was a good afternoon to stretch his legs, and to sort his head out at the same time, if he could. Fred walked across Boston Common, muttering.

If Franklin Tilley and Suzette Shaughnessy were blind weavers, weaving, together, this "tissue of lies," could the fabric hold together? Could it hold the new lies Fred was dropping into it? The lies in themselves were seductive, and threatened to distract from the end at which Fred wanted to aim: protection of his unwitting client, and the discovery of further information about what he had purchased, which had no business even existing, much less being purchased.

Tilley's only hope of retrieving the chest lay in the fact that the man he called Reed might turn up for the three o'clock appointment. So Franklin would be there. He'd have to be.

Halfway down Pekham Street, there was Franklin Tilley, dressed in that same blue suit, coming down the front stoop of his building. Fred slipped into the alley in time to let Franklin go on his way without interruption. The man was walking with such speed that the chances were good he would not notice Fred in any case. He had turned uphill, in the direction of the State House, and in five minutes was out of sight.

"Might as well wait inside," Fred said. "He can't say he's not expecting me. Or, well, he's expecting Clayton."

After he'd rung Tilley's bell to no response, the front door opened to him with relative ease, as did the door into Franklin's quarters. The emptiness of the apartment was speedily confirmed; an emptiness accentuated by the smell of dead cigarette smoke. Fussy as the management was about shoes being worn in the premises, did nobody care what cigarette smoke could do to a painting? There was less on the walls of the big front room, though the change was not significant. Fred noted two empty hooks, one of them in the place where the not-Cézanne *Bathers* had hung: the one thing Franklin had said he couldn't sell.

This was Fred's first opportunity to look the collection over without interruption, and he took his time, starting next to the entrance door where the painted chest had been until early Monday morning. Here hung a watercolor as aggressively Northern European as it was nineteenth century, representing a port scene with sailing ships at anchor, with stevedores busy either loading or unloading casks. Because the action was frozen in time, like that between Leonardo's infant and the ape, it was not possible to be certain in which direction the casks were passing. Just as, in the busy crucifixion scene, an oil painting two pictures over, one could as easily assume that those soldiers and the mob were a well-meaning group which, coming upon three men on crosses, was hastening to cut them down as gently as they could, and carry them to the nearest hospital.

The watercolor was executed in a variety of browns and tans, with an occasional hint of vermilion. It was signed, with a signature that would be legible only by someone who already knew what it was. The painting, in its mat and frame, occupied almost two by one-and-a-half feet of wall. Its glass looked dusty on the inside, and its mat was stained and foxed. Therefore it had not recently been jazzed up, cleaned, and re-housed for the kind of sale that might call on a decorator as intermediary.

"Whatever it is, it's the genuine article," Fred concluded. He took the picture down from the wall and turned it over. Its brown paper backing was splotched and dark, nicked here and there with dings where it had been bumped against sharp corners. It carried an old label from a London gallery, on which the artist's illegible name had been recorded in a spidery script, along with the painting's title, *Shipping, Dordrecht.*

The painting might have a soul back of all that dust, but Fred did not feel it burning or struggling in his grip. The workmanship seemed more a matter of schoolboy obedience than the disciplined rebellion that had gone into the work Clay was convinced was Leonardo's. "Shouldn't I be stunned and amazed," Fred asked himself, "at the idea that an unknown Leonardo sits ten minutes' easy jog from here? It's as if we'd discovered a new planet, and stuck it in the fridge. What's wrong with me, that I don't stutter and stumble with excitement? And what a cool customer Clay Reed is, isn't he, so cool that a stroke hasn't carried him off. Instead, as if I'd been used to handling such things all my life—it's like slapping a fistful of plutonium in your pocket—I have been speculating over the painting as if it had no more significance than what I'm holding. Sure I'm amazed, but it's the painting that amazes, not who it might be made by."

A Leonardo, to accomplish the intimate finish of a painting like Clay's *Madonna,* or the Louvre's *Virgin of the Rocks*, needed months, even years, of well-protected and well-fed man hours, during many of which he was spending much of his time and mental energy thumbing his nose not only at the competition, but also at those who were protecting and supporting him. And, as the day spent reading up on him in the library had confirmed, Leonardo was forever going off on tangents, inventing this or that machine that wouldn't work unless someone else invented the internal combustion engine.

With the brown English watercolor still in his hands, and still looking at its back—an approach to the study of paintings that had never occurred to him until he saw Clay Reed working the room three days ago—Fred ruminated on the size of his ignorance of what went on in the commerce involving works of art. He'd fooled himself up to now, allowing his interest to be limited to the face, the form, the structures, and what he thought he could grasp of an artist's spirit while he looked into a painting, whether in a museum or a shop. Often, when he found himself with the opportunity to stand entranced, and even lose himself in a painting, he'd been recovering from an exercise that craved to occupy his entire consciousness for the rest of a life that threatened to be brief. That day in the Louvre, as he recalled, when he had allowed himself to be sucked into Leonardo's *Virgin of the Rocks*, he'd been a week out of the hospital, and moving around with a good deal of discomfort.

What had entranced him? A rage that was either his, or the painter's, or that might be shared, in the same way as a jolt of electric force leaps out of the earth to meet the stroke of lightning. It had nothing to do with commerce, or so he had thought until now, holding this object in his hands, he considered, "Whether the picture's good or bad, in its day, and even now, it has been and it can be reckoned in terms of hundredweights of turnips, or spare parts for assault helicopters, or raw furs. It has a history, and part of that history is commerce. One day it was wet and being worked on. One day it was dry and the painter's wife or mistress said, 'Willie needs shoes.' In the two hundred fifty years between then and now, where has the watercolor been? Who framed it? How many times has it been framed? What is this London gallery? Was the owner of the shop a friend of the painter's? What's his story? Who bought it? Or was it still in the painter's estate when he died in a ditch, or was hanged for some crime, or poisoned by his lover, or drowned in Dordrecht harbor?"

The Grand Street Gallery in London must have a history also. Its label signified something. Did its presence not add reassurance to the picture's initial buyer, like the presence of the Treasurer's signature on a bank note? Even to today's buyer—supposing Fred decided that he wanted to own a dismal scene of Dordrecht

Harbor to give class to the vestibule of the place in Charlestown, if he asked Franklin Tilley to give him a price on this picture, wouldn't he himself be reassured to find this old label fixed to a work so firmly that its seals (in a manner of speaking) had not been broken? But if he asked for a price, how much would he not have to know about the commerce in works of art, before he could judge whether the price demanded matched the going rate for such objects in the world at large?

Clay Reed had made a truly remarkable leap of courage, trusting in his own eye, disregarding all appearances, proceeding past the double-triple fake of Franklin's subterfuges, and exchanging currency for what might still turn out to be no more than what it seemed to be, a box with an odd top.

Chapter Twenty-eight

But why, for an object as old as the watercolor he was holding, were there no other markings to give him an idea of its history? No fond mother had written on its back, "Happy Christmas to Benny, Dec. 25, 1837." No auctioneer had written a lot number on it in yellow chalk. No signal hinted at the picture's transition from one set of hands to another, by inheritance, by gift, or by exchange for fourteen pounds sterling, or seventy thousand dollars, or for a barrel of salt horse on a Dordrecht dock.

"God, I'm an ignorant cuss," Fred said, hanging the picture back where it had been. He gazed around the room to see where his instincts might lead him, and his general sense of ignorance increased. It was like looking at the crowd at dawn in a Calcutta street, in which each human, living or newly dead on the roadside, had a complete or pending invisible story, in addition to the surface appearance that presented itself, and which might or might not be a fair indication of the underlying story.

Tilley had set up something resembling a gallery or shop, but without providing any of the signals of reassurance that a shop uses to keep its clients docile. Nothing informed you, The good stuff is in this corner. Nothing was priced. There'd been that little flap last Sunday night/Monday morning, in which Clay Reed, beating Franklin at his own game, had pretended interest in the painting of the penitent Magdalene (complete with breasts, her own, and presumably someone else's skull), while Franklin pretended the painting might be by Mantegna, might have belonged to his great grandfather, and—because that's what he wanted for it—might be worth three million dollars. Or, according to Suzette Shaughnessy, two million. It was, in its own way, not unlike the Great Game in which, not long ago, Fred had been a player in Southeast Asia and points north, south, east, and west. With the exception that in the present game, Fred's ignorance was almost encyclopedic.

You had to believe a profit motive existed in the equation. Thinking, therefore, solely in terms of the object as commodity, what could the *Magdalene*'s initial value be to Franklin Tilley? One million? Seven hundred dollars? There was nothing to give any guidance at all as to any one of these paintings' realistic fair market value. If they were houses, they would have to be *somewhere*, and that somewhere would have a lot to do with their value. The same house, same number and quantity of bathrooms, kitchens, et cetera, would be worth seven times as much in San Francisco as it would in Cheyenne. Pictures, though, were portable. Their values, whatever they were, were inherent, and depended a good deal on the knowledge both of the buyer and of the seller, each of whom, by convention, was apparently expected to set out to lie and to outwit the other.

Fred found that he'd crossed the room to look at the purported Mantegna again. All these considerations had nothing to do with whether the painting was any good. Nor even whether it was from the hand of Mantegna. A signature might help, if the boys had been signing their pictures in those days. But a signature, in any case, would be easy to fake. Much easier than a painting.

As far as Fred could feel it, the painting was the product of an honest impulse on the part of its maker. It was the result of weeks, maybe months, of effort, as well as years of training. If the subject was not original, originality was not regarded as a necessity in the time and place where the picture had been made, whoever made it. And the identity of the maker may not have been that big a deal. Or else the maker thought to himself when he was finished, "Only I could have made this. The object itself is proof."

It wasn't from humility that a painter such as Leonardo didn't stick his name in the corner of the *Mona Lisa.* "It wouldn't hurt Franklin to provide a chair," Fred grumbled. No, Leonardo knew that his name was all over what he had painted. The whole thing, in his day, blazed his identity. How could he imagine the tide of ignorance that would sweep over the world after his death, so great that somebody had to write his name onto the *Lady with an Ermine* in the Czartoryski Museum, doing his best in Polish, *Leonard Dawinci*, making the whole thing seem a fake if you wanted to start from the authenticity of the purported signature. But then you looked past the signature at the skin of this painting in which the woman held a weasel who looked so much at home in her arms that you could imagine it licking the drops of water from her eyelids after she showered.

Fred made a detour to the bedroom to get a pillow he could sit on while he waited. The bedroom was without pictures. Their absence, next to the over-supply in the front room, was disquieting. How could the man pretend he cared about these things if he wouldn't sleep with them? Wasn't everyone supposed to believe they were all his?

Fred pried a pillow from under the Aztec spread as the sound came of the key in the apartment's door. A rough male voice, "Over there, wiseass," followed by a scuffle and the sound of a blow.

Fred wandered into the front room holding his pillow. The large man who had entered with Franklin paused, his right fist raised, glaring at Fred as Franklin, who'd been knocked off balance, struggled to convey equanimity and poise.

"Since I was expected," Fred explained.

"Misunderstanding," Franklin blurted at the same moment, in the direction of neither of the two men who had invaded his space. The stranger, interrupted, was lowering an arm that had been dressed for warmer weather, instinctively measuring Fred's size, weight, and possible style. The T-shirt was light blue, the skin burned dark, and in choosing to wear baggy shorts, he had also elected to stand out in Boston as an interloper or tourist. He conveyed an air of brutal confidence.

"Shock troops from Atlanta," Fred guessed aloud, plumping his pillow.

The man's attack was sudden, subtle, and supple. But it was based on barroom rules Fred knew too well. The start was the kick to the heel, meant to unbalance him, but Fred, seeing it coming, stepped aside and simultaneously grabbed the striking left arm, twisted it up and behind his opponent, fast, and ran him, not gently, into the wall next to *Shipping, Dordrecht.* The picture shook at the near impact, making the room's reflection in its glass wobble.

"This wilderness needed more monkeys," Fred said.

Chapter Twenty-nine

He kept hold of the man's arm and maintained his position doubled over, head shoved into the wall, a good old-fashioned Boston wall made of lath and plaster. Plasterboard, the man's head would have kept going unless it lucked out and hit a stud.

"Friend of yours?" Fred asked Franklin.

The man in the shorts heaved and twisted. Fred shoved him tighter against the wall.

"More like an acquaintance," Franklin said, rubbing his left shoulder and wincing.

"Carl, meet Fred. Fred's a client. An *important* client."

The man in Fred's grasp grumbled something, the tension lapsed, and Fred relaxed his hold, letting the man stand upright, his face red with fury.

"I was early, you weren't here, I came in," Fred told Franklin.

Carl's red face worked. His breath reeked of alcohol. He bunched his fists, heaved his broad shoulders in the tight blue T-shirt. Humiliated, he wouldn't stop being trouble.

"A lucky break," Fred said, picking the pillow up again. He'd been obliged to drop it. "Sorry, Carl. I'm nervy. Too fast to pull the trigger sometimes, and I apologize. I should have held off, waited to get acquainted."

"Important client," Carl said to Franklin. "Should I care?"

"It's complicated, Carl. This isn't like tending bar. Like I told Mitchell...."

"Mitchell," Fred said. "Another monkey."

"Mitchell is next," Carl said. "Franklin, get this. You say it's complicated? For you, maybe. I go through life, most everything boils down to the bottom line. Life and death, Buddy. Simplify your mind. Stop caring about the suit, the skoozy apartment, the *important* Boston contact. You've got a package for me." His attention was all for Franklin. Fred might as well be the maid, standing there with the pillow.

"Right," Franklin said. "I'll get it."

"I'll stay behind you while you do," Carl said. He glared around the room, disregarding Fred. "Skoozy apartment," he said. "The rug."

Franklin looked automatically down at the rug and saw he was standing on it, wearing his shoes. He blushed and knelt to unlace them, explaining, "House rules."

"For chicks I take off my shoes," Carl said. "If I have time. When I climb into bed with them. If *they* have time." Everyone looked at Carl's brown leather Nike high tops, and at the protruding cuffs of the white athletic socks that hugged his ankles, striped with a blue that matched his T-shirt.

"Mitchell says, on this carpet, nobody wears shoes," Franklin insisted.

"Speaking of Mitchell, where's Mitchell?" Carl demanded, swinging his head belligerently on a neck whose width was more than sufficient to support it. He jerked the head toward Fred. "The tough guy, your *important* Boston client, has his shoes on, wiseass."

"Medical condition," Fred said quickly, before Tilley could make a mistake.

"Like infected feet," Carl helped. "Ringworm?"

Fred said, "Which, once it gets into the rug, the carpet, it's there forever. You gentlemen are busy. I'll come back."

Carl, with reluctance, and operating in the shadow of the invisible Mitchell, had knelt to unlace his Nikes, which he put next to Franklin's shoes by the door. In his athletic socks, and keeping within arm's reach of Tilley, he moved across the breadth of the carpet and toward the bedroom.

"The rest of this, I could give a shit," Carl told Fred. "The rest of it, the setup, the shoes, the carpet, the rest of it, the suit, I could give a shit. You got that? I get what I came for, I'm out of here."

"I'll wait, then," Fred said. He pitched his pillow against the wall and sat on it, leaning back, as Franklin and Carl went into the bedroom and closed the door behind them. A minute passed. Two. Three. Whatever the men were up to in there, it was quiet. The sound of another blow. Carl opened the bedroom door and stood there holding a small blue gym bag. He said, over his shoulder, "That's a message. And you can pass it along to Mitchell. If you see him before I do. Wherever he is. You say you don't know? So I stick around. I'll find him." He crossed the enormous carpet in his white sport socks until he stood in front of Fred, studying the situation and looking for an exit line. "You want a medical condition?" he said, after sufficient study. "Next time we meet, I'll give you a medical condition." He strode for the door.

"Your shoes," Fred reminded him, making him stop to pick them up.

"Asshole," Carl told him. He picked up the shoes and marched out, one hand encumbered by the shoes and the gym bag, the other with the stage business of opening the door. He slammed it after him. He'd have to sit on the top step and put the shoes on. You can't tie bows in your shoelaces while working to intimidate the man who has already run you into a wall.

In two minutes more Franklin staggered out of the bedroom. His left eye was swelling already, and blood showed on the cheekbone under it. "You're still here," he said, staring with disbelief.

Fred said, "Put ice on that." Tilley probably hadn't been hit since seventh grade. He made free of the bathroom and the kitchen's refrigerator and put together a cold pack for Franklin to hold to his face. Then he sat again as he had been.

"Not my business," Fred said, "but you could use different friends. Unless—maybe Mitchell is a sweetie? Based on what I've seen, and not for the first time, and not that I like you in any way—just, as one monkey to another—you might want to watch out for the guys you're running with."

Chapter Thirty

"Fuck them," Franklin said. He was still standing in the center of his private gallery, in his socks. Black socks with a gold toe. He held the cold pack to his face and winced. "Thanks, by the way, for playing the guy along. When there's a misunderstanding, a gap in communication, they don't have the sense to send someone with a brain."

"They," Fred remarked. "Incidentally, who answered your phone? In Atlanta?"

Franklin narrowed his available eye and sat against a wall perpendicular to the one Fred had chosen, allowing his head to rest under the painting of the gentleman in the red waistcoat. He said, "These guys have a confidence problem. How you got in I don't know. I don't care, since I guess it's a good thing. Sorry about the interruption. Let's get on with it. You want the money."

Fred allowed what might be a look of encouraging sympathy to seep into his face. "The money," he prompted.

"For the chest. According to Suzette…."

"Ah," Fred said. "You've talked with Suzette. Already?"

"We're working together now. Keep it simple. According to her, you can deliver the chest."

"No kidding," Fred said.

"The problem is," Franklin said, "in terms of the money, you'll have to…."

"Yes?" Fred prompted.

"Crossed wires. My working capital…. It'll be a couple days more," Franklin said.

"You mean Friday." Franklin said nothing. He winced and adjusted his compress. "The day Agnelli gets into town," Fred went on. A pause extended between them. "What do we say next?" Fred continued. "Small world?"

"You happen to know some of my business," Franklin said. "That doesn't make it your business. Your business is the money Reed Gingrich sent you for, if you're with him. If you're on your own, fine. Don't bring the chest here. Better I go to it. You'll have to trust me, now, like I trusted you, for the money…. I'm good for it."

Fred yawned a lazy yawn. He'd learned how quickly Suzette had passed along the fictitious name Reed Gingrich. But this new bluff was based more on hope than on anything Suzette might have told Franklin. Fred had promised nothing. Why let them imagine they had a prayer of getting Clay's Leonardo back? When he had put the yawn away again Fred observed, "We spend a lot of time talking philosophy, you and I. Sometimes, before you take that leap of faith, you ought to look where you're going. Reed Gingrich doesn't send me, as you put it, anywhere, or to do anything, anytime."

"But I offered…." Franklin closed his mouth on the rest of the sentence his frustration was causing him to blurt out.

"Talk to me," Fred invited.

"Suzette's telling the truth? You're working together?"

Fred yawned again. "We've talked before about asking questions. You are not learning. Unless you have your correspondent physically overpowered already, as soon as you ask the question you reveal your own vulnerability. You ask my connection to Reed Gingrich. But it gives me no advantage to answer you. I just drop into my wallet the fact that you want to know."

"What do you want, then?"

"Another question. Does it mean, How can I help you?" Fred said. "I don't think so. Suzette drew a mistaken conclusion. I didn't come to sell back the chest. I want its provenance, that's all."

"My business is confidential. My clients demand that. My clients on both sides of each transaction."

Fred said, "Clients like Mitchell and the lovely Suzette Shaughnessy. And Carl, of course. Carl is a client?"

"The eye's closing up," Franklin said.

"The name Franklin Tilley may already be associated with some funny business," Fred said. "People who don't know your face might recognize the name and shy away from the person it goes with. I would. Or the terms of your probation don't allow you to leave the state of Georgia. Or you are hiding out from Mitchell, and/or from Carl and whoever Carl represents, and now Carl, since he had this much trouble finding you—how did he find you is another of the questions I am not asking—and Carl is pissed off, and...just some random speculations. I don't care about all that, understand? The money Carl took with him? I don't care. I just want the object's provenance."

"Listen," Franklin said. The interruption stopped Fred's flow of thought. He waited while Franklin Tilley wrestled with what he wanted to say. "Listen," he decided. "Frankly, I'm in a jam."

Fred asked, "Have you noticed that whenever a politician, for example, uses the word 'frankly,' the next thing out of his mouth is always a lie?"

"You can help me," Franklin said. He shifted the cold pack on his face and groaned. "I said I'll pay ten grand in cash, but listen, between us, the chest is worth more. Could be."

"I ask myself, How come it's worth so much money?" Fred said. "You I don't ask." He let the observation rest.

"Shit," Franklin said, disgustedly. "It's not even worth what Gingrich paid. It's just, this other guy wants it."

"And my mission?"

"Convince Gingrich to sell. For whatever. There's ten thousand in it for you. The profit you make off Gingrich, that's up to you."

"I'm bad with numbers. Didn't Suzette Shaughnessy say twenty?"

"Twenty then," Franklin said.

"I mean that she'd pay twenty for it. Commission. On top of the ten."

"I'm confused," Franklin said.

"You are," Fred agreed. He studied the situation a moment before he continued, "The problem with your plan, or *a* problem, as a plan, is, *if* Gingrich still has the chest, which he denies, if a person like me goes to him with an offer like that—twenty thousand, fifty thousand, whatever—it makes him think it's worth five times as much, whereas *we* know it's not worth what he paid for it. If he has it. He says he doesn't."

"We'll find out. Suzette Shaughnessy's tracking him down."

"What if the chest is already mine?" Fred asked.

"Shit!" Franklin said.

"And what if you have accidentally informed me that it is worth a good deal more than thirty thousand dollars? Serious money. Another question I don't ask."

"Shit!" Franklin said. "Listen, we can work this together, can't we?"

"Here's one we can both answer," Fred said. "Is that the doorbell?"

Chapter Thirty-one

The bell rang again. Franklin rose to his feet and crossed to the intercom next to the front door, held the receiver to his ear, and told it, "Yes?" He listened and added, "I'll buzz you in." The questions in his visible eye as he looked over at Fred remained unspoken.

Fred shifted on his seat, but it did not make him more comfortable.

Franklin opened the door to Clayton Reed's elegant self.

"Mr. Gingrich," Fred exclaimed.

"Your conservator—if that's what you call him—is already here," Franklin guessed aloud. Clay's face, as he took in Fred's presence, revealed nothing. He inclined his head slightly and, unbidden, knelt to unlace his shoes. The gray suit he was wearing fell into perfect line as he stood again. He walked to the center of the room and looked slowly around at the four walls. He sniffed the air in disapproval. The tension stretched as it does in a poker game the moment before someone loses a great deal of money that he may not have.

"Cigarette smoke," Clayton complained.

"I control what I can," Tilley said. "What I can't, I don't. Some people are incorrigible."

"A couple of developments," Fred began.

"An advisor," Franklin kept on. "Not someone you want to cross."

Clay held up his hand. "The Mantegna," he said to Tilley.

Franklin, the improvised ice pack held against his dripping cheek, began to speak but was cut off.

"Couple of developments," Fred pushed on.

"I want that chest back, Mr. Gingrich. I'll pay good money for it," Franklin said.

"The one with the monkeys on it," Clay said smoothly. "It has been sold."

"This man, Fred, says that he bought it."

"Indeed." Clay let his eyebrows rise to a lofty height. He shrugged. "The issue is closed," Clay said. He was poised in front of the painting of Mary Magdalene now, looking it over with a quizzical eye. "Mr. Tilley has hurt himself," he observed, in a voice that struggled to suppress its satisfaction.

"A friend or associate named Carl," Fred said. "A messenger from an as yet un-named associate. Who is also looking for a mutual friend of theirs named Mitchell."

"You know Mitchell?" Franklin blurted. "Where the hell is...."

Clay shrugged the interruption off as if it were no more than a light breeze ruffling the pile of his white hair. The hair was too white for whatever age Clayton was. Was it real? Did he have it done? On purpose?

"I want to examine it under a black light," Clay said. "The Mantegna, as you call it."

"Black light?" Franklin asked. "Isn't that for growing...?"

"You have none?" Clay scolded.

"I don't have a clue what you're talking about," Franklin said.

"He's confused about many things," Fred said. "But I have to say you've lost *me* now."

"The black light reveals paint that is not original," Clay explained. "Because newer paint fluoresces differently. Some of the later additions to the *Magdalene* are clear to the naked eye. Here, for example." He crossed to stand closer to the painting. Fred got to his feet and joined him, and Franklin moved in closer, tipping his head in order to focus with his good eye. "Under the breast here," Clay pointed to Magdalene's left breast, "in the shadow, someone has filled in for lost paint. It was clumsily done.

There are areas, too, in the sand, the sky, the skirt. This is all to the naked eye. A painting with this much age has usually been retouched many times. How much of the original paint surface is left...I cannot say. Mr. Tilley, you offer to sell, at a premium, an object not only whose identity you cannot guarantee, but whose condition you do not know?"

Franklin, without responding, turned and crossed to the hallway leading to the bathroom, disappeared into it, and came back a few moments later without the cold pack. The left eye was swollen shut, and taking on color. "It's up to the client," he said. "Decide for yourself. Examine it any way you want."

"I shall take it only on approval, subject to further examination," Clay said. "Naturally I shall give you a receipt."

"Are you out of your mind?" Franklin exploded, before he remembered himself, and the league in which he was attempting to feel comfortable. "Under some stress," he fumbled. "Sorry. No can do. The consignor won't let the object leave the premises until it's sold."

"Also," Clay said smoothly, "I shall need the work's history."

"I noticed metal folding chairs in the bedroom closet," Fred interrupted. "If anyone wonders where I am, I'm getting them." When he brought the two chairs back into the room and started to set them up, Clay was saying, "Surely, for an item that purports to have this much importance, you keep a file. Provenance. Exhibition history. That's what I wish to see. As is common. I shall take it with me to study." He sat in one of the two chairs Fred had placed on the rug. Fred took the other and both of them faced the *Magdalene* as if it was a television set.

Chapter Thirty-two

"You mentioned a consignor just now," Fred prompted. "Though you also said you yourself bought the picture. Or inherited it? In any case, the bill of sale...."

"Exactly," Clay chimed in. "That will be helpful too. The bill is in the object file." He sat expectantly. Franklin shifted uneasily from one foot to another.

"The service I provide is confidential," he said finally, repeating himself. "I don't reveal the name of the painting's present owner any more than, you being the purchaser, I will reveal that fact to the present owner. This confidentiality is a crucial part of the service I provide."

"Suzette Shaughnessy," Fred said. "You seem to share a good deal of information with her."

"Yes. She is working with me. Partners. In a single restricted project. You know the project, Mr. Gingrich, though you claim the issue is closed. She called on you?"

Clay said, "Unfortunately, I have not had the pleasure."

"Never mind all this," Franklin insisted. "And I'm talking to both of you, or either one of you. What will you take for that chest?" His urgent tone, along with the damaged eye, made the plea almost pitiful.

"We have no further business," Clay announced, standing and crossing to his shoes. He knelt to put them on, adding, "I want nothing further to do with you, Mr. Tilley."

"I'm about done here too," Fred said.

"Think it over, Mr. Gingrich. I'll call you," Franklin pleaded.

"Regrettably, my number is not listed," Clayton said. Fred followed him out. Once on the stairs Clay said, his tone tinged with regret. "You did not do that to Mr. Tilley?"

"Carl is visiting muscle from Atlanta, representing the power behind the operation. He walked out with a satchel of cash, I assume. I saw the satchel, not the cash."

"My name has become Gingrich?" Clay said. "I can't say that I like the name Gingrich."

"They were bound to look for you, given how much they want the painting back. So I gave them a name," Fred said. "Which we can bet Suzette Shaughnessy at this moment is hunting for."

The afternoon had turned chilly and damp. They both turned down the hill, walking side by side as if they had the same destination. Charles Street, when they reached it, was bristling with foot traffic and choked with cars whose drivers cruised with an eye for nonexistent parking places that might open up in time to be nabbed just before the meters stopped functioning, in which case they'd be set until morning. Clay finally broke the silence. "You were in the neighborhood," he said.

Fred said, "Let's hang back and make sure Tilley doesn't try to follow you. He's dumb, but he's desperate, and he may be sly. I might as well let you know, I dropped the hint to Suzette Shaughnessy—we lunched—that the chest went from you to the Agnelli Collection. She's not working for him at all, to judge from her response. Hoping to sell to him, she pretended to be *with* him. You and Agnelli cut her out of the loop, is her conclusion. If she believes that. She can go to Agnelli and ask him but he'll deny it, and she won't believe him, is my guess. And if she asks him, she loses a lot of face, and maybe the customer. Then I dropped the hint, both to her and to Tilley, that in fact I own the thing. When Suzette and Tilley compare notes, there's going to be confusion. That can't hurt."

Clayton waved his hand for silence. "The reason I kept the appointment."

"Yes? I wondered since you said you wouldn't."

"Very well. No matter. At least six of the paintings in that room come from the Brierstone collection. Shall we go now? I take it you are going in my direction?" Clay sounded resigned.

They walked in silence for ten minutes, as far as the antique store above which the woman with the snake tattoo lived. His woman. Fred's woman. Her name tugged at a vanished cord in a dark part of his brain. "Brierstone," Fred said. "That so-called hypothetical yarn you were spinning about the *Diana de Milo* the other day. You were fishing. Testing. Looking for what I knew."

Clay said, "It would have been instructive to see your face indicate an awareness of the Brierstone name. I could not rule out the possibility that you and Tilley were acting in collusion. It would have been a clever ruse: you, the worse villain, snatching me from the jaws of the first villain, and using the occasion to gain entrance to my home." Clay took hold of Fred's arm with his long fingers and stared into his face as if he were considering it as a possible addition to his collection. "I was confident that I recognized the *Magdalene* and one other," he said. "The *Bacchus* by Titian. Not in good shape. It's why I came back this afternoon. To check. To be certain. If it was a risk it was worthwhile, because now I am almost certain that I will confirm the Leonardo's provenance.

"I am a suspicious man by nature. I suspect the veracity of almost everything except my instincts. Although I may on occasion have misread my instincts—a reading may be diverted by folly—my instincts themselves are never wrong."

"I am happy for you," Fred said, "even though you change the subject."

Clay started walking again, his hand, at Fred's elbow, propelling him forward in company.

"I have made a decision," Clay said. "Come to my house. We'll discuss it. That is, if you are free."

"I have nothing pressing," Fred told him.

Nothing more was said until after Clay had opened the big front door and led the way into his parlor. The *Madonna of the Apes* was where Fred had seen it last, propped on the love seat. Fred's eyes flickered to the other paintings hanging on the walls. The walls had been painted a dull deep green. There was too much, and too much variety, to be taken in quickly, although it was nothing like the almost meaningless clutter of the collection in Franklin's apartment. What put Fred off balance here was the odd juxtapositions of works. It was as if, in the zoo, the rhinoceros, the sturgeon, and the brown recluse spider were presented in contiguous cages.

"Sit," Clay invited. Fred found a chair that would accommodate his size, took off his windbreaker and sat, the jacket across his knees. He'd chosen a place from which he could keep his eyes on the *Madonna* and on the apes as well. While Fred studied the painting, Clayton sat in a flimsy chair that had been designed for one of Marie Antoinette's off moments, and studied Fred.

"Where would he have seen an ape?" Fred asked, after the silence had lasted long enough.

"In Milan," Clay said. "Leonardo had come to Milan, after difficulties in Florence. Difficulties, I say. It could have been a mortal difficulty. He was accused, with a young musician, of sodomy, for which in those days burning at the stake was the legal remedy prescribed, although said remedy might have been more honored in the breach than the observance. He must have had friends in Florence, colleagues, who were jealous. I forget the outcome of the accusation but he must have been acquitted because, fortunately for the world, Leonardo was permitted to live. You ask about the apes. Leonardo studied animals. He studied everything. The duke of Milan, Ludovico Sforza, would have kept a zoo. In the 1480s anyone wishing to maintain any degree of pretension was obliged to keep a coterie of exotic animals. Not to mention musicians, armed guards, and mistresses. You mentioned one of them earlier, downstairs."

"I did?"

"Certainly. Cecilia Gallerani. It was she who modeled for the Krakow painting you spoke of, *Lady with an Ermine.* By the time she was fourteen years of age, that ambitious young lady was in Ludovico Sforza's bed."

"Nowadays we'd call that statutory rape," Fred said. "We'd blame the duke."

"Indeed."

Chapter Thirty-three

"I spend hours studying my painting," Clay continued. "Thinking about it. Doing research. Anticipating what will be said and published in the years to come, after I am dead. Even when we make allowances for habits of style and execution, there is a striking resemblance between the head of the *Madonna* before us, and that of the *Lady with an Ermine,* and even, when you look, of the head of the angel Uriel, who appears in the Paris *Virgin of the Rocks.*"

"What became of her?" Fred asked.

"The angel?"

"Cecilia Gallerani. The job of a strongman's mistress isn't easy."

"By 1493 she had been set aside, along with a son—the duke's—and a husband the duke chose for her. She had a dowry large enough to allow her to commission her own castle. It amuses me to think that my painting may have stayed with her. That's one hypothesis. The painting displays more than a hint of wickedness, wickedness suitable to an illicit alliance. But this hypothesis is fueled in part by my own conservatism in such matters. Neither Sforza nor any of the thousands of public figures of his day, including cardinals and popes, saw anything out of the way in keeping a mistress. She was no more than a necessary piece of stage business: an expensive prop."

Clay paused, distracted. "How did we get onto Cecilia Gallerani?"

"You were speaking of the zoo you either know, or think, Ludovico Sforza kept in Milan," Fred said, "when I mentioned the apes. That's not why I'm here. What you are actually doing, while we converse, is to mark time while you organize your thoughts, putting off whatever you really want to say."

Clay twisted his hands together, thinking. "It does not matter that you see a painting differently from the way I do," he said finally. There being no useful answer, Fred let the observation go. "I notice that you have the ability to be candid," Clay continued. "That's rare." Fred let that pass unanswered also. "You were there again this afternoon. I should be enraged and suspicious, yet I am neither. Why? You are working with me," Clay said finally. "I repeat myself, but I can't think why."

"Join the club," Fred said.

"You will find I am not inclined to pry into matters concerning your personal life or past history," Clayton said.

"Suits me," Fred said.

"Will you require time to settle your personal affairs?" Fred spread his arms. "As long as it suits us both," Clay continued, "the office space downstairs can be yours. The couch—you have a place to sleep?"

"I do," Fred said.

"As for salary...."

"I'll tell you what I want," Fred said. Clay tilted his head inquisitively. "I said there is nothing I want and it's not true. Candid, but not true. I've been thinking about it. I want to see the other sides of those paintings downstairs. The ones you have turned to the wall. That's what I want. Salary, sure, we'll figure that out, and the rest. Until one of us says to hell with it.

"Now. The Brierstone collection. Tell me about it."

"Very well," Clay said. "I am pleased. Delighted. There is no time to waste. As you say, the operation on Pekham Street is clearly temporary. Equally clearly, not legitimate. Thank God we brought at least the Leonardo into safety. At any moment, all the rest could vanish. As I told you, I thought I recognized the *Magdalene* that first visit. I'd thought about it before, having seen it reproduced in an old issue of *Adonis*, an article about the Brierstones' country house in Kent. There had been collusion between the family and the editorial board of the magazine, because within the year the estate was put up for sale and the contents, apparently, dispersed. The *Magdalene* appeared, with others that are presently a few blocks from where we sit, in photographs showing the drawing rooms and staircases of the house. Such images stay in my mind. In particular the *Magdalene* had caught my attention because the caption reported the authorship of one of the Brierstones' paintings to be attributed to Mantegna. The caption seemed to relate to this painting, though it was not clear. I remembered because it was easy to see, even in the photograph, that the painting could not be by Mantegna."

"Did your chest show up in any of the photos?" Fred asked.

"I did not recall it. I took time yesterday, in the museum's library, to go back to the old issue, find the article, and study the photographs. Though I still could not resolve the issue of the purported Mantegna, not even to ascertain whether it was the *Magdalene* at issue, as I say, I identified six paintings: six paintings from the Brierstone collection, that are presently on the wall of that man Tilley's apartment. The inference is plain. Unless he has already sold to Tilley, Brierstone's last heir is quietly and secretly selling what he can, the least notorious objects from the family collection, here, outside of England, clandestinely, in order to evade the taxes due to the governments of both countries. I don't know for a fact, but I presume, until further notice, that the chest was part of the Brierstone collection which, in its time, was varied and considerable. I have already set a researcher to work, in England, to find pertinent records. Wills. Inventories. In the big families such records are always kept."

"So it's a tax dodge," Fred said.

"My purchase was made in good faith," Clay said. "It is up to the seller to collect any sales tax due. I have no knowledge that Tilley does not mean to pay the Commonwealth of

Massachusetts its five percent, even though he was so generous as not to require it of me."

"I mean, as you just implied, whoever is selling the material now, in the U.S., is avoiding British taxes. The obvious next question…" Fred said,

"Exactly. Who is the heir?"

"Is, Who is the heir?" Fred said.

"According to the article, when it was published he lived in South Africa. He does not set foot in England, according to what I can learn, on account of legal matters. His name is Peter Hartrack, and, reading between the lines, he may well be a scoundrel. Though my sources in the world of art are multifarious, when it comes to doing research in the world of scoundrels…."

Fred said, "There are people I can call…."

"I thought as much," Clay said. "Good. Excellent. Proceed. I am pleased, Fred."

"The office downstairs?" Fred asked.

Clay, nodding, said, "I'll leave you to it, then. I am obliged to go out for dinner. The door locks itself as you leave. I notice you do not smoke. I cleared out the desk drawers, anticipating this eventuality. May I say again how pleased I am. I placed a blanket on the couch, should you wish to nap. A nap often clarifies the mind. Anything you wish to look at while you are down there, by all means, do. You are most welcome. I have taken note, also, that you understand how to handle a painting.

"I must dress, or I shall be late. I suggest that for the time being you not answer the telephone. People would be confused. Well, then…."

"About the phone," Fred said. "One thing. The calls I make, for information about Hartrack—you'll be billed for them as usual, but only the charges will appear. At least—the numbers that show on your bill next to the charges, those numbers, if you call them, will get you only the recorded message that they are temporarily not in service."

"Ah," Clayton said, his face breaking into the first smile Fred had seen on it. "I am delighted." He paused, hesitating as if before giving away his deepest secret. "Incidentally, Fred. As long as we are working together now. You should know: I am no thief, nor do I condone or abet thievery. Should it be proved that the Leonardo was not properly offered to me, I shall take what recuperative measures are indicated. Be under no illusion. It will have been an honor merely to house the work, and to protect it, however briefly. When driven to it, I am capable of nobility."

Chapter Thirty-four

Ten-thirty. If Clayton Reed had returned, he'd come through the upstairs entrance and he'd been quiet about it. Fred left his notes on the desk, took a look at the old leather couch, gave it a smack, and made for the street.

Though his office provided a window through which he could see the feet and lower legs of passing dogs and pedestrians, he had not noticed the fine persistent rain that had developed. It was cold and smelled of new leaves. Also it pierced directly through his short hair and ran down his face and neck. If he'd thought to do so, he might have picked up one of the umbrellas from the blue and white vase next to the entrance door. But he hadn't thought of that until the door was closed, and he was locked out.

His buzz at the intercom bell next to the antique shop's front window got him a sleepy "Hey?"

"Amnesia?" he said. "It's Fred."

"Just a minute," she said. "I'm on the phone."

Fred took what shelter he could in the building's doorway until, ten minutes later, she came down and, seeing him through the glass door, gave him a wave. She was enveloped in a large terry-cloth wrapper, bright yellow. She opened the door and told him, "You're wet," as she stepped aside for him, put out her hand and said, "You have suffered enough. My name is Mandy. Short for Amanda. Come upstairs. I've been watching a truly stupid monster movie with the sound off while I talk to my mother. God!"

Fred followed her to the fourth floor. Mandy. "So, I'm forgiven?" he asked.

"Hell no. It's just easier," she said. "I'm in bed. It's the only warm place there is. The heat's off." She ran through the apartment's single room, throwing Fred the yellow wrapper and climbing naked into bed. "Hang your wet stuff in the bathroom. Maybe it will dry by morning. Put on the robe and don't come near me until you are dry."

A television the size of a breadbox, on a table on her side of the bed, was pullulating with vague maggoty monsters that had likely been conceived in Japan. While Fred took off his loafers she was turning the sound up with the remote. Sounds came from the film, resembling slobbering, growling and, distantly, human speech.

"God, that woman," Mandy exclaimed as Fred made for the bathroom. He hung his clothes on the shower rod over the tub, and dried off before he pried himself into the yellow robe. It had been huge on her and barely did for him if you did not count the inches of wrist it did not cover.

"I wanted to see you again. I didn't think—I should have brought something, Mandy," Fred said.

"I've got everything," Mandy said.

"A house present I mean. Nothing was open, and besides, I didn't know I would stop until I was here. That sounds...."

"Random," Mandy said. The TV gulped. "Random and episodic."

"Like a bottle of wine," Fred said. "So I'm not empty-handed."

"There's Scotch someone gave me," Mandy said. "Or, I know, make us some tea." The TV gulped again. "God! The idea is they eat the people alive, but slowly, a lot of them at once, and they have gotten mixed up with bees somehow, so there's a queen monster maggot who gives the orders and there's a good chance they'll take over the world, which I could tell them is a mistake but they're not asking me. There's Lemon Zest and Red Zinger and something else that has no taste at all with chamomile in it. Mugs in the cabinet. I want sugar and milk."

Fred began fumbling in the kitchen alcove. "Do you care which one I make?" he asked.

"They're all the same."

The TV gulped.

"God!" Mandy said. "Someone told them about my mother."

Fred found a saucepan in which to boil water, and two mugs with mottos on them: *Fuhgeddaboudit* and *The Boston Globe*. He looked for real tea and, finding none, elected the Lemon Zest and the Red Zinger and put a bag of each into the saucepan. The TV gulped. After the water had boiled he filled the mugs, added sugar and milk to Mandy's, and carried it to her. She sat up, letting the bedclothes fall to her waist. The left arm, reaching out for the tea, brought the snake's tail writhing forward.

"Come," she said, glancing beside her to the unoccupied side of the bed.

"I'll spill everything," Fred warned.

Instead he hoiked a chair from the little dining table and sat by the bed, across from the TV. The maggots continued eating what, it appeared, had been an honest and well-meaning newspaper reporter. But there was another newspaper reporter, even more honest and well meaning, and with a girlfriend, who would probably come out of this Okay.

"Random and episodic," Fred said.

"With a monster movie, what else do you expect?" Mandy asked. "I was talking about my mother, though. In this movie everybody's got a prevailing motive. The maggots want to take over the world. That's dumb, but it makes sense. Take it over, eat it, I guess. The other people—the reporters, the girlfriend, and now the army—see how those bullets just kind of ploodge through the maggots without hurting them? What do you do to a creature that has no organs, after all? No brain, you can't shoot it in the head. No, I've seen it before and a wise and kind old scientist who has discovered a gene that everyone thinks could destroy the world, instead it's going to purify the world by infecting all the maggot monsters. It's, well, a kind of anti-Nazi movie as I read it."

Chapter Thirty-five

"What I was going to say," Mandy went on, "the good guys—the girlfriend is a student of the wise and kind old scientist. Their motive is to save the world and also, obviously, have sex—I mean the girlfriend—though the movie is too old-fashioned to mention sex beyond rolling their eyes. Which I'm not up to tonight, do you mind?"

"Fact is, don't be insulted, I came for your company," Fred said.

"Okay. So really, it's not that random and episodic, it's just—you run into someone, who knows what's in their mind?"

Fred said, "The wise old scientist looks like Einstein."

"I wasn't listening," Mandy said. She sniffed at her tea and drank. Her dark curls swept briefly across her forehead.

"When I was a kid, I spent time on a farm in Iowa," Fred said. "Cows. Dairy. A herd moves around its territory in a regular, predictable way. The beasts have habits, and those habits take them beyond their private, individual motives, like eating or copulating or swishing flies with their tails. You get odd birds who are good at spotting weak points in the fencing. But for the most part, after you live with them long enough, you know pretty much what they are going to do next. But if you were on the farm for one day, and happened to watch them, random and episodic is what you'd conclude."

"The tattoo," Mandy said. "I thought about it for six months before I did it, saving my money. Yet everyone, when they saw it, assumes you don't do that except as an impulse purchase."

"Exactly," Fred said.

"The snake has a bad rep, I figured, among Christians anyway. You know, how the Virgin Mother is going to crush its head beneath her heel? Seemed awfully bloodthirsty for the mother of God. This isn't India! And the nuns used to threaten me with her when I was little? So I figured, I was about twenty-two at the time, and the idea didn't leave me until I acted on it: 'Crush this, Baby!' Ever since then, the Virgin Mary and I have gotten along just fine. She doesn't mess with me, I don't mess with her.

"Everyone thought this tattoo was random and episodic, whereas in fact, once you get to know me, it's only the tip of the iceberg." Mandy drank again. The queen of the maggots said, "They shall all be destroyed. No one shall live." She slurped and smiled in a maggoty way. "My mother," Mandy said. "She still won't talk to me. She was on the phone with me for an hour."

"Complex woman," Fred remarked.

"Not really talk. You don't know what they want," Mandy said. "Unless someone writes them a stupid line to say like 'They shall all be destroyed.' But you're right. Mom's more complex than that by a mile. They've already tried diplomacy."

"You've lost me," Fred said.

"The U.N. When the first reporter, the dead one, realized the maggots talked English, being genetically modified by radiation. It's really more than you need to know and I wouldn't be watching it except, well, hell, it's on."

"Talking about motives," Fred said.

"We were?"

"In a way. I was going to make an observation about someone, but I lost track of what the observation was going to be. In my experience, sometimes while you are watching the main character, the one in front, figuring out what he or she might want, you lose sight of what's happening in the background—let's say for example there's a bunch of monkeys running around."

"This film's gonna blow a gasket if you add monkeys," Mandy said. "There's a scene coming up I like, then I'm turning it off. Take *War and Peace* for example."

"Okay," Fred said.

"Sure there's a lot of monkeys running around, all with the same name, or all the same person but with different names. You choose. Then there's the maggot monster, Napoleon, who says, 'They shall all be destroyed. No one shall live.' And there's another guy, Pierre, who's like the wise old scientist except he hasn't got a clue and he doesn't have a formula either. Well, he has a formula, but there's nothing to go with it. It hasn't been developed. So when the whole thing's over the monkeys have pretty much taken over and there's Pierre in a rocking chair, still with no clue. The rest of it I didn't follow but it wasn't going anywhere. Now watch. This is the scene."

The maggots had withdrawn from the screen. The wise old scientist had gotten onto a plane, along with the surviving and handsomer reporter, Tad, and the handsome female student, Monica. A storm was shaking the little plane up and down, lightning played outside the windows against which stagehands were throwing buckets of water. A stewardess bounced down the aisle and teacups and glasses flew off the tray.

"I love it," Mandy said. "The maggots aren't enough. They get to the White House, the President is in bed with pneumonia, it turns out the Vice President is in league with the maggots, has been the whole time."

"Complex," Fred said.

"Exactly. Yes. Like my mother," Mandy answered. She killed the thing with the remote. "If I ever have children, which I won't," she said, "it will only be to get my revenge."

She'd emptied her cup and Fred took it, with his, to the sink. Outside the window the rain was stronger.

"You're not married, are you?" Mandy asked.

Fred shook his head. "Never. I told you that."

"Although you make a good cup of tea. Will you join me? In a minute." She slid out of bed and half-closed herself into the bathroom, from which watery sounds emerged to join with the rain.

When was the first time that a painting made in the Western world depicted falling rain?

Chapter Thirty-six

At four-thirty in the morning Fred's eyes opened and it was clear they would not close again. He stared around the room, listening to the regular breathing of his companion. The air on his face was chilly. They'd burrowed under two blankets. Then Mandy had turned the TV on again. The maggot movie had been supplanted by a similar one about spies from an unnamed Middle-European country, and Fred slept to the familiar sounds of gunfire.

He couldn't just leave again. Not for a second time. Not after she'd promised to make him eggs for breakfast. But neither could he happily sit in her straight-backed chair for three hours or so waiting to do the right thing by a pair of poached eggs. Using the street light coming through the window, he searched a table that had papers on it and found the back of an envelope addressed to Amanda Mont, on which to write, "Dear Mandy: Gone for a stroll. I'll be back for breakfast. Love, Fred."

Where would she look first? The toilet's cover might be inappropriate. He found a spot in the kitchen alcove next to the sink and put it under one of the mugs they'd used for tea. No, that wouldn't do. It was the one that said *Fuhgeddaboudit.* He replaced that with the one advertising the *Boston Globe.* He dressed in his damp clothes and went out and down the stairs into a night that dripped intermittently, but whose rain had stopped.

What had awakened him had been a general, if palpable, misgiving, as if he'd been trapped again. Any building could do it. Anyone's house. Anyone's bed. But that wasn't it. It hadn't been this pleasant interlude in an attractive woman's house. No, he'd wakened with the realization that he'd been blindsided by Clayton Reed.

The older man, odd as he was, apparently cowed by his ingrown mannerisms into a parody of incompetence, had already proved himself more than Fred's equal twice. No, three times. He'd acted with speed, courage, and finesse, and walked out of Franklin Tilley's trap, carrying a treasure that might be worth millions, if anybody cared. He'd proved himself almost as impervious as Fred was to the painting's possible value. His statement that it was worth more than the gross national product of Latvia had been made for dramatic effect, not because he imagined cashing it in. And, finally, he'd bettered Fred because he'd sucker-punched him. Clay had known what Fred wanted better than Fred himself did, and therefore he'd landed Fred.

Fred, barely aware that he wanted anything at all, had swallowed the hook along with the bait. Because he wanted to see, and get his hands on, Clay's collection, without confronting the issues of ownership that allowed him no peace. And now Fred had fallen into a game in which only Clay's presence allowed him the rationale to participate actively. He'd thrust himself forward and Clayton Reed, with stealth and dexterity, had not only sized him up but reeled him in.

A dog's whining brought Fred out of his reverie. Without thinking about it, he'd reached the river, walking the wet grass of the Boston side, away from the city's center, and toward Alston, Brookline, and points west. A piebald dog without collar and tags—a loner, like himself—was fretting over a bloody suit that once had held a man. What was left of the man was still in it, though the head was gravely wrong. Fred squatted to look closer. Lights from infrequent passing cars, not far off on the parkway, flickered across the bloody face, black eye and all, of Franklin Tilley. A bullet fired up through the roof of his mouth had taken off the back of his skull. It had happened here, and not that long ago. The body was warmer than the night, though its feet lay in the river. The bridge they were under dripped on both of them, the dead man and the body.

"They'll look for the gun in the river," Fred mused. "That's the plan. And if they don't find it, they can blame the river. That's the plan."

Franklin Tilley had been returned to his lowest common denominators. "Your curiosity wants to know what it's like after you die," Franklin had said, continuing, "There's no ham sandwich waiting. You turn off." If there was in fact a ham sandwich waiting, Franklin Tilley knew now whether it included mustard.

The dog whined again, asking permission to lap at the blood and brains that lay around the dead man's head.

"Go ahead, friend," Fred told her. "You need it more than he does now."

Twelve minutes later Fred, in a public phone booth on Charles Street, at the circle under the MTA station, doing his best to control his rapid breathing (he'd been running) was reporting, "…under the overpass. Looks like suicide."

Eight minutes later Fred, wearing the yellow terry-cloth robe, was sitting in the closest thing Mandy had to a comfortable chair, letting the street's lights fall where they wished, into the room, and onto the crags of his face. There was nothing to read in here, and if there was, there was no reason to read it. Nothing to read but the message he'd written Mandy, and that was already torn into many pieces and flushed away. He'd be here when Mandy wakened, and in that way he would have been here all night. "Jeekers," he whispered. "Clay Reed's prints are all over the man's place. So are mine."

Once he'd warmed up he went into the john again, checked that his clothes were hanging as they had been when he first took them off hours ago, gave a final rub to his head with a towel and flushed the toilet again. Then he climbed into Mandy's bed. She nuzzled his neck in sleep and wrapped him with an arm and a warm leg. "Mmph," she said.

Fred stared at the ceiling, then at the window and the walls. He learned everything on the walls: the mirror, the calendar, the photo of Mandy with an older man, in a frame. That could be her dad. The colored picture of cherubs lying on their stomachs, their chins propped in their hands, saying to one another mischievously, "I'll show you yours if you'll show me mine."

Chapter Thirty-seven

Mandy's poached eggs were not bad. It was distracting, in a pleasant way, that she cooked wearing nothing but an apron, and that the apron said *Be Cool* on it. Fred had again been assigned the yellow robe, and that would allow his clothes more time to get closer to dry.

Having cooked, and before they sat at her table with instant coffee, toast, and her poached eggs, she'd removed the apron and put on a blue robe that was either silk or nylon. They chatted over breakfast, a comfortable pair of strangers, until Mandy remembered, "I have to be in front of a mess of over-aged teenagers at ten. Business Math, they call it. It's how to do your taxes. In hopes they ever earn enough. So I'm back Sunday night," she added, around an impending forkful of egg and toast.

Fred remembered, "The wedding. Cleveland. The dress with long sleeves. May I see it?"

"Not unless you come to Cleveland. I'm not taking my run today. Unless you want to."

"Not today," Fred said. If he started running he might not stop. "Sirens last night," he added.

"Most nights," she said. "If I'm awake I hear them, but when I hear them I don't notice them."

"Around five. This morning, really," Fred corrected himself. "Unless you object, I'll wash the dishes."

She mopped up a spill of egg with the last of her toast and handed him her plate, telling him, "You wash the dishes and I'll wash me."

"What time Sunday night?"

"Nineish, I guess," Mandy said. "Move your clothes. More like ten-thirty."

Fred walked to the drugstore on the circle and bought a better cup of coffee. He stood in the area where people did that, next to the newspapers, to drink it, keeping his ears open. If there was any place where local news developments might be mentioned, this was it. But nobody brought up a local sudden death, and Fred wasn't about to accentuate his profile by bringing the subject up himself with what couldn't help but be a memorable question. "Anyone found dead in the neighborhood last night?" would raise eyebrows.

Sudden death in a big city is not that big a deal. Not news. He strolled back to the corner of Pekham Street and, seeing no commotion in the vicinity of Franklin Tilley's last stand, he walked uphill to the mouth of the alley. Did anything connect Franklin Tilley's body to this place? If so, there should be activity in Franklin's building. Aside from a mournful visitor entering the dental surgeon's office for his nine-thirty appointment, there was no sign of life. No sign of bustling institutional interest or concern. Had Franklin's body carried his ID? If so, the inquiries would be directed to Atlanta.

A man's shape passed back of the curtain in the front window of Franklin's apartment. A heavy, sturdy shape.

Fred took himself to Mountjoy and rang Clayton Reed's downstairs bell. In two minutes Clay appeared above him on the front stoop. He was at leisure in the blue robe, and was holding a teacup in a distracted hand. "Bright and early. We'll get started. Apologies," he said. "I recalled last night, coming home, that I had neglected to give you keys. There will now be three sets: mine, yours, and those of the couple who clean. The big one is downstairs, the two smaller ones up. You won't need those." He tossed a set of keys in Fred's direction. "I'll join you shortly."

When Clay came down the spiral stairs into Fred's office, Fred was on the couch, checking the notes he'd made the previous evening on the index cards he'd found stacked on his work table. Clay sat on the edge of the table and waited. His feet rested next to the side of the chest, sitting vacantly on the floor there, its angels and flowers in their puzzling, stilted choreography.

"Some calls I couldn't make last night," Fred started, "on account of the time difference. I got enough info for the big picture. Peter Hartrack. But first—don't go back to Pekham Street. Tilley's dead. It'll be on the radio by now, and the TV news if you have one."

Clay shook his head. "Great heavens!"

"In the papers tomorrow, I guess," Fred went on. "If it seems interesting."

"What happened?" Clay's pale face had gone paler.

"Looks like suicide. I emphasize, *looks* like. I was sleeping nearby," Fred said. "A friend. In the early morning, restless, I took a stroll, and the stroll took me along the river. Four-thirty. Tilley's body was on the grass, fully clothed, his feet in the water almost as if he'd been standing in the river when the bullet went through his skull. Shot through the roof of the mouth, which looks like suicide. Though a friend can threaten you, shove a gun in your mouth to make you obedient, and then, once the trusting soul believes the gunman has been appeased by all this obedience, pop! The world turns off. The discharge from a .38 wants a lot of skull."

"The gun we saw there?" Clay hazarded.

Fred nodded. "That would do it. My guess is it's murder. I don't see Franklin Tilley doing that job on his nice haircut. No, a friend got him."

"Friend," Clay repeated. "You are thinking of—what did you say his name was? Carl?—who was there yesterday in that man's apartment, and took money by force."

"Yes. Carl, but acting for someone else, following orders. For Hartrack we assume, given what we've now learned, who has to keep himself on the far side of the Atlantic."

"These are dangerous times," Clay said.

"Dangerous people," Fred corrected him. "Dangerous *people*, if Franklin was playing them for suckers, as I think he was.

"We can get back to it, but this kind of trumps the rest of what I gathered for you. Last night, on the phone. On the other end of the story, and assuming you are correct that the chest comes from the same collection, the reason Peter Hartrack does not appear in England is that if he does, he'll be arrested. And he can't come here to the States, either. Yes, he's the heir to the Brierstone fortune. The problem is anything out of that fortune that gets sold in England, like the Bronzino you mentioned that was sold at Christie's, London: the crown wants all or most of it. Tax problems, the rest of it. And the only reason the government of South Africa does not let Britain extradite him is that he's tied to the right people in the right places, in South Africa; which he knows can change any day since governments change. So he's cornered. Stuck in South Africa. And unsure that South Africa will work for him indefinitely."

"Why would he be arrested? What's his game?"

"Arms," Fred said. "Above the table and below the table. He's an international arms trader and there's no such thing as an international arms trader who is not also an international arms smuggler. There's no such thing as an international arms smuggler who does not, at the same time, interest himself in one side or another, or both, of any revolution that's building.

"It's up to someone to supply machetes to the Tutsis and the Hutu, and shoulder-fired missiles to the rebels in Kashmir and Kandahar. In addition to all the sales to be made in the open market, to the governments of Iraq, Sudan, Libya, Pakistan, Indonesia, Syria, and other pleasure spots around the world."

Chapter Thirty-eight

"I don't know anything about the international trade in arms," Clay said, "beyond that it's one of the ways the richer nations have to strip from the poorer countries what little wealth they have. As for Hartrack, you conclude...."

"He's trying to raise a lot of clandestine money, in cash, in this country, so as to make a purchase. That's what I hear. The people I talked to had a pretty good line on this monkey. He can't sell what he inherited in the UK, and we have to assume he hid as much as he could from the authorities there. Reading between the lines, unless he sold it there to someone who's fool enough to pay for it first and try to smuggle it out later, he's found an agent to spirit what's left of his family's collection out of England. Tilley is, or was, part of the selling end. Working under cover this way, illegally, and being ignorant anyway, they can't help being stupid. Hartrack can't do the sale in person because we normally suck up to Britain and if we found him here we'd send him back to the UK to face the music.

"So he's got to work with scoundrels. And, not knowing how to latch on to scoundrels who know the ropes and can be trusted, he latches on to scoundrels who don't know what they're doing. Which he figures may be all right, since every dollar he makes is tax free, and worth double. Being scoundrels, of course they don't tell each other what they're up to. Everyone has a dodge. Tilley made a mistake. What that mistake is, or what they think it is, I don't know. Maybe he kept money he shouldn't have. All that cash blowing around? What was that about? Maybe he spent Hartrack's money stupidly, like for the fake Cézanne. Got the bit between his teeth, thinking he'd turn a profit for himself before he got found out. He wouldn't be the first idiot in the history of the world to go down that hole. Maybe he sold something he shouldn't have sold, for not enough money. For example, to you."

"Right," Clay said, with surprising equanimity. "And you assume these people, Tilley's friends as you call them, would kill for such a mistake?"

"A mistake the size of the gross annual product of Bolivia? Are you kidding? Yes, we operate on the most prudent assumption: these people kill for the right mistake, but not until they have decided what to do next," Fred said. "We know they want the Leonardo back. At least Tilley did, calling it a chest. Nobody admits what it is. So Tilley was being pushed. Do they know they lost a treasure worth the gross national product of Serbia? That was last seen disappearing down Charles Street on my shoulder?"

"Still, murder is a dramatic response to what may have been no more than an honest mistake," Clay observed. "Though Tilley was a violent man. He struck me. Why would his colleagues be any better?" He folded his long hands and tipped his head to one side, speculating.

"Interruption," Fred said. "For what it's worth. Who's Mitchell? What was Tilley waiting for? The big deal painting he tried to promise you. What is it? Where is it? End of interruption."

"We don't need to know that," Clay said. "Much better ask ourselves, what do we want? That has not changed, despite the distractions. I still need provenance. With Tilley's sudden unfortunate exit from the story, that becomes more difficult."

"Also, and more important, dangerous," Fred said. "First, we want to stay in front of *their* speculations. On Sunday night we discovered, almost by accident, a clandestine fortune, illegally in this country, and destined to serve as barter in a large purchase, by a ruthless man. We ran off with the best part of that fortune. The amount of money I saw in Tilley's place, upward of fifty thousand dollars, is peanuts in the arms trade. Peanuts to a Peter Hartrack, even though when it's cash, and nobody knows about it, it's worth twice that. But it sets the stage. That and the art. Which I'll get to. Sure, Tilley was a fool. Still, he found you. Who else did he find? He reached Agnelli, if we can believe anything that comes out of Suzette Shaughnessy's mouth, by way of Suzette Shaughnessy.

"Keep it simple. Hartrack needs a lot of money. It was up to Tilley to get the money by selling paintings. Tilley didn't have to know all that much. As long as he got the total, maybe it didn't matter what individual pieces brought. He tried for three million on the supposed Mantegna. He knew something in the group was worth that, is one way of looking at it. He just got the wrong thing. What would you have done if he had demanded three million for the Leonardo?"

"Ah," Clay said, "but how could anyone be so ignorant? To confuse a Mantegna—even a false one—with a Leonardo?"

"Try this hypothetical," Fred countered. "We drop you into an arms bazaar on the outskirts of Tripoli with a few million bucks to spend. You want to choose between—let's make it easy. You're shopping for missiles. Do you select the American AIM-54A/C Phoenix, the much older Sparrow, or the Sidewinder? Maybe you want the UK's Skyflash, it's brand new, but how do you check on the Marconi XJ521 guidance system? When push comes to shove, will it work? Maybe you go with the French R.550 Magic or a Russian Acrid. They're on offer two for the price of one. Or maybe you want the Aphid, if you can tell the difference between them…."

"I take your point," Clay said.

"And yet you are an intelligent man. Maybe in the top twenty percent."

"I *have* taken your point," Clay said. He slipped off the edge of the desk and, dodging the chest, began to pace in the area in front of Fred. "You turned the three paintings around," he said.

"Something to enjoy while I was on the phone," Fred said.

"What do you think?"

To shift from the morning's concerns to the three paintings was like stepping from a parched landscape into a cool glade full of rushing water. Fred had turned them around the previous evening, even before he confronted the task he had taken on. Two of them were studies of clouds, each radically different from the other. One was filled with an angry and windy sunset, the other with a gliding pomposity of cumulo-nimbus buoyed up by summer breezes. Neither was signed. Both were extremely dirty. The third painting represented an Italian hill town, probably in Tuscany. It was designed with clean discipline, the architecture of the town as clever, almost as godlike, as the architecture of the hill it stood on and the hills around it. The architecture of the sky and of its clouds spoke the same hand of God, and in the case of all these architectures the god involved was neither Christian, nor classical Greek, but probably an outright atheist. The colors were laid on precisely, as if to give guidance to the designer of the real world. The small C in the lower right-hand corner confirmed the authorship.

Fred said, slowly and hoarsely, "You mentioned last night that we don't see paintings the same way. If you mean this as a test, it's a waste of your time and mine. The Constable on the left is made of righteous anger. The one on the right, of puzzled self-satisfaction. Between them, they do a whipsaw. The Corot—for the life of me I can't understand how a man who could see such logic onto the land, wasted his late years in that exorbitant fluff of chocolate box designs. True, a lot of those fuzzy, vapid landscapes are fakes. But a lot of those fakes Corot made himself.

"We don't have time for this. Listen, I don't know the values of paintings. There's a man dead, which I do understand. Since you and I are involved, and we still need information so the painting you bought doesn't implode, I have to go out asking questions. I need to understand the environment. I'm as dumb about the art market as you are about the price of sidewinders. The collection we both saw at Franklin Tilley's. In broad terms, what's it worth?"

Chapter Thirty-nine

"I've been puzzling over that," Clay said. "In the first place, there's more to say about the value of money in a transaction that is not reported. You say his fifty thousand cash is worth a hundred, and that's true. But. Everyone knows it. Therefore when the man says he wants—take the William Anderson, for example...."

"William Anderson?"

"A watercolor. British painter. Dutch harbor scene. Near the...."

"I saw it. *Shipping, Dordrecht.*"

"My point is," Clay went on, "if he asks for five thousand and I offer him two and a half in cash, he and I both know he's got his price. Therefore, because everybody expects to bargain, if I offer cash, I might start at one and, depending on how much I want the picture, and how much he wants the money, we tug back and forth until we have a price.

"I should not have given him five thousand dollars for the Leonardo. It made him suspicious. No, if I had played my hand correctly, I should have had it for three."

"I wouldn't complain," Fred said.

"It is the principle of the thing." Clay had been pacing all this while. Now he took up his perch again on the edge of the desk. "To return to your sensible question. There are too many imponderables to hazard a guess at the black market value of the collection. If you were to purchase them at a gallery, the premium would be overblown because it must necessarily include the gallery's costs in rent and personnel, in the form of commissions.

"I mentioned the William Anderson. If it were an identifiable American port, and especially if we saw a *Stars and Stripes* on one of the ships, it might bring five thousand at auction. That's what American collectors want, and that's who has money. If it were purchased by a gallery for stock, the asking price might be twelve thousand, leaving the gallery ample room to bargain. But it is not an American subject, and it is not at auction. Its condition is good, as far as I could see. If I wanted the painting I would offer two thousand dollars and be willing to pay three.

"For a sidewinder missile I could give you a pretty firm price," Fred said.

"But, like lettuces and cans of tuna fish, within each brand name, the missiles are identical," Clay said. "Are they not? If they work. Of all the other paintings by William Anderson, each is unique."

"Try it this way," Fred said. "Say the guy dies. The government knows about the collection and wants its death duties. Somebody puts a value on the collection. An appraiser. Where the appraiser's values come from I don't know, but...."

"They take the auction record into account. Those are published. The prices realized by all the creditable auction houses. You can look up William Anderson and see what his view of Dordrecht should bring, more or less, barring unforeseen events. But by tradition an estate appraisal's a good deal lower than, for example, an insurance appraisal or an appraisal made for the purpose of a gift to a charitable institution. There's room...."

"Give me a guess," Fred said. "How much does Hartrack want for the whole shebang?"

"If he knows it included a Leonardo?"

"We assume he doesn't know. Give me a ballpark."

"Too many imponderables," Clay complained. "I don't know what half the pictures are. And I don't know what they *think* the pictures are. Some look like tourist frauds from two centuries ago. Some, like the Dierck Bouts, appear to be honest and excellent pictures. For the Bouts, if I had three hundred thousand dollars to spend, I would spend it."

"Which was that?" Fred asked.

"The little *Crucifixion* next to the fraudulent Cézanne that has since disappeared. For that, incidentally, if it were not a fraud, the retail price to be expected would be in the neighborhood of two hundred thousand. But for other pieces on the wall the values would be some in the thousands, some in the low ten thousands. On the other hand, what I took to be a late Titian, the *Head of Bacchus*—You spotted it?"

"Maybe not," Fred said.

"If I am right, though damaged, probably three million. Overall...." Clay squeezed his eyes shut and calculated, using his fingers. "Let's level the field and hypothesize that these works, with a published provenance, were legally offered at public auction. The estimated hammer price might fall—don't hold me to it—between fifteen and eighteen million. That's counting the Titian as a Titian, extracting the false Cézanne, and leaving the Leonardo out of the equation."

"Not much in the arms market," Fred said. "Therefore they want the Mantegna to be a Mantegna, and they sure as hell want that *Madonna* back. What's it worth? Don't give me the gross annual product shtick."

"The Leonardo alone, properly vetted and published, should realize between a hundred and a hundred fifty million. Easily. There has been nothing like it on the market. What would the *Mona Lisa* bring? More or less than the Taj Mahal, do you think? On that score things have changed, I have to say, drastically, and recently. Just twenty years ago or so, in the late '60's, the Metropolitan Museum in New York passed up a chance to contend for the *Ginevra de' Benci* we've talked about already between us. Too expensive, they thought, when the National Gallery scooped it in for six million. If it came on the market today, you wouldn't get near it for eight times that figure."

"At those kinds of numbers, you just stop thinking about money, don't you?" Fred said.

Clayton looked demure. He twitched. "If I valued my collection for its monetary equivalents," he said, "I should be a bundle of nerves. I do not."

"It would be like valuing Bulgaria for its monetary equivalents," Fred helped.

"Meanwhile, there is our duty as citizens," Clay pressed on.

"Duty as citizens," Fred repeated.

"Regarding the death of a fellow citizen. Regardless of the fact he was a villain," Clay said, "the authorities must be informed."

"I did that right away, but quietly," Fred said. "I don't like the anonymous telephone call, but our prints are all over that man's apartment. We could help them with what we know, but our civic duty to a dead fool won't make him less dead or less of a fool."

"Our civic duty is to the living," Clay scolded. "We don't want them here, as they would be, were we to interfere. You made a wise decision. Prudent. Meanwhile, your research last evening. The next step may be to make direct inquiries at the source. Did you find an address, perhaps a telephone number, for Peter Hartrack?"

"Jumping Jiminy," Fred exclaimed. "Think!" His exclamation had brought him to his feet, within inches of Clayton's perch. Clay winced but held his ground. Fred turned, took a few steps, and sat again.

"Not a good idea, you think?"

"The man's a major force, involved in a shady transaction in which he wants his involvement to be secret. The reason for the transaction is shady, and secret. He's a merchant of death already. And five hours ago, here's a violent end to one of his team. Now you want to telephone Hartrack and ask him to explain his part in these events?"

Clay clasped his hands and studied the proposition. "He is free to deny his connection."

"That advances our cause not one inch, and puts a collector who lives on Boston's Mountjoy Street square in his sights.

Take my advice. It's what I'm here for. Say nothing to anyone. Do what you're good at. Work from Leonardo's end. It's where your talents lie. See what you can learn about this painting's past, if you can do it without being seen to be looking. Let me work among the living," Fred said. "And, if need be, the very recently dead."

Clayton was adjusting to this demand while Fred put on his windbreaker and headed for the door, adding, "We have no choice. Things are moving. We have to know what they are. I'll go and talk to Suzette Shaughnessy. No. Better. I'll make her come and talk to me. But I need bait. With your permission, since it belongs to you."

Chapter Forty

Fred waited on Bolt Street, outside Bernie's place. There was no way anyone not prepared for it would believe this was a living space, and not some tiny version of the Old Abandoned Warehouse so beloved of movies that have nowhere else to go.

The bones of the building were brick, and a dingy side door next to the two rolling overhead garage doors might have been stolen from the seediest of grocery stores in a bad part of town. Though there was a button to push that seemed to lead to a bell, nobody would believe the bell was in working order. "Join me for lunch at my place," Fred had told her and, such as it was, he had it with him, in a paper bag.

Suzette Shaughnessy was dressed in a blue summery outfit that was premature, and that had required her to throw on a sweater as well. Her golden hair sparkled with damp. She carried a large black bag and a dazzling smile that was, this late morning, a bit off center. She'd come on foot.

"What do you, live here?" she demanded, disgust and dismay struggling to break through the ambient jocularity of the question.

Fred said, "I'm watching the joint."

He led her in through the garage and watched her dismay darken and waver as, turning, she saw evidence of the security systems Bernie had installed to protect his cars. The one hooded vehicle, under its tarp, brooded as they went past.

"Upstairs," Fred directed her.

He drew back to let her precede him up the staircase and they jostled on the landing as he pulled out the key to Bernie's living space. Once in, she threw her bag on the floor by the couch and begin to deliberate whether to take off the sweater. It was a thick knit, of dull rust color. It was chilly up here and she concluded that she needed it. When she sat on the couch and crossed her legs, most of the dress disappeared under the sweater, and most of her legs emerged, clothed in sheer white.

"Shall we talk first or eat?" Fred asked. "There's subs. Your choice. Tuna or Italian. I can make tea, I think."

"Business first. It's good you called," she said, patting the couch next to her. Fred pulled a chair from Bernie's small all-purpose dining and worktable and sat where he could see her. "You're probably the only one who can help me," she said. "I have a thing about people and I know when I can trust them." She crossed her legs the other way. "Where is Franklin Tilley?"

Fred's silence, accompanied by slightly lifted eyebrows, invited elaboration.

"I stopped by," Suzette continued. "To pick him up. On the way here. I knew you wouldn't mind, since naturally Franklin is interested too, and you're working with Franklin, and...but... and so am I, naturally, now...anyway, Franklin wasn't home. Another man answered the door. Carl. Told me Franklin had been called away suddenly. His mother is critical. Carl doesn't know where. Not only not what hospital, not even what city or state. 'It was real sudden,' is all he would say. So Franklin's got cold feet, and he's hiding out, maybe. Unless the mother story's true. Carl wouldn't let me in. He made me real nervous, I have to say. He was nice enough, but he made me afraid."

"Did he have his shoes on?"

Suzette's outpouring came to a sudden halt.

"Sorry to interrupt," Fred said. "Go on. That no shoes business gets to me. Did you happen to notice, Carl, did you say his name is? Is it a rule of the house? Or just Franklin's rule. Was Carl wearing shoes?"

"Scaggy white socks," she said, and tittered. She smiled, almost like her old self.

"And the shorts with the bags on the sides, and a T-shirt. He looked, I took him for the janitor or the cleaner. No, he said, he's a friend of Franklin's, watching out for the stuff until Franklin gets back. Him and those paintings...." She paused.

"Yes?"

"They don't go together at all," she said. She crossed her legs the other way. The dress couldn't ride any higher. It was gone. She kicked off a shoe and wriggled the toes. "You, since you're working with Franklin, know how to reach him," she said.

Fred scratched his face.

"Or if you don't, you can find out from Carl. Carl might respond to size. Ask him. We can ask him together. Later. First things first. You have a line on that chest," Suzette said. "According to what you said on the phone. Yes?"

"'Let's talk about it over lunch' were my exact words," Fred corrected her.

"It's been a god damned wild goose chase so far," she said. "And I hope to God—listen, Agnelli's coming tomorrow. We're expecting. He's expecting...."

"Not the Mantegna," Fred exclaimed.

Suzette snorted. It suited her. "You know and I know what Agnelli wants. Why should we play games with each other? We're on the same side."

"We are?"

"Once the chest got away—and Agnelli swears he doesn't have it. 'I'd never do that to you, Sweetie,' he says. Which is why I come back to you. Because there's a market for it. There's only the one other thing over there that Agnelli would care about. A lot of what's left isn't even Italian. And I want my commission. There's enough to go around. Unless—is this collector you're working, Gingrich, hot for the Titian as well?"

Fred shook his head slowly. "We don't like the condition."

"Hell, if I could look that good in five hundred years...." She leaned toward him and looked piercingly into his eyes. "I mentioned your name to Agnelli and he said, 'Who?' Then I mentioned Mr. Gingrich and he said, 'Don't bother me.'

"Therefore, knowing Reed has an inside track—Franklin told me he had to hold up on selling anything else until I don't know what—here I am." She smiled and shimmied out of the sweater, which she laid on the couch next to her. She patted it into place like a large and embarrassingly obedient dog. She noticed where her dress had gotten to and pulled at it, without much result. "Tell me about you and Gingrich."

"He and I are not close," Fred explained. "We happened to have a project that interested us both. Nothing in your league. To save time and money, we decided to work on it together."

"Sounds interesting," she invited.

"These things never are," Fred demurred. "They start interesting, everyone's filled with hope and excitement, and then they peter out. What you thought might happen doesn't, or what you thought might be something turns out to be something else."

"You're talking about that chest," she said. "Which you bought together. Or you bought from Gingrich. Franklin told me. So, where is Franklin?"

Fred offered, "If I hear from him, I'll call you."

"You can do better than that," she wheedled. "Get Gingrich over here. I want to watch him while he answers the question what he did with that chest."

"Let's lunch," Fred said. He stood.

"Franklin. Tilley," Suzette insisted. "Where is he? Shit, who cares? You want to talk about that chest? Forget about Tilley, then. I'll handle that end. Maybe it's simpler. If he's gone, he's gone. Sell me the chest."

"There are some issues I wonder about. Mitchell. Where is he? And, as long as we are doing business together, you and I, who are you? I asked for your card before," Fred said. "You'd forgotten it. Remember? In the other bag? Isn't this the other bag?"

Suzette bit her lip and studied the situation for thirty seconds before her face broke into a dazzling smile and she exclaimed, "Of course! I remember now. I thought it was a *déja vu*. At that horrible restaurant, yes? I'm telling everyone—everyone I hate—to go there. I should have made you meet me there today. It would have served you right. But I wanted to see…." She swept her bag off the floor and pulled a card case out of it, from which she extracted a pasteboard rectangle that she turned over to Fred along with the tail end of the dazzling smile. Fred took the card and sat again to have a look. *Suzette Shaughnessy Fine Art* it read on the first two lines, in large print, serious, not florid. Then, below, almost as if in parentheses, *Consultant,* with an address on East 83rd Street in New York, and numbers for telephone and fax.

Fred tucked the card into his shirt pocket and gave his version of a dazzling smile, stretched out his legs and crossed his feet, ready to listen. Suzette had quailed somewhat before his dazzling smile, which tended to show teeth. "Yes?" he prompted.

"First, I've only told Agnelli about the collection," she started. "It took me a week to get through the god damned secretaries. There's six in a line, like the cartoon where the fish are lined up, the little one followed by the bigger one and so on, all with their mouths open, until the biggest one, Agnelli, swimming along, is just smiling and saying to himself, in bubbles, 'I can wait.'"

Chapter Forty-one

"Let's start with how you learned about Franklin Tilley's pictures," Fred said.

"No. We start by we shake hands and agree, scout's honor, we split the commission."

"The commission," Fred drawled.

"Sure. Anything we sell to Agnelli. Anything else. Since we are working together. We work as a team now. We sell to your man Gingrich, we're together. The chest—I assume you're not just bullshitting me. Anything else. The Titian. You can get the chest, am I right? Agnelli swears he doesn't have it."

Fred held out his hand. Hers was small and warm and dry, with a firm grip that did its best to encompass his, and failed by two thirds. "Fair enough," Fred said.

"Okay," Suzette said. She folded her hands in her lap. "Forget what I may have mentioned before."

"We'll file it with what the Nixon White House classified as *inoperable.*"

"They did? Anyway, now I'll level with you. A friend of a friend of mine was in school with Franklin Tilley. My friend was…."

"What school?" Fred asked.

"Art school. Savannah. My friend was into restoration. Architectural. What Tilley was into…." She paused. Fred let her arrange whatever it was she was arranging in her head. "Franklin Tilley. He was from down south somewhere. Charleston? One of those. My friend…."

"Your friend's name?" Fred asked.

"Not important," Suzette assured him. "It's a gay thing. They all know each other. It doesn't mean anything."

"Mitchell," Fred said.

"And I want to see that chest. Mitchell was a professor there. Dr. Mitchell. Really, my friend you couldn't care less about. Like most of my friends. Which is why I decided to change my life.

"My friend heard Franklin had gotten involved in the picture business, which surprised him. Franklin was asking around, Who did our mutual friend know in the art world who was in a position to make fast decisions for big money for pictures, guaranteed not to be stolen, but that were needing a low profile until some time after the transactions were completed, if ever.

"So our mutual friend, being in New York, knew me, and introduced me to Franklin, and I asked him to keep the thing quiet, and I told Franklin, which is true, that I have the exact client who can commit to buy the whole thing in five minutes. He has the money, don't worry. But I had to see the collection first, get an idea of the ballpark, the rest of it. You got any coffee?"

"Maybe," Fred said.

"This is five weeks ago. I only got in at the tail end of this. Which I hope is not falling apart. Mitchell had done the expertise, telling Franklin what everything was. That bunch of stuff—well, you saw it? It would take a professor to figure it out. I met him in New York, and I was convincing, since the next thing was—Why Boston, I don't know. Meanwhile Franklin was on his way north in a U-Haul truck, all that stuff, can you believe it? Wrapped in bubble pack and blankets and strapped to the walls like it was used refrigerators. Franklin had the apartment rented already, and I guess he was handy enough to hang it, since he'd been to art school. It looked all right.

"I came up right away and my teeth about fell out. I printed some cards...."

"What?"

"Well, *got* them printed."

"You're not in the art business at all," Fred said.

"I am now. Before I was doing interior design," Suzette said. "If there's a slower way to make money, they haven't told me about it. So I know pictures all right, besides studying it in college and a year in grad school. More than you want to know. Besides all the people you have to suck up to, the client, the dealer, the other people in the field who all have a partner or spouse who's a doctor. Suck up to or, you know, worse. We could go out."

"We could."

"For coffee."

"I'll make some. You printed some cards," Fred reminded her.

"And started working to get through to Agnelli," she said. "Because I could see we were in the big leagues. Franklin didn't have a clue what he had. I mean, Titian? And in spite of that he wanted big money."

"He gave you a figure for the whole thing?"

"Sure. Fifty million. But cash. So that left out most people. I didn't know anybody like that. Not close. Except Agnelli, who is notorious. And because he does so much overseas, with governments that don't necessarily.... I have to drink coffee."

"See what I can do," Fred promised. "I could use some myself. Keep talking."

He rummaged through the dinky cabinet above Bernie's sink and found a jar of instant coffee, mugs, and sugar. The contents of the "Creamer" jar had hardened. He lit the fire under the kettle.

"So, I had a week to study the collection," Suzette said. "I've put my savings into that fucking room at the Ritz, so I'll look like I know what I'm doing. Which I do. I've handled old pictures before. I put a Goya into a private collection in New York. Lived four months on the commission. And I have people I can call. And while Franklin wasn't looking I snapped some pictures. And listened to Mitchell go on, him and Franklin snuggled up barefoot on that fucking carpet, and Mitchell telling him about painters so dead and gone their own mother wouldn't care. Mitchell thought he should try to educate Franklin because when the time came, Franklin was going to have to make the sale, or what he was after was only quality time with Franklin. You tell me. At first Franklin insisted the collection had to stay all together, which was not going to happen, and he couldn't sell it anyway, being so ignorant. Then, as I got their trust, and I had Agnelli primed and with the room reserved at the Ritz, the bastard started selling things one at a time after all. Couldn't wait. And buying, too. Did you see that Cézanne?

"The thing is, Franklin is such an idiot," Suzette said, taking the mug Fred offered her, "and then he and Mitchell fell out, which left him with pretty much me. And he never guesses when I'm winging it."

"Franklin's waiting for something," Fred said. "You've seen it, of course."

"You be careful of Franklin," Suzette warned. "He's very seductive."

Chapter Forty-two

"Tuna or Italian?" Fred asked her.

"Tuna, if it has pickles."

"Take a look." Fred handed her the wrapped sandwich and they sat together at the table while she unwrapped it, opened and approved it, and started eating.

"The collection," Fred said. "Franklin and Mitchell told you where it comes from."

"I pushed pretty hard," Suzette said. "I wanted to know for myself. That kind of money, Agnelli wanted to know. Who wouldn't. Also for me it's harder. It's not enough, especially if you don't have your own gallery space, just to tell people it's legitimate. You drop hints. The one I like is it belongs to a prominent member of society, a Lloyd's of London 'name,' who has to make good on some big loss, but he doesn't want his friends to know.

"So even if Agnelli's interested, we're not home free. Mitchell, who's never kept a secret before in his life if you ask me, says his client must be kept in confidence. Franklin won't say anything except they are from overseas, it's a willing seller who's changing his collection to the moderns, he says—de Kooning, Jasper Johns, Francis Bacon—but the client doesn't want help on the buying side, Franklin says, because I told him I know a de Kooning that could be made available. Not that Franklin would know de Kooning from Balthus."

"Why cash? Did he mention?"

"But enough about me, as they say. What's the plan?" Suzette swerved.

"The plan?" Fred said.

"To move us to the next plateau. I didn't just come for the tuna. Here's the program so far. Let's try to save this. Agnelli arrives tomorrow. We have drinks at the Ritz, he and I, and get acquainted. We'll find out how acquainted he wants to get. Saturday I am supposed to take him to Franklin Tilley's. How I get him past Carl I don't know. Or the guy Carl says is taking over from him. Unless Franklin shows up again, with those people I am back to square one. Or I wouldn't be...well, but, next step, the point I was trying to make an hour ago, we call Franklin now, right?" She looked expectantly at Fred, letting the steam from her coffee cup accentuate the squint in her eyes. "The chest, though, we'll keep that just between the two of us."

"My guess is as good as yours where Franklin is," Fred said.

"Shit. Then my next point, as long as Franklin is out of the picture, and since I know Agnelli wants the chest, the two of us sell him the chest. Anywhere you want. My room at the Ritz? Even if the whole Franklin deal is a washout, that way we have something left."

She'd eaten half her sandwich. She wrapped what was left, pushed it aside, and rose to search in her bag for a pack of cigarettes, from which she pulled and lit a volunteer.

Fred took the last bite of his sandwich and worked on it, sorting and filing the wealth of new information Suzette had brought, any part of which might or might not be true. The trouble with a good liar is that truth comes from the lips as easily as the lie. "Before we proceed further," Fred said, "I need to confer with Mitchell."

"Who said I could...?" she started.

"Forget it," Fred said. "Mitchell is in this game. You're working with Mitchell since you're too smart not to. Franklin's too dumb to put this together. And you're too smart to be working with Franklin anyway. So. Put Mitchell where I can see him, or all bets are off."

"After all this, you have nothing to contribute?" Suzette demanded. She put her lighter and cigarettes back into the bag. "You fooled me. I trusted you. The deal is off."

"No commission," Fred said. "Rats. How much was it going to be?"

Without another word Suzette turned for the door. She'd reached it before she turned again to see Fred, sitting where she had left him, at the table, his hands around the empty mug.

"Let's say, as a hypothetical, I can find Mitchell, even produce him," she said. "If I can do that, might you recall something about the chest that for the moment may have slipped your mind?"

"Not impossible," Fred said.

"And in the meantime, since we are working together, and you don't know where Franklin is, maybe you want to prove it by coming with me and asking Carl. Since we are working together."

"I could do that."

"Let me think," Suzette said. She came back to the couch, where her heavy sweater was still lying (that would have wrecked her exit! Sweeping back to pick it up or, worse, having to ring the bell to come back for it), and sat down.

Fred said, "You've come a long way on bluff. Congratulations. Problem is, there's only so much bluff you can sell. Though you are very good at this, you have nothing. You are in the void that exists between stuff that is real, and the people who own it, and/or the people who represent the people who own it, and the people who want it, and/or the people who represent the people who want it. You have to separate all those people from each other because if you don't, you get left out. No commission. Meanwhile, all you have to your name is a business card, a room at the Ritz, a lot of gall, and a great nightgown. You've got Agnelli interested. That's a plus. But you've got nothing to show him. No art, anyway. That looks like a real minus to me. Don't we need each other?"

"We add your bluff to mine?" she said. "The chest you may or may not be able to put in front of me?"

"What else do we have to sell?" Fred asked reasonably.

"We split fifty-fifty."

"That's agreed already," Fred said.

"And we'll go talk to Carl?"

"We'll do it now."

"Can I use the phone first?"

"Cut off," Fred said. "Since my friend's traveling."

Her face changed as she made her decision and said, "If I find Mitchell, you should know he's keeping a low profile. He and Franklin had a falling out, I told you. Mitchell won't speak to him. Go easy with Mitchell on the Franklin subject. Promise?"

"I hear you," Fred promised.

Chapter Forty-three

A steady rain had developed out of somewhere. Fred poked around the garage area until he laid hands on an umbrella he could offer to Suzette. It was a sad object, more than ready for the knacker's yard, and certainly no match for Suzette's outfit—but it would keep her more or less dry.

"Boston," Fred told her. "You want to expect rain. Especially during the spring or any other season."

"Not unlike New York," Suzette said. "I left the hotel in a hurry. Someone told me they had something I'm looking for."

The rain pattered earnestly onto Fred's head, and onto the windbreaker. He'd become wet, but he'd been wetter.

"If that isn't your place, where does a person find you?" Suzette asked. "Your piano, your goldfish, the rest of it. The things you have to sell. What do you have? You're not listed with Information. What are you looking for? I know a de Kooning we could pry loose for the right customer. You and I…."

Rain had darkened the steep brick sidewalks and made them slippery. The trees interfering with pedestrian traffic, or planted in the small yards in front of the brownstone and brick townhouses, were inching their leaves into the weather eagerly, and one could almost hear the pollen popping. Suzette slipped and Fred grabbed an elbow, keeping her upright.

"Where *do* you live?" she insisted. "You have an office? Gallery? Work out of your car?"

"Where you found me today is where you'll likely find me," Fred said.

Fred asked, "What's the approach with this guy Carl? If he's still there." They'd reached Pekham Street and started on the steeper downhill stretch that would lead them to the building Franklin Tilley had abruptly vacated.

"We get inside, ask him where Franklin is, and go from there. In other words, wing it. I'll talk on the intercom, since he's already met me, and disregarded me. You'll be the surprise."

"Gotcha," Fred said. He stood back while Suzette rang the buzzer and waited for the gruff "Yes?"

"I was here before?" Suzette said into the grill. "Looking for Franklin? Something came up. It might be important." The growling buzz clicked the door open to Suzette's self-congratulatory smile.

"I'll go first," Fred said. "In case he's ugly."

"He's ugly all right," Suzette said, falling back behind him as Fred trotted briskly up the stairs. Carl, standing in the doorway in his stocking feet, was taken enough by surprise at Fred's sudden appearance that Fred could shove past him, letting a heel land squarely on Carl's toes. Carl spun, swinging. His fist caught the back of Fred's head and jarred it sideways and he followed up fast, staying close and pounding at Fred's head, the windbreaker, and kicking with the sides of his feet. An all-in scrapper, making up for lost time.

Fred answered in kind, but making no effort to do more than protect himself. One canny blow, placed right, would put Carl into a sudden sleep or, worse, crush a windpipe or nose, or neck, and kill him. Not what Clay wanted, most likely, from his new colleague.

"Carl." The voice from the bedroom door was male, and sharp, and filled with easy authority. Carl swung his right fist into Fred's gut. "Let's ask what the gentleman wants."

"He wants to talk," Carl said, swinging with his left against Fred's shielding arm. "I've seen this fucker before. Talk. It's all any of them want. Watch this." He dropped as Fred's blow connected with his forehead.

The man in the bedroom doorway came forward, glared at Carl and held out a hand, glancing beyond Fred at the place where Suzette, until quite recently, had been standing. Carl, on the floor, snored. The man's suit, long hair, and white shirt placed him on the white-collar side of the entertainment.

"Likely he's been unconscious so often," Fred said, disregarding the hand, "he gets to that state efficiently. I'm looking for Franklin Tilley."

"The sales representative. Called away," the man said. "Your business?"

Fred's gesture encompassed the contents of the room. "We're negotiating. If he's gone, who takes over? You?"

The man held out a card. Carl snored. JOWETT EDOUARD PEASLEE, Attorney at Law, with an Atlanta address. "I don't take over. I hold the fort until the next representative arrives," Peaslee said.

"I've been wasting my time? Tilley has no executive authority?" Fred demanded.

"He did. No longer," Peaslee said.

"So you can't make the sale?" Fred demanded. "This is a pain in the ass. Tilley made the appointment. Now what? What can you do, if you can't sell?"

"I represent the status quo," Peaslee said. "I'd offer you a chair, but they don't seem to do that." He was in his stocking feet, Fred noted. "Come back later. Tomorrow evening. Call first. Better, give me your name and number."

"As long as you're nobody, Peaslee, I'll reserve it," Fred said. "I'll drop back unless I get bored with the whole thing. What's the situation? The owner's getting cold feet?"

"I'm out of my depth," Peaslee said. "Your negotiation with Mr. Tilley has to be placed on hold. I can't comment on it. Was Dr. Mitchell included in the conversation?"

Fred said, "What this looks like to me, I have to tell you, is a god damned mess."

"It's being straightened out. Call back tomorrow," Peaslee said. Carl stirred. "How do we reach you?"

"I'm off," Fred said. "Give my apologies to Carl."

~~~

Suzette was waiting on the sidewalk, several long paces toward Charles Street. "You were right," she said. "He did turn ugly. What did you find out?"

"Nothing about Franklin. The other man, an Atlanta lawyer—you know him?"

Her answering look gave away nothing.

"He can't make commitments," Fred said. "Says a new guy will be there tomorrow. Call first. So the next thing is Mitchell."

"If I find him, and if I can get him," Suzette said. "I have to make him believe I have that chest."

"You have the talent," Fred said. "You want to simplify this and tell me where he is?"

"I'll bring him by that place around six," Suzette said smoothly. "Six-thirty. You'll be there?" Fred nodded. "If I'm not there by seven, I couldn't swing it. Or no, well, I'll be there in any case. I might not find him. Anyway, I can't make promises for Mitchell."

"Good enough," Fred said.

"You see me with an old man looks like he's put together from cigarette butts, that's Mitchell," Suzette said.
~~~

Chapter Forty-four

"Franklin Tilley is not only dead," Fred remarked, musing as he headed back to Mountjoy Street. "If he's been identified at all, it's as a tourist from down South who strayed from the Freedom Trail. The strong arm, Carl, who knows better, tells the world Franklin left town to visit a sick mother. Correction. Suzette told me Carl said that. And here's surprise backup from Atlanta, the lawyer, Peaslee, who found out that things are in such a mess up north he has to come up himself until whatever. His line is, Franklin's called away; not the sales rep any more. Nice epitaph."

Clay, hearing Fred enter, came down to meet him in the workroom. He sat on the edge of the worktable. "Have you lunched?"

Fred told him, "I Italian subbed."

"And were you able to get satisfaction from Ms. Shaughnessy?"

"Suzette Shaughnessy is a bundle of contradictions wrapped up in the enigma variations," Fred said. "She's mostly a waste of time. Still, if she can do what she says, she might be useful. Let me think how much she said is worth repeating."

Clay twisted his hands together. His fingers had been designed to execute Chopin mazurkas on reluctant keyboards. Elegant strength, they suggested. "Start with this," he said. "It's where people betray themselves most quickly. What does she want?"

Fred said, "She wants the chest you bought. You know that. Says she's trying to find Franklin Tilley. She stopped to see him this morning, went up, found the bruiser who came in yesterday while I was there. Carl gave her the dog-ate-my-homework story…."

"Please?" Clay said.

"Fed her a line. Told her Tilley was called out of town to help a sick mother. So Carl knows he's dead, and is covering for his absence. Shaughnessy's not genuinely in the art business…."

"They never are," Clay said. "They see places to insert themselves between moving forces."

"Exactly. She smelled the situation and, since Franklin was a rube, she weaseled herself into it, expecting to collect a commission down the line, of which for a brief shining moment I was supposed to expect I would collect half," Fred said.

"As I see it," Fred continued, "the forces at issue are the collection, A. The people marketing it, B, who are now visibly represented by Carl. There's the owner, C, Peter Hartrack, unless Hartrack's already sold his interest to an unknown letter, call it X. Discount. That didn't happen. Hartrack's in Johannesburg, but a moving part in an annual thirty-some billion-dollar industry. And moving into town tomorrow is force D, Agnelli, with international stature and resources larger than the gross national product of Estonia and Latvia put together. Among the forces in play, Agnelli is a large unknown. I may not know the art world or its market, but I do know Agnelli doesn't drop whatever he's got to do in Toledo and fly to Boston just because he hears a pretty voice over the phone. You don't get where he's got that way. When you're at the Agnelli level, you expect things to come to you. You're not that rich without being ruthless, and you can't be ruthless without…."

Clayton interrupted, "You're not accusing Agnelli, are you? Don't we assume that if there was indeed murder, the murderer, Carl, is quietly sitting ten blocks away?"

"Not sitting. Lying on the floor when I saw him last," Fred corrected. "It's why I may look a little banged up. I was just there again. It's a long story and you don't need it, beyond there was an Atlanta lawyer there, Peaslee, who I'd say represents Hartrack, and had gotten wind of the fact that things under Franklin's administration had gotten out of hand. For our purposes, I don't care about accuracy: whether the killer is Carl or a friend of Carl's called in for the job, or Peaslee, it doesn't matter; or Tilley himself under pressure and not able to face the music. There's E, the wild card, Suzette Shaughnessy. And Mitchell. *Doctor* Mitchell, she told me. None of this may be important...."

"It is important to Mr. Tilley's mother," Clay protested. "Mrs. Tilley. If he has one. His friends in Atlanta if he has friends. His lover, grieving, if he has one."

"Spoken like a civilian," Fred said. "What I'm here for is to tell you that to us, for the moment, it doesn't matter. In terms of your objective. Of course the story itself progresses, as a story, in many ways, in many places. Every one of these apes has a mother, a father, a place to go next, a favorite nut, a wish to get laid. What we want is what *we* want. That's my job. I'm trying to keep it simple."

"We have what we want," Clay said, gesturing toward the stairs that led to his *Madonna*.

"Not unless we can both understand and protect her. My next point," Fred said, "and I don't remember where I am in the alphabet...."

"It doesn't matter."

Chapter Forty-five

"Your next point," Clay prompted.

"My next point is what I went out for. I may be close to a meeting with one of the other wild cards in this mix. The man Mitchell. Dr. Mitchell. Suzette Shaughnessy might be able to produce him. Dr. Mitchell is the inside expert they called in to tell them what the collection was, and appraise it."

"Some expert," Clay snorted.

"Here's one place we differ, you and I," Fred said. "I assume everyone is smarter, or stronger, or at least more unpredictable, than me. I assume everybody wants something I can't see and probably never heard of. The reason I'm still alive…."

Clay cocked his head.

"Don't underestimate your opponent."

"Very well. Dr. Mitchell," Clay said, speculatively, "is presumably someone with credentials. Doctor as in Ph.D. What else do you know about him?"

"Likely on the faculty of a college or university in Savannah. Looks like he's put together from old cigarette butts, according to my informant. I gather he has some age."

"I'll see what I can find out. Excuse me," Clay said. "We'll go upstairs."

He led the way up the spiral staircase and into his parlor, motioning Fred to sit while he used the telephone at the small table next to the kitchen.

"I'm doing what I can," Fred said, in the direction of the painting.

The *Madonna* gazed with an absent, indulgent, quizzical expression, at a point somewhere between the viewer and her unruly child, whose squirming insistence was distracting her from some meditation such as, for instance, the question, "What if I'd said, 'We'll see' when the angel asked me?"

It was impossible to look at her without wondering about her author, Leonardo, the man himself having receded so far into the past, but leaving so vivid a proof that he had lived.

It was a brown river before her, of uncertain depth. You can reflect an entire mountain in an inch of water. The aridity of the landscape she sat in was so extreme that it was impossible to imagine where the fig might have come from. The heraldic plants, sparse as they were, made their unlikely livings out of not much soil, even though the wilderness supported a good quantity of apes, and they seemed robust.

But the matters under discussion in the painting did not involve natural history, any more than Leonardo was really interested in natural history. His studies, his drawings, his speculations, all revealed his passion to impose onto the world the order, and the logic, he demanded of it. He refused to admit to chaos, or—chaos is a logical extension based on despair—he refused to admit to the possibility of a power that has no shape. It would be for him like imagining a God without a face.

In his drawings of torrents and deluges, for example, which Fred had paused over in the library recently while he struggled to become less pig ignorant about this painter, Leonardo insisted on presenting the forces of rushing water in intricate organizations of parallel lines, as if water, animate and vertebrate, could move of its own volition. Whereas in reality water falls because A, it's heavy, and, B, the bottom's been pulled out.

No, it was Leonardo's mind that was orderly, even in the machines he invented, which would not work at least until the advent of steam on a larger scale than the system he imagined for turning a spit.

"My ignorance is almost absolute," Fred murmured. A man's life was embedded in the painting, as well as the world that life had been a part of. All of it vanished, but for this shocking remnant, and some thirty others. It was as if a man and his mortal wound had disappeared, leaving only the scar. Fred went across to study the edges Clay had described earlier, the ones that had been aged artificially. He could not see the artifice.

"I'm as out of my depth as Clay would be, trying to buy those missiles I teased him about."

Clay put the telephone's receiver down with a crack and crossed from the post where he'd been conversing in low tones, pausing, and jotting notes on the small index cards he kept in a top drawer of the table.

"The news is not good," Fred guessed, seeing that fact in his demeanor.

"Two possibilities," Clay said. "Based on a quick search at the reference desk in the library of the Museum of Fine Arts. One, John Malcolm Mitchell, if he is living still, would be *emeritus.* We don't know what his present affiliation is. He is the author of numerous learned articles and catalogues, and of several books including the frequently reprinted *Italian Masterpieces of the Seventeenth Century.* That's fine. No more than one academic in twenty thousand can handle an appraisal, though many claim the ability. Those who live in ivory do not recognize that ivory is a commodity like any other. We can hope that it is he. But I fear not. He would be eighty-nine, if he still lives.

"It is the other, Fiorello Mitchell, who fills me with disquiet.

"First let me tell you something. This will amuse you. I learn from my own research into Leonardo's *oeuvre* that there is another instance where a genuine Leonardo was brutally cut from its matrix and used as the top of a wooden box."

"You don't say," Fred said. "Among the few Leonardos known, that happened twice?"

"A portion of the *Saint Jerome in the Wilderness,*" Clay went on. "At one time the head of the saint was cut away and used as the top of a coffer. By great good fortune it was discovered in a Paris antiquary's, and ultimately joined again to the panel it had come from. The result is in the Vatican collection."

Chapter Forty-six

"So there is ample precedent," Clay concluded.

"There was a time when the wood was worth more than the painting," Fred said, "is your point. If the vandalism occurred a while ago. Whereas, with your painting...."

"More recent, yes. And I cannot be simply relieved at finding the precedent, since anyone else in the world who looks could discover it also. You are about to point out that the vandalism against my painting was carried out recently, at a time when the painting should have been regarded as of more value than the wood."

"Which means no more than—" Fred began.

"We note the fact, and do not pervert our minds against the fact by drawing premature conclusions," Clay said. "Otherwise we see only what we expect to see." He'd come to stand near the painting and was gazing at it as he spoke.

"Okay. Now that you've had a chance to get your breath back. Who's the other possible? The other Mitchell. Fiorello."

"It is both wonderful and alarming how quickly one can get such information," Clay said. He sounded like someone who has very recently encountered a tidal wave.

"Spit it out. Let's not pervert our minds against facts by drawing premature conclusions," Fred quoted.

"Very wise. Thank you, Fred. Your point is well taken. Fiorello Mitchell would be in his mid-sixties, of retirement age. We were not able to find him on any present faculty. He is the author of numerous articles such as the following, published in a learned journal ten years ago. Its ungainly title: *Masterpiece and Forgery: Can Art or Science Detect the Difference?*"

"Oops," Fred said. "A buck says that's our boy."

They both stared down into the gaping hole that yawned so suddenly between them and the Leonardo. Only a tidal wave might fill it.

Fred said, "Let's change the subject while we get our bearings. I've seen no sign or evidence, so I assume it is cutting edge. Tell me about the security system that protects your building."

"There is none," Clay said. "It alerts them." He sat in the chair he had placed three days ago, from which he could survey his *Madonna.*

"If we continue working together," Fred said, "we visit this subject again."

"If you wish. You, like me, are capable of suspicion. Good. I must go out. I wish to consult the record of Professor Fiorello Mitchell's publications. If you are to meet him, it might be useful for me to have done that beforehand. During these unsettled times, would it inconvenience you to remain here in my absence? What time did you say?"

"Six o'clock."

"Ample time. I shall return by five-thirty."

Fred stood back in the hall and let Clayton open and close the door for himself. He had, he realized with a rush, the place to himself. Not for the first time, no—but when Clayton had left him here to work, a few nights back, he'd stuck to the downstairs office.

He came back into Clay's parlor, alone now in this room, as he had not been before. He was alone with these large beasts, with no bars to separate him from them.

"Is it money?" he asked himself. "Because I don't want it? The mask of money, that gets between us?"

But he didn't know where the question led, or where it came from.

It was high time he got to know the man into whose game he'd thrown his hand.

Chapter Forty-seven

"I don't think it's the money," Fred said, crossing the room. "Although I hate it as much as I hate purposeful cruelty."

Fred went first to the Hopper, and the Hopper sucked him in. He'd marked it from his first moment in this room but had never been closer to it than twenty feet. The Leonardo had gotten in the way, as well as the natural diffidence that came with being an intruder on another man's turf.

The Hopper hung over a mantelpiece setting off a fireplace that clearly was never used. The subject was roofs and chimneys silhouetted before a sky that had so much impending weather in it you could not guess what it portended. Normally when a form is seen against the light, the insistence of the luminous background forces the form into the illusion of two-dimensionality. Since the painting is already two-dimensional, this makes for a disorienting sense of double illusion, the viewer being forced to perceive an illusory two-dimensionality in an illusion of three dimensions that has been built on the two-dimensional plane. Though the paint was not really flat. Never flat. It was as rough as a city.

Here, though, the roofs and chimneys were so insistent with presence that they seemed almost pregnant. They blocked the light, defied it, and in their threatened substance claimed, to the advancing sky, "You think *you've* got something up your sleeve." Fred stood in front of the painting, reaching his right hand out to within an inch of the surface as you might with a banked fire, to test its heat.

To anyone with an interest in such things the room's rugs, curtains, furniture and so forth might be worth noticing. Overall, the room—double parlors opening into what must be a small kitchen—felt and almost smelled of Old Boston. Though nothing was shabby exactly, none of it had been polished up for sale within the last hundred years, and nothing had been new for longer than that.

The walls were green. The heavy curtains hanging at the windows were a deeper green that, if it wasn't brocade, was something worse. They were tied back with gold loops that sported tassels. The view of the outside world of Beacon Hill was masked by a scrim of white net, so that nowhere did direct daylight strike into the space. The light in the room seemed to come from the paintings, which in turn were illuminated by spots set into the high ceiling.

"What else do we have?" Fred said, although he had already done a hasty inventory the moment he first walked in, in an involuntary gesture he feared resembled the appraisal performed by what women knew as "elevator eyes."

"The Canaletto was my wife's," Clay had told him in passing, when they entered with the *Madonna* that first day. Clay's tone of voice he had not been able to read; and in any case he was not really listening. Was it dismissal or affection or, perhaps, a mingling of the two, with a tinge of regret added? The Canaletto looked as if it must have come with the house, and had been hanging between two tall windows overlooking Mountjoy Street since it had first arrived in Boston. It was a horizontal view of a Venetian scene, a gondola builder's yard, maybe two-and-a-half feet wide by a foot high. A person who knew Venice, or who had known Venice in 1740, would have been able to tell you at which juncture of which canals the painter had been standing when he made the preliminary drawings; the name of the church whose spire was seen over a peculiar rectangular building with Moorish trim; would have been able to tell you what that peculiar building was used for. The boats and the business and the scurrying people were presumably made up, or were a composite of activities the painter had jotted down in a notebook. If you were little, and sick, and stuck in bed with the thing on an opposite wall, it might amuse you to speculate over the lives and projects of the men; to count them; to note the variety of their clothing, and to ask why so many men appeared, and so few women.

Though what intrigued the painter was none of that. He loved the stage set, the gliding grace of the square-rigged buildings made almost to float on glass. The cruelty of the Venetian civilization was beautifully masked by the elegance of its commerce, and by the fact that, like the cruelty of all civilized constructions, it protected many decent humble people too busy, most of the time, to indulge in the small cruelties their natures invited them to try.

The Canaletto was a good picture. The fact that it came with the house, that Clayton had not chosen it purposely, made it no less a picture. It was, though, a badge of Bostonian generations, like the Gilbert Stuart portrait of a young woman hanging on the wall opposite. Fred studied her, but with less patience. She was presumably an ancestor of the wife Clayton had lost. What was her maiden name? Clay had mentioned it with a passing caress, but too much had been happening.

Chapter Forty-eight

Next to the Gilbert Stuart virgin or young wife, the top of whose bosom was as rosy as her cheeks, and painted with the same formula, hung a shocking shriek of obscenity that was what, in fact, had pulled Fred across the room: a woman's head contorted in a scream. It was, it had to be, one of Gericault's studies of mad women. The paint was as tortured as the strokes in the Stuart were smug. There was cruelty in the face, cruelty in the world, and a compassionate answering cruelty in the artist's eye.

Gericault had painted studies of the heads of guillotined prisoners. This was worse. Anyone looking could tell you, "This is Granny. She's been like this eight years. She'd pull her clothes off if she could. We have to tie her to a chair and change her every day. She'll only eat when we feed her by force. Threaten her? With what? She's already on fire."

Fred knew her. He'd been there. He didn't need to reach out to feel the searing heat that lurked back of the gray background. "Does the man have a sense of irony?" he asked. "Or does he hang them side by side because the background color of the Stuart portrait is almost the same gray?"

Then—was it still an ironical procession?—next to the Gericault, but separated from it by a whatnot bracket on which a whatnot made of blue and white porcelain was sitting, there hung a Dutch cow. Fred could not put a name to the painter, and couldn't read the signature. Clay Reed had the tact not to stick brass plates on his picture frames to tell himself what he was sitting on. In any case there were probably twenty Dutch painters, in the mid-1600s, who could have painted this cow this way, and this well. She was at ease on the crest of a green hill, chewing her cud and, all twelve hundred pounds of her, compressed into a rectangle barely a foot wide. The carved black wooden frame around her might as well be the "little black dress" intended to package her to the best advantage. Her charms included a coat of almost poisonous buttery creamy yellow, and a placid eye that regarded the viewer with outraged disbelief, as if Fred were saying, "Don't get up."

"Don't worry," she'd say, in cow. "I'm doing what I'm doing, and I'll keep on doing it long after you're dead."

It was all about gravity, and light, and the transformation of frail green tendrils into butterfat, and the present if waning triumph of the Dutch maritime empire. She owned it all. She wasn't moving.

A phone rang at the end of the double room, next to the kitchen. Clay kept a desk there, on which was nothing but the telephone. Fred crossed to it but let it ring. As far as Clayton's world was concerned, nobody knew that Fred had entered the picture. If Clayton was trying to reach him, they hadn't planned for it. The guy had a whole life after all, independent of the matter at hand. The phone stopped ringing. No answering machine. What had he said? "It lets them know what we are doing."

Clayton had hung a mirror over the desk, grudgingly, no doubt, since it took wall space. Except that it reflected, once the unruly lines and crags of Fred's face were out of the way, the small luminous gem from far away. From here it was only lines and color, backward: primary colors.

Fred crossed the room again, dodging furniture, including the grand piano on which sat the portrait, framed in silver, of Clayton's wife. Prudence? Lucy? Yes, "Stillton," he'd said. Fred stopped and looked at the photograph with amused surprise. She looked, didn't she—and you had to make allowances for the casual mists of loveliness thrown around their subjects by portrait photographers—but didn't she bear some resemblance to Leonardo's *Madonna?* No wonder the man was smitten with his painting.

Strange, the night of their first meeting. Fred had assumed, out loud, that the conjunction he'd happened into, between Tilley and Reed, had been an assignation. Reed, accused of the indiscretion, had responded with a surprising lack of affect. The normal response of any man would have been vigorous and, if the suggestion did not apply, vigorously negative. But for Clay, beginning from that first encounter, sexual orientation seemed to be a non-issue. Though he spoke of it, he seemed, simply, to have no dog presently in that hunt. If it was an issue at all, it was only an issue because Fred had made it one, as Tilley had. And Clayton had simply dodged away.

If the stage set tells the story, what was Clayton's story? It needed more than one mind to understand the stage set. Put a woman here, in this space, and ask her what was the story. A woman would read it better. How would Mandy understand it? Mandy coming out of the shower into Clayton's parlor, her hair wet, in that yellow robe? She'd done pretty well, figuring out *War and Peace.*

She'd look at the photograph of Lucy Stillton and say, "What do I know? The man comes from somewhere. He's obviously not from here. Chicago? California? He's done well. Princeton, he said. Then Yale. Or the other way around. Whatever. So his family had money, some, enough to send him to school.

"Then he comes to Boston. Not law. Not government work. But his business—I know—his business is Money. He works for a firm and he does well, meets other people in Money. Goes to the opera with them, maybe gets into one of the clubs, even though he's from somewhere else. Then—what makes sense? He's a fish out of water here, in a way, but he fits right in. He's a convert, is what. It's all his more than if he was born to it. And it's not his by inheritance, either, because he's a proud man. Odd bird he might be, but he has what he has because he gets what he wants."

Chapter Forty-nine

Mandy wandered the room, her bare feet leaving damp tracks on the carpets. "I know. He makes money, but not that much. Also his dad, who believes in supporting the kid just so much, stopped with the allowance one year after he got out of Princeton, or Yale, whichever came second. He didn't flunk out. Not him. So it's graduate school. Where there were other people so much like him he didn't know he was out of the ordinary.

"Anyway, he's here in Boston, doing well. Then he comes into real money. Sudden money. Which can only be crime or tragedy and since it's Clayton it isn't crime. His parents—no—his brother. His *elder* brother. Because the guy's a man in the world, and he knows he's a man in the world, but he's had the role in some way thrust upon him. He's diffident with it. So the older brother, the heir apparent, older by six years, so Clay really looked up to him—he dies in a tragic way that's also unseemly. He's murdered, maybe in a gay bar, and everyone had assumed he's straight including the girl he was engaged to. He's, whatever he is, or was, amazingly successful and he left pots of money, and all of it to his little brother Clayton, big surprise. Now suddenly this guy's a millionaire, with a brother he loves who's dead in disgrace. His parents are living still? I can't see them. They die maybe later, but they're not important because Clay's moved on."

She lifted the hem of the robe to dry her hair, bending in the diffuse light of the bay window. She was enjoying this, getting into it. "He's already fallen in love, or he's already met, the woman he's going to marry, this Lucy Stillton, from an old Boston family. Though he doesn't have much experience of love, he's suspicious of this one because he's been to Princeton and Yale and he's read the books and he can see that, for the outsider, a way to move into the social system is to marry into it, and he wants to be part of it. But he also knows that it's the woman who moves most successfully. A man moving into the tribe doesn't take on its color the way a woman does. With a woman, unless you really look, you don't know where she comes from.

"But he's rich now, because of the unseemly tragedy of his brother's death. So nobody can suspect him of being after Old Boston money, and besides in this case though the family is old, it turns out there's no money. Nothing more than illusion.

"Lucy Stillton is younger, she's pretty and she worships the guy. She's been out of Wellesley two years already, where she was good in French. She swims well. Was athletic. The family has a place on the North Shore. Manchester maybe, or a small town near there whose name I wouldn't know because I haven't been invited. She's been used to go sailing with her brothers and their friends, and they go skinny-dipping in the ocean. She's good with a boat and she's strong. She meets Clay—at a wedding? A garden party? On the neighboring boat when they tie up in Gloucester to buy lobsters? Does she take Clayton Reed skinny-dipping? Somehow I can't get there.

"Anyway she's in love, he's in love, he's the only kid left in the family now and his scruples are overcome when he understands that the family home, where he was invited last Christmas Eve, is in hock, mortgaged as far as a mortgage will go, and the family—the parents are dead? The father is, only the widow's alive and Lucy's brothers, all older, because they are MEN, have taken on or been bequeathed the family finances. And wrecked them."

"Wait a minute," Fred objected.

"Don't bother me. I'm rolling," Mandy said. She sat on a sofa, the yellow of her robe singing against its blue upholstery, and crossed her legs. "The brothers—do the scene that Christmas

Eve, with one brother raising his glass to proclaim drunkenly, This is the last time we'll be together in the old wreck, so drink up. He's tipsy but not too tipsy, since he's used to it. Let's not overdo this. It turns out the brothers have decided to sell the family place and divide whatever's left after the mortgage is paid off. They think it's worth more than it is. They always do.

"So Clay steps in, buys the house as a wedding present to Lucy, and Lucy and he move in. (Never mind that what Lucy wanted was an apartment over the harbor.) Mama stays on upstairs until she fades out of the picture, which has to be soon because Lucy is gone pretty soon herself.

"They're in love. She's young. He's innocent. They are elated when the symptoms begin, because they believe, everyone does, she's pregnant. Clayton's amazed, out of his mind. This business of carrying on the race, and the family name, he had been leaving to the elder brother and now it's he, Clayton, who is presiding at the bud that's to become a new branch on the family tree.

"But the symptoms are of something else, devastating and wasting. In four months the woman who had been strong enough to swim through waves in sea water sixty degrees, and towing a dinghy with a rope she holds in her teeth—in four months she can't walk by herself, and in six months she's dead."

Chapter Fifty

"Clayton Reed never knew what hit him," Mandy continued. As a wraith she had remarkable staying power. "How long they were married I don't know. Two years? Could he have even known her? Did she suspect, when they married, that something was wrong with her? I don't think so. She was more surprised than anyone.

"Clay was devastated. If she hadn't been so determined in the first place, they'd never have been married. And if she hadn't been three times as adaptable as he was—women are—they'd have never stayed married. He woke one morning like a man who'd had a cathedral fall in on him. Lucy'd been buried in the family plot in Manchester or nearby, and here he was in this house, this present he'd bought her, with the mother upstairs, the brothers, the nephews and nieces, the furniture and the Canaletto.

"The whole thing makes sense as a monument to Lucy Stillton. Lucy wouldn't have bought the Hopper, or the Gericault *Mad Woman*, or that cow. Or…."

"No," Fred said, "you're right. She wouldn't buy it. But Clay would, in her honor." The telephone rang again, and when Fred looked back from it, Mandy, the illusion of her, yellow terry cloth robe and all, was gone.

Fred had wandered on to the small and intense canvas that had earlier caught his eye. About eight inches by ten, the painting was the only thing abstract in the room. A slab of rust red jostled against a slab of midnight blue. Jostled was the wrong word because the edges between the two colors were clean and hard. But the two colors were so antithetical one to another that they made friction, as two well-bred people might who had hated each other for years, but who found themselves seated next to each other at the funeral of a person both had loved.

One of the Russian Constructivists? Malevitch?

Or, "Why not finish the story," Fred said. "The painting is by Lucy Stillton herself. She was one of those accidental geniuses who makes a stunning work of art, stands back, grins, says, Look at that! and never does it again. Never tries to. Never needs to. Never wants to. It's done."

The telephone stopped ringing.

Fred checked his watch. Four-thirty. Let Clayton not lose track of time in a library, the way Fred did! If Fred had any chance of confronting Professor Mitchell, there wasn't likely going to be more than the one chance. He checked that the front door was secure before moving downstairs into the space that he'd so quickly, easily, and comfortably begun to think of as his office.

While Fred had been occupied with a very living Suzette Shaughnessy, Clayton had lost no time scratching among the dead. He'd made remarkable progress fleshing out possible background for his painting; convincing circumstantial evidence that might tie the painting upstairs to the hands of the long-dead painter. Clayton had left his research lying around in the form of books with markers in them, and note cards on which he had written in pencil, in a hand that was most easily classified as "insufferable." Somewhere between Greek and Cuneiform, it was made up mostly of vertical marks running parallel, most with a slight bend sinister. Fred found that the only way to read them was to get a running start and to let the eye roll along at exactly the right speed, neither too fast nor too slow. The words had to be read more quickly than speech, but more slowly than reading. Still, except for the odd word, Clay's questions and observations were not impossible to get around.

He'd concentrated on the period of Leonardo's first stay in Milan, after he'd arrived there from Florence in 1481. He was thirty years old and, though he'd had some success in Florence, he'd had to dodge that scandal. Then he'd been passed over for a big commission, and decided to try his fortune in Milan, under Ludovico Sforza, known as *Il Moro,* The Moor.

What he'd presented himself *as*, when he got to Sforza's court, was a confusing jumble of possibilities. Jack of a lot of trades, not all of them useful. He was carrying with him a lute he'd made, or invented, or found—house present for the duke—of a lyre in the shape of a horse's head. He, supposedly an accomplished musician himself, was traveling in the company of another musician, Atalante Migliorotti. This man, ten years younger, and said also to be Leonardo's pupil, was a singer. What Leonardo was supposed to be teaching him never became clear although by the end of his life Migliorotti had become the Vatican's inspector of architectural works. It would be easier to assume that they were lovers than that they were not.

Leonardo had trained in Florence, in the studio of Verrocchio, who, like the other masters of his time, was equally able to paint, to sculpt, to design you a building, or to make a complicated wedding presentation in cast gold. Leonardo learned all these trades, and was assigned portions of some of Verrocchio's paintings to execute, to correct or complete. But it was not as a painter that he offered himself to *Il Moro,* Duke Ludovico Sforza.

"Take that, Peter Hartrack," Fred said. What Leonardo da Vinci offered, in his letter to the duke, was arms. He described the weapons he wished to make with a lavish and optimistic assurance that promised to bless, with bloody chaos, all the military adventures his patron might ever contemplate.

Chapter Fifty-one

A copy of Leonardo's self-introductory letter to the duke existed, in which his abilities as a painter were mentioned only, almost, as an afterthought. After the nine categories of services he offered, all of them military, he had added, *in peacetime I...can...be the equal of any man in architecture...or conduct water from one place to another.... I can carry out sculpture in marble, bronze, and clay; and in painting can do any kind of work as well as any man, whoever he be.**

So, even in the unhappy event of peace, Leonardo suggested, there would be a use for him. But what he really wanted to make for the new patron was, 1, Strong but light bridges, by which to pursue or flee an enemy; 2, Scaling ladders to use during sieges, and means to drain the enemy's defensive moats; 3, Systems that could be used to destroy enemy citadels in cases where bombardment was not effective; 4, Practical mortars, easily transported, to rain stones down on the enemy, filling him with terror, hurt, and confusion; 5, He could direct the digging of underground tunnels, even under the enemy's system of moats; 6, He offered what we would call tanks, covered vehicles, safe and unassailable, to destroy the most powerful troops; 7, Bombards, mortars, and fire-throwers "of beautiful and practical design." ("Beautiful and practical fire-throwing machines," Fred noted. "What's practical

*For this and associated material, see Serge Bramley, *Leonardo, the Artist and the Man*, tr. Sian Reynolds, Penguin Books, New York and London, 1994, pp. 174 and following.

is also beautiful. The concept of beauty and practicality, for Leonardo, may be interchangeable. Talk to me, Mona Lisa.") 8 and 9 offered the prospect of further engines of destruction, to be useful on land and sea, mostly in the hurling of missiles, but also, Leonardo claimed, he could make boats that would resist *even the heaviest cannon fire, fumes and gunpowder.*

Aside from the instruments of war, Leonardo's biggest selling point, in this work of self-advertisement, was the claim he made that he could design, and cast, a colossal bronze equestrian statue to *the immortal glory and eternal honor of the lord your father and blessed memory of the illustrious house of Sforza.*

"Einstein played the fiddle," Fred recalled. "And he invented relativity though he couldn't do a goddamned thing with it once he had it except pull out his fiddle and play it lullabies. So it figures Leonardo played the lute."

Two thirds of the people living in the world would recognize Leonardo's name, and tell you who he was. Two thirds of those (the others being snobs) would welcome the chance to have their photos taken standing in front of the world's most famous painting, the *Mona Lisa.* And maybe twelve hundred people in the world (of whom Fred was not one) knew enough really about the man to give you more than a paragraph about him.

It was amusing to chase Clay's notes and observations, and to speculate over where his interests had been directed. Was he trying to demonstrate to himself why his painting, against all likelihood, must be the genuine article, an autograph painting by Leonardo da Vinci, unknown all these years, and not even the subject of speculation? Was he trying to assign to it the likeliest putative date of composition? Difficult for a painter whose finish could require not just months, but years, to achieve. Leonardo, it appeared, hopped from one horse to another at mid-stream or anywhere else. He had completed almost nothing. Given the pile of promises he brought with him in his otherwise empty poke (well, empty except for a silver lute in the shape of a horse's head), why did Duke Ludovico keep him around? Why not drop the fellow head first into one of the mangonels he promised, and see how far he'd fly over the battlements?

The big bronze "horse" was never finished. Other commissions petered out. That huge *Last Supper* started flaking away even before it was finished, because the arrogant bastard—and he was a bastard—was using his biggest commission ever to experiment with a new medium he was inventing that, like so much of what he invented, just didn't work.

Whatever else he was good at, he had the gift of gab, like the tailors who sold the credulous emperor that new suit, but twenty times over. Look, he'd say (this was all in his notebooks), here's a good idea for a tank, except it's powered by the men running along inside it, and after the first one trips on a rock, or log, or severed head, the rest of them topple over him.

There are people like this: people who sell you hope, who start things nobody else can finish. People in government love them.

Imagine this scene. The tailors, getting wind of trouble, tell the emperor they have to go elsewhere for a week to get fresh supplies only they can find for the magic garment. The week stretches out to a month, then six. The emperor's nervous since he's already invested in the new suit, and the occasion is coming when he wants to wear it for the first time. He's angry, he's concerned at the size of the investment he's already made, he's full of delight at how wonderful he's going to look when the suit is finished, if it is, which he starts to doubt. How do the tailors phrase it when they come riding back? "Forget the suit, your excellency. We have a better plan. Would you like to fly? All we need (except how could Leonardo know it?) is for somebody else to invent the internal combustion engine."

Chapter Fifty-two

Well and good. But Leonardo was no fraud. An optimist, maybe. If he promised something, it was at least within the scope of everyone's imagination. Who hasn't imagined flying? Who could not envision, happily, the sight of flaming rockets falling like rain into the enemy city and setting fire to the enemy women and children in their thatched houses? Who could not imagine a colossal horse made of bronze?

The man was a think-tank. He was, whatever else he might be, and however useful, at least a worthy decoration for an ambitious court. He was Ludovico's own private Institute for Advanced Studies. Like Einstein, once he was enshrined, he was never obliged to produce. To anyone asking, "What the hell are you doing all day?" he could show his notebooks. And indeed all day and every day he was thinking, drawing, speculating. Why did God put shells made of stones on the tops of mountains? What are the qualities of certain animals that allow us to perceive them in symbolic ways? How does a horse move? Look how, when I place certain aspects of fish, lion, ape and bird together, I get a griffon or a dragon. And look, when I take my knife to the willing corpse—at least it makes no objection—see the articulation of the bones, the placement of the blood vessels, the interaction of the organs in the ventral cavity.

However, his observations were distracted by preconceptions. "How on earth did he justify from experience, what he drew, a direct line of communication, in the form of tube-like vessels, between a woman's breasts and her uterus?" Mandy asked. Fred hadn't realized her phantom was still with him.

"Only Mona Lisa knows," Fred said. "And she ain't telling."

Or was Clay's special interest the question whether the model for his painting might indeed be Cecilia Gallerani? He'd tried, and hadn't gotten very far with this line of inquiry, to see what had become of Cecilia's son, who was also the bastard son of Duke Ludovico, legitimized by the man she'd married. To chase that down you'd have to go to Milan and hire a wizened gentleman covered with scraps of Latin and cobwebs.

But there'd been a more fruitful line of inquiry.

By the time Leonardo had been adopted by Francis I, the king of France, until he died at sixty-seven, he had become little more than a think-tank, partly paralyzed, although he could still draw. Clay's notes hinted at the merest outline of what could be years of study. Leonardo had never married. Acknowledging the inevitability of his impending death, he had disposed of his worldly goods, including the few paintings that remained of the few he had ever made.

Testament, Clay had noted on another card. *Half of a vineyard to Salai, as well as the house Leonardo built him. The house had paintings in it? The rest of the property, clothes, books, writings, and "all the instruments and portraits concerning his art and trade as a painter" were left to his executor, Messire Francesco Melzi.* Clayton had underlined the word *portraits*.

A separate card headed *Melzi* set out to track the fate of the collection of Leonardo material that had gone from Melzi, who died in 1570, to his son Orazio. The dispersal of manuscripts to Lelio Gamardi (if Fred was reading Clay's hand correctly), the family tutor; a monk named Mazenta; a sculptor named Pompeo Leoni employed by the king of Sardinia; Cardinal Borromeo; a painter; Charles-Emmanuel of Savoy.

"So this is what Clayton Reed is up to while I chase around in the rain," Fred said. "Leading what we may call the active life, collecting bruises in my solar plexus."

These were the starting points of the tracks that led, after impossibly convoluted and infuriating twists and turns, into the history of the possessors of the various notebook manuscripts alone. Enough to entrance. Enough to drive anyone crazy. Except that, if you owned a work thought to be by Leonardo, you'd want to be able to say, if you could, where it had been since the old man died. Not so old as that, Fred reminded himself, at sixty-seven.

What of Salai? Clay had written at the top of one of his cards.

Who the devil was Salai? Everywhere Fred looked in the real world, and every bush and outcropping Clayton peered behind back in the record, there was another monkey.

Envy rose in Fred's gorge. Clay Reed was free to roam among his paintings and his books, while Fred must push into the rain again, to see what new surprises Suzette might have in store.

It was twenty after five. Fred scrawled a note including the telephone number at Bernie's, and cast around for a place where Clayton, in his large establishment, was bound to see it. He could prop it against the *Madonna* and earn Clay's horrified contempt into the indefinite future. There would be many little things to work out for this uncertain future, including what was Clayton's telephone number? Not only was he unlisted, the number wasn't recorded on the telephone itself.

He roamed again through Clayton's first floor, checked the kitchen to make sure nothing was on, made sure the front door was secure, and went down again to the office floor, where he looked once again at the chest. "The marks of the saw," he said. "We can have those analyzed, learn what kind of saw, hand or mechanical, and when the work was done." Then he stepped into the rain, grabbing an umbrella as he went.

Chapter Fifty-three

The rain was now of the kind that doesn't seem to fall, so much as to hover in the air. It was not so much a visitation as a presence. It managed to find the undersides of leaves. It insisted on fecundity, seeming to be an undeserved blessing distributed by the vegetable gods. Fred opened the umbrella above him, though that made little difference since the rain was suspended in the air he walked through.

The people on the late afternoon sidewalk seemed not so much oblivious to the rain as enlivened by it in a way they were not aware of. Everyone carried more light, or speed, or grace. Fred walked uphill, beginning the meandering ascent that would take him finally to Bolt Street. He'd avoid Charles Street this time, and the corner at Pekham where he could not prevent himself from looking upward at the building out of which Clay's painting had come, so surprisingly and so recently. Four days it had been.

He'd checked a few times out of the windows, during the afternoon, to see if there were overt signs of anyone taking an interest in Clay's house. But you couldn't tell that from inside. That was the trouble with being inside. A house is a trap, and the only way to watch it is from the outside. There was no reason to expect a watcher, any more than there had been reason to expect Franklin Tilley's body beside the river early this morning, adding its quiet stinks to the morning air.

From all appearances Clay, his person, home, and possessions, were secure. There was no sign, as Fred walked uphill, of any interest. No standing vehicle whose driver showed a sudden unnecessary concentration on yesterday's newspaper. Nobody searching with tedious methodical slowness for a lost cat or earring. Nobody leaning frankly against a telephone pole and whistling into space. And there were no shops in which a watcher might sit. The alleys were empty. It didn't hurt to be prudent.

Bernie was not a reader; nor did he keep canned food in his pantry. He'd stripped the place down past its skivvies before heading off to Mumbai and points north. More for something to do than out of hunger, Fred devoured the half sandwich Suzette had left on the table at lunchtime: tuna fish with pickles. Then he paced the length of the room's wall where Bernie kept both the indecipherable sound system and his massive collection of records and tapes. He studied the jackets and labels without taking anything completely out of its place on the shelf. Everything was in Bernie's idea of meticulous order, and Bernie's idea of meticulous order could not be understood by anyone else. Bernie was his own uncrackable code.

At a little after six-thirty the telephone rang and gave him Clay. "Give me your number there," Fred suggested. "Then tell me about Salai. No, that can wait. Give me your number. Then fill me in on Mitchell."

After postponing Clayton's apologies, he wrote the number on a scrap of paper he tucked in his pocket.

"If Fiorello Mitchell is our man, he knows a good deal in a highly restricted field," Clay started. "Never published a book. Small potatoes in the academic world. Apparently he spent his career shuttling between short-term positions in various American academic institutions, and taking grants to work or teach or study overseas, usually in Italy. Fiorello Mitchell, as his name implies, is the result of the union between an American serviceman and an Italian woman, who met during the First

World War, married, and produced this child some time later. His field…."

"In case we're interrupted," Fred said, "streamline this."

"His field of expertise is a group of Sienese master charlatans who produced works in the manner of the Italian fifteenth century, between the late eighteen hundreds and the early. I believe I mentioned, in passing…."

"That's the door," Fred said. "If I don't get down there, I'll lose him. Stick around."

Chapter Fifty-four

A male contraption constructed of cigarette butts and wire stood at the door, next to Suzette, under that umbrella. Suzette had put on her black raincoat again, down which the rain was chortling in brisk rivulets. Fiorello Mitchell, slightly behind her, was halfway between five and six feet, wearing a trench coat and a hat from a bad 1930s movie about spies. His brushy mustache was of the kind that sticks straight forward, seeking to snatch out of the air more than its weight in crumbs.

"Fred, Dr. Mitchell," Suzette said. "Let's for God's sake get out of the rain. Mitchell, Fred Taylor."

Mitchell, looking around him furtively, gazed with misgiving into Bernie's garage before he screwed up his courage and followed Suzette inside. "Where is it?" he asked.

"Leave your things down here," Fred suggested. "There's no room upstairs." He helped them hang their wet coats on nails poking out of the exposed studs of the garage walls. Mitchell handed over his hat reluctantly, as if it gave him more valuable access to the world even than a library card. He smelled strongly of the cigarette butts he was made of. Under his coat, the suit, which had once been blue, had worn itself down to a color that almost matched, but not quite, his shirt. There was a necktie, and it had been red. Fred followed them up the stairs.

Suzette sat on the couch, homing to the indentation she had left that morning. Mitchell gazed slowly around the room, fondling his moustache, bristling it clear of crumbs. He said, "I was designed, by the good lord, to be a wealthy man." He smiled sadly, waiting for the applause of sympathy he knew from long experience would never come, and went directly to the wall where Bernie kept his music. There was nothing else on the walls to look at, not even a calendar.

"And is the good lord disappointed?" Fred asked. Mitchell might be sixty-five but he could pass for ten years older.

"The lord has considerable patience, evidently. Billions of years of it." Marshall's observation, funny in itself—at least self-deprecating or wry—was not accompanied by any change in expression. Both statements had been made with the simple flat tones that might accompany the statement, "There are six eggs in this bowl."

"You are an expert in forgery," Fred said.

"Start somewhere else," Suzette interrupted. "Maybe more neutral."

"It looks like rain," Fred said.

"A forger is a lazy man," Mitchell said. He looked at the couch, thought better of it, pulled a chair out from the table, sat on it, and rested his head on his arms before he lifted it again. "A lazy man, and a fool. I've had enough of fools. Still I'm no expert." He put his head down again and kept it there.

"He's been staying in a hotel," Suzette said. "Where he says he can't sleep."

"The pigeons," Mitchell said, raising his head. "They disturb me. They interrupt my prayers."

Was this a joke? It was impossible to tell either from Mitchell's or from Suzette's expression. "And yet they are God's creatures," Fred hazarded. "Pigeons, I mean. Like the rest of us."

"Mitchell did the expertise, I told you," Suzette said. "The appraisals, all that."

Mitchell raised his head. Were those tears? "This man challenges my good faith," he announced. "I am finished." He made no move to leave; simply sat, looking hopelessly offended.

"I better warn you," Suzette interrupted. "Which it took me a long time to figure out, because I've never run into it in this business, before or since. Dr. Mitchell tells the truth. What he says, it's always what he believes or what he knows. It's disorienting, like he's hiding in plain sight. Like he's an honest man disguised as an honest man."

"And yet he's in the art business," Fred said. "Mitchell, I meant no offense."

"None taken," Mitchell said: a man insulted so often that he took no offense from insults?

"My special interest," Mitchell said, "my avocation, concerns a small group of artist craftsmen who went to great pains to learn, and to use, the materials and methods of their ancestors. I am weary."

"Tell me about it," Fred invited.

"Mr. Taylor, are you are willing to be educated?"

"Fred," Fred said.

"Fred, then. A forger is a lazy man who finds, for example, a brown Dutch painting of a miserable old man, signs it Rembrandt, or R van Rijn, and rushes it to market. There is a difference between that charlatan and the true craftsmen who are the object of my study. These men are imitators, but not forgers. *Are,* I say, but I should say *were.* Though their work lives, the great ones are dead. Are you listening?

"In the late nineteenth century a school of master craftsmen developed in Siena whose journeyman members, following the old traditions, were skilled in many things. Italy had recently awakened to the value of its previously despised artistic heritage; the thousands of works of art and decoration that had been produced, many of them in the fifteenth century, for churches and other wealthy patrons. Book covers, frames, portraits. These things had been moldering and falling apart, neglected, for years. In the churches the frescoes sifted into ruin. The great gilded tabernacles and altarpieces, the carved and molded fretwork decorating walls and ceilings...."

"Fred gets the picture," Suzette said.

"Almost within living memory," Mitchell persisted, "in certain towns and villages, fires were sometimes built in the public square, in which old paintings, furniture, were burned so that artisans could retrieve their gold. But in the late eighteen hundreds this was changing. Churches, towns, noble families, began suddenly to appreciate what they had disregarded. They came into vogue. Craftsmen were needed to repair them. These craftsmen were obliged to discover, to imitate, or to duplicate in some way, the methods of the ancients. Suppose the gilded frame around an altarpiece had been carelessly charred over the years, by candles? Now the cathedral suddenly saw a purpose to repairing it. The restorer must fill and match the portion that had been harmed.

"This involved labor, complex, often excruciating labor, paid at a service rate. Even so, the work required, and it developed, true genius.

"I shall quote for you the very words of the greatest of these craftsmen, Icilio Joni, speaking of just one of the processes involved in the sort of repair I speak of."

"Oh, Jesus," Suzette grumbled.

"*We had now an established method of producing a patina on frames and tabernacles. The patina used to give an antique effect to the gold was composed of well-ground soot, turmeric, very light chrome yellow and a little gilding gesso, all mixed with a little Arabic gum. A good glaze for the gold was also produced by keeping the stumps of Tuscan cigars in water for several days. To fix the patina, we added a coating of spirit varnish, glazed on with turmeric, pyric acid and a little Prussian blue. Then we took some ashes, put them in water to get rid of the potash, and gave them a tone with raw umber; this substance was thinly mixed with Canada balsam, and laid on with a brush; and the surface was wiped with a damp sponge, so that the stuff remained chiefly in the hollows. The effect was modified with a cloth, so that the surface parts had a certain polish and brightness, and then the parts that had been most worked* *upon were touched up with a piece of pure wax, to modify the effect once more. By this time the illusion was almost perfect.**

"Illusion was the aim, in a worthy cause, and at the cost of considerable labor."

"Not forgery. Illusion," Fred said. "Got it."

"Now it is true," Mitchell pressed on, "that at the same time as the owners of old things were valuing them suddenly, and causing them to be restored, other people, who did not have such things—many of them from England or America—cultivated a taste for them. A market developed for paintings and other decorative items that either were, or resembled, these old things. The same craftsmen who were doing the restorations of their country's heritage also restored or created reproductions and imitations. How else would they learn? Because they were craftsmen, they were despised by the same marketplace that came to profit, often illegally, from their efforts. Their imitations sold for a song to dealers who then made great profits, selling to credulous collectors, simply by adding fictitious provenance, and the reassurance that might attach to their own reputations."

"That's all beside the point. Please, for the love of God, get on with it," Suzette complained.

"I respect God's name," Mitchell said. "You have twice taken His name in vain. You are offensive."

*J.F. Joni, *Affairs of a Painter*, London: Faber and Faber, c. 1936. On this subject see also Gianni Mazzoni, *Quadri antichi den Novocento*, Vicnza: Neri Pozza Editore, 2001 and the liberally illustated catalog *Falso d'autore: Icilio Federico Joni e la cultura del falso tra Otto e Novecento*, Siena: Protagon Editore, 2004. See also the review of the exhibition for which this catalog was prepared, by Roderick Conway Morris, *International Herald Tribune*, Saturday, July 31-Sunday, August 1, 2004, p. 8.

Chapter Fifty-five

"Okay. Let's get to what we're here for," Suzette demanded. "I apologize. Okay? To you and God, Dr. Mitchell. Okay?"

"A specialist makes a mistake, believing his specialty has importance in the world. I know, Ms. Shaughnessy, I am a bore, in love with a bore. Give me a glass of water," Mitchell demanded. Fred went to the sink and complied, as Mitchell went on. "To be brief. A lawyer approached me. I give no names. My service was obtained in confidence. Confidence is part of the service I provided. If it was not deserved, still I am obligated to the terms of my agreement. I was asked to catalogue and appraise a collection of paintings overseas. The owner planned to ship them out of the country and offer them for sale. He was utterly dependent on me to describe them. They were to be sent—a harmless subterfuge—along with, and as a part of, the returning household effects of an American diplomat who was being posted home. The collection...."

"Spare me. Fred's seen the collection," Suzette said.

"A container that holds the effects of a returning diplomat traditionally is not subjected to more than a cursory examination by customs officers, whether in the country of origin or the destination. This collection was such...."

"Fred *saw* the collection," Suzette repeated.

Mitchell pressed on, "...that unless it was examined by a true expert in fine art, such as myself, even though it had significant value, it might well pass as simple household goods. The diplomat, I may say, had already a fine collection of things. But we could not take the risk, that is my client could not, of close examination. And one piece stood out."

"Here it comes," Suzette said. "What has it been, a quarter of an hour?"

"Among the objects was a *cassapanca nuziale,* what in this country used to be called a hope chest. A wooden wedding chest. I recognized it as Italian of the late fifteenth century. My heart stopped when I saw it, I can tell you." He drank from his glass of water and blew the collected droplets from his moustache. "The chest was carved and gilded as these things are, not as elaborately as is often the case. What struck one first was the painted top, which I recognized immediately."

"A wedding chest," Fred said.

"About which I say no more," Mitchell said, closing his mouth tight on the words.

"See, if you can't lie, the only thing left is, be silent," Suzette explained.

"I want the chest," Mitchell said. "I have come for it."

"*We* want it," Suzette corrected him. "We are partners, Mitchell and I. Just in this project."

"Ms. Shaughnessy told me you have the chest," Mitchell pressed on. He sounded like a man who has spent many years on Death Row in Texas, anticipating the inevitable response to his plea for clemency.

"As per your instructions, Fred," Suzette continued, with brisk dispatch, sounding like that prisoner's attorney who expects to be paid only, if at all, ever, by the hour.

"I have a question," Fred said, changing direction so as to come back from another angle. "Some of the things I saw. You identified the Cézanne, to take one example."

Mitchell shook his head angrily. "Nothing to do with me. If Franklin gave my imprimatur...."

"So, the Cézanne comes from another source," Fred said smoothly. "Nothing you worked on. The Mantegna?"

"That is an attribution only," Mitchell said. "I don't accept the attribution. They know that."

"Ah," Fred said. "Smoke, if you want, Dr. Mitchell."

"The Mantegna is a gray area," Suzette chimed in while Mitchell took a limp pack of Camels from a side pocket of his suit jacket. Suzette reached for one and the conversation lagged until two plumes of smoke flavored the room.

"Franklin Tilley was expecting an important painting," Fred said.

"We're done here," Mitchell said, jerking to his feet. He stalked from the room, clattering down the stairs.

"Asshole," Suzette said. She stubbed her cigarette out in that morning's coffee cup. "What's wrong with you? Are you crazy? Look what you've done now. We're back to square one."

She clattered out herself.

Chapter Fifty-six

"New ballgame," Fred told Clay, before starting to fill him in.

They had enough to talk about. He'd gone back to Mountjoy Street, and they were sitting in Clay's parlor, facing a *Madonna* who was not quite facing either one of them. She had her own concerns.

"Not that we care. But do we care?" Fred said, picking up. "Mitchell was hard to play, and I screwed up. He pranced out in a snit. He described what you bought as a wedding chest, Italian, fifteenth century. Said he recognized it immediately, from its top."

"That's ominous," Clay said. He toyed with his snifter of brandy.

"Then he high tailed it out of there so unexpectedly, and with Suzette in tow, that it didn't occur to me to follow him, even if I'd wanted to. Eventually, though, I can find him again, I reckon, if there's any reason to." He was contenting himself with beer, and he swallowed some.

Fred said, "He's an exhausting man. Rancid with piety, unless that's a fraud. But I don't make him out as a fraud, though his dear love is this specialty of his, the craftsman forger Icilio Joni. While I run around finding dead bodies in the rain, and talking to half-naked women and old men made of cigarette butts, you spend your days where it's dry indulging your taste for research. From your notes, you're making progress.

"Of the paintings he did, the ones everyone agrees were his, and that we can find now, and counting yours, how many paintings did Leonardo actually finish?"

"Something like twelve," Clay said. "And of those twelve, the *Last Supper* is a wreck. The *Mona Lisa* was cut down. Aside from the spurious signature, there is argument whether another hand appears in the *Lady with an Ermine*. The cleanest, clearest, most finished, most perfect Leonardos number five in my opinion: Washington's *Ginevra de' Benci*, the Louvre's *Virgin of the Rocks*, their portrait called *La Belle Ferronnière,* the *Mona Lisa,* and mine. And mine was intact until some monster cut it down. But to your report. Your conversation with Mitchell was not in vain, Fred. Though he withholds the name, he obliquely confirms the source of the chest; therefore, presumably, of the *Madonna. Presumably* is not enough, you say? Far more important, my research has exposed the possible, nay, the *probable* source of the *Madonna.*"

He looked as smug as Casanova must have after a good evening.

"I hope you don't mind, since your notes were on my desk," Fred said. "For my edification, I figured. You've covered a lot of ground in a short time. Who is Salai?"

"Here we must glance into Leonardo's life story," Clay started. "Although normally I would wish to protect even the dead from prurient prying, in this instance it is inevitable. I will do what I can to be discreet. After he had settled in Milan, in 1490, beginning when the boy was ten, a youngster, Giacomo, called Salai, or Little Devil, lived with, worked for, plagued, stole from, apprenticed to and, presumably, shared the bed of the master—almost until Leonardo's death in 1519.

"Salai was a constant in Leonardo's later life, although Leonardo was some thirty-five years his senior. At the time of Salai's own sudden death five years later, he was described in the inevitable legal papers as a painter. Salai's death was ruled accidental. He was killed by the bolt from a crossbow."

"So," Fred interrupted. "What Suzette Shaughnessy calls 'a gay thing.'"

"Gay?" Clay asked. "Ah. Gay as in an intimate relationship between two persons of the same sex. In this instance, two males. That's a distraction."

"Except that Salai inherited property from Leonardo," Fred said, "according to your notes. A vineyard, a house, paintings? Leonardo was into everything, wasn't he? Didn't he work on improving the crossbow's firing mechanism?"

Clay waved the question away. "What kept me," he said. "Why I am later than I intended. I was able to find a copy of Salai's last will and testament."

"Jeekers!" Fred said. "From 1524?"

"The Italians throw nothing away," Clay announced sententiously. "At least, no document. Salai left paintings indeed.* To his legatees, his sisters Angelina and Laurentiola. But because Salai was a painter himself, an *indifferent* painter, the inventory preserved with the will, of his worldly effects, is murky. Is your beer holding up?"

"I know where to find more," Fred said. "Don't interrupt a good thing." Clay's extended hospitality was little more than an occasion to prolong the pleasures of anticipation. "The inventory included paintings. Go on."

"Listen to this," Clay almost chortled. "When Salai died, he even owned the *Mona Lisa.* This monkey whom Leonardo had brought in off the street! Also in his studio was Salai's own copy of the *Mona Lisa.* In 1525, one of the sisters sold Leonardo's *Saint John as Bacchus*, now in the Louvre. You'll have seen it. It's the traditional depiction of Saint John in the wilderness; young man dressed only in a loin cloth. But now Saint John wears a wreath of vine leaves. The easy guess is that Salai, the widowed Ganymede, perhaps bored, perhaps drunk, perhaps prompted by indifferent malice, desecrated this part of his inheritance by painting the vine leaves onto Saint John himself."

*Salai's *Last Will and Testament*, including the inventory of paintings mentioned in my text, is frequently quoted in the literature.

"Which makes the work as we now have it a joint effort," Fred pointed out. "Unless—I doubt it—did Salai goad his aging lover into painting the wreath himself, one rainy night? Keep on. What other treasures did the old boy leave Salai?"

"A hoard simply breathtaking to contemplate. Leonardo's *Virgin and Child with Saint Anne,* never finished, now in the Louvre; the *Saint Jerome* in the Vatican, about which we spoke earlier—an unholy mess, but the saint's head has been restored to the painting; and other works now lost. A *Leda and the Swan* was described by the appraiser as the most valuable of the works left to Salai by Leonardo. There was a so-called *Portrait of a half nude,* said to be a nude Mona Lisa," Clay said.

"It keeps on coming," Fred said.

"But listen to this," Clay continued. "One of the entries, which I have simply not seen accounted for, was this: a *Madonna cum uno filiolo in brazo?"*

"If I make sense of the dog Latin," Fred said, "that translates *'Madonna with her son in her arms.'"*

"Precisely," Clayton exclaimed. *Madonna cum uno filiolo in brazo.* Why is this painting never mentioned? It is listed in Salai's estate. The appraisal gives no authorship, no clue. But consider the relative values assigned by the appraiser. *Leda,* supposed to be the best of the paintings, was assigned 200 scudi, and the *Mona Lisa* 100 scudi. These figures indicate a certain value, which unfortunately I cannot interpret without further study. The *Madonna cum uno filiolo* is fobbed off at 20 scudi, one fifth the value of the *Mona Lisa.* My conclusion is that first the appraiser, and then all scholars since, assumed this entry must be by Salai.

"Suppose the appraiser looked at my Leonardo, considered the apes, and decided, That will never sell."

Clay went to the sideboard and refreshed his brandy. Fred took the opportunity to find another beer.

"Cast your mind back to 1525," Clay demanded, when they were settled again. "The painting I have acquired, this painting, *Madonna of the Apes,* may have been so heretical in its implications as to compel not disregard, but the dangerous attention of armed religious authority. Not only are the Madonna and her divine offspring shown without haloes; their only attendants are, not angels, but the animals that most closely mimic man. Heretics were burning in those days. So, often, were known or accused homosexuals. A gay heretic wouldn't have a prayer unless he had truly powerful friends."

"Your theory is," Fred suggested, "that if Leonardo's friend Salai was willing to paint a wreath of vine leaves on Saint John, turning an ascetic into a roué, did the apes come from his brush too? After Leonardo died? No." Fred's gorge rose at the thought. "They are too brilliantly painted, and too much part of the painting's original conception."

"You say brilliant now," Clay interjected. "But how would this painting have been seen in 1525? If Salai's sister had wanted to sell the *Madonna of the Apes*, whom could she have sold it to? Who would dare be seen with it?"

"So if the painting belonged to Salai, it was a joke," Fred said. "Is that what you're saying?"

"Does it feel like a joke to you?" Clay asked. His eyes traveled across the room to the painting and he shook his head firmly. "All I suggest is this. It must be kept out of sight and enjoyed only in secret, in the company of persons not in the mainstream, who could appreciate the outrageous."

A *"gay thing,"* was Clayton suggesting? The work passed down from hand to hand for centuries, but underground? The "*gay thing*" made for its own web of clandestine allegiances that, since it factored into Leonardo's life, might well factor into the painting's history. A line of descent through a secret society like the Masons, but whose constituents were gay? That would be interesting.

Fred said, "If this is the painting you found recorded as *A Madonna with her son in her arms*, we have a long way to go to prove it."

"I find the possibility intriguing, and encouraging," Clay said. "And I look forward to the search."

Chapter Fifty-seven

"Salai would have known her," Fred said.

"Who?"

"Sorry. I was thinking, but not out loud," Fred said. "It's all so long ago and out of sight. Yet so real in the presence of this painting. The woman who sat for your *Madonna.* Cecilia Gallerani, if it was she. Salai would have known her. According to you he would have been underfoot, in and out of the studio, grinding colors, stealing fruit, washing the dishes and breaking them, pissing out the windows on passers by. He was ten when he came to live with Leonardo, you said, and that's about the time, 1490, when Leonardo painted the *Lady with an Ermine.* We agree, don't we, that that is the portrait your *Madonna* should sit beside?"

"There comes a time when thinking threatens to replace looking," Clay said. "When that time comes, I stop thinking."

The observation fell into the room and went nowhere for a minute or two. They sat like men who find themselves, strangers, seated next to each other in a bar, on a day when nothing is happening, not even on TV. Except that here the *Madonna* occupied the room, and filled it with more event than a World Series.

"Sorry to be so slow," Fred said. "There's too much going on. You say there's a nude *Mona Lisa?"*

"Was. Yes, apparently Leonardo also painted her nude, whoever she was, and if she was anybody. The *Mona Lisa*'s much later than the *Madonna*, of course," Clay said. "Maybe as late as 1503. It's been turned into such a myth by so many observers that it is as hard to think about that painting, as it is to get near it at the Louvre. The tourists flock around her like apes. Too many people have thought about her, and have then published what they think. She's practically invisible.

"Leonardo is said to have worked on her for more than four years."

"If that's true, most of his time was spent just staring and worrying at her," Fred said. "There can't be more than a quarter pound of paint on the whole thing. Hell, not even that."

"I am diverted from the direction of my musings," Clayton said.

"Which were?"

"How prone we are to assume that there must be a basis in reality for an image that takes such a hold on us. We crowd to cast a story against the object simply because the object fascinates, and our time must be filled with white noise."

"Mona Lisa, Mona Lisa, men have named you," Fred sang, not well. Nat King Cole's tune was barely recognizable. Fred's singing voice went up and down at the right places, but it avoided notes. "And other happy horse shit," Fred continued, no longer singing.

Clay declaimed, "Like the vampire, she has been dead many times, and learned the secrets of the grave; and has been a diver in deep seas, and keeps their fallen day about her, and trafficked for strange webs with Eastern merchants; and, as Leda, was the mother of Helen of Troy, and, as St. Anne, the mother of Mary."

"Jeekers," Fred said. "Who produced that gloomy wet dream?"

"It's Walter Pater,* but it could have been any one of a hundred other critics in the 1800s. They get so excited trafficking in the strange webs that come out of their own mouths, they can't see past them."

***Studies in the History of the Renaissance*, London, 1873.

"I notice that you have a little Latin," Clay said.

"And less Greek. What, if anything, do we do with the knowledge that Professor Mitchell is in the mix?"

"I must think about your question," Clay said. "I am presently inhabited by strong emotion. Because that can sometimes be indistinguishable from instinct, I am capable of making a mistake. What do you think?"

"I think don't stir the waters. Last I heard, you were claiming the box was a fake."

"I have been reading in Leonardo's notebooks," Clay announced, swerving away from the matter at hand. "*The Notebooks of Leonardo da Vinci,* Edward Mac Curdy's definitive, if outdated, edition." Clay crossed the room and took a fat, squat book from the table where he kept the telephone, next to the kitchen door. "There were few subjects he did not touch," Clay said. "Among the subjects he never touched—I don't know why this occurs to me—is that of Mary Magdalene. Not a mention. Perhaps the pretended Mantegna in Tilley's collection brought her to mind and I wondered, off-hand, if Leonardo gave her a moment's thought.

"But my study as you came in concerned what he might have had to say about the ape. Here," he riffled pages with his long fingers, "on one occasion, he has taken the trouble to dissect the arm of a monkey in order to understand the comparative musculatures of man and monkey. Elsewhere, again by dissection, he seeks to understand the differences between the structures of the foot of man, bear, and monkey. Here again is a drawing of a monkey's hand, so like our own. And here, finally, he directs himself, *Write of the varieties of the intestines of the human species, apes and such like; then of the differences that are found in the leonine species, then the bovine and lastly in birds; and make this description in the form of a discourse.*"

"Busy man, busy mind, busy pen," Fred said. "I'll bet when you asked him a question he'd talk about something else."

Chapter Fifty-eight

"No, what interests me," Clay said, "now that I own a spectacular example of his finished work, is the quality of the man's mind. All genius is flawed. But listen."

He opened the book to the place marked by his finger. "From the *Quaderni d'Anatomia,* now in the Royal Library, Windsor—illustrated as appropriate—*If you cut an onion down the center you will be able to see and count all the coatings or rinds which form concentric circles round the center of this onion.*

"Similarly if you cut a man's head down the center you will cut through the hair first, then the skin and muscular flesh and the pericranium, then the cranium and within the dura mater and the pia mater and the brain, then the pia and dura mater again and the rete mirabili and the bone which is the foundation of these. Do you see?" He put the book down again, his finger removed now so that he could clasp his hands. "Do you see?" he repeated.

"Frankly, no," Fred said.

"Simply deliver to the man an onion, a human head, a knife," Clay said, "and he will do the rest. His mind works by comparison, not even by metaphor. Metaphor is the morass into which Walter Pater would lead us. The Romantic's sublime avoidance of all issues. The *Mona Lisa* a vampire, indeed! Did the man have no respect at all for his mother?

"The apes in my painting are being compared to humans. Leonardo is painting apes because he has studied them. He knows them inside and out. He paints humans because he has also studied them. Again, he knows them both inside and out. He boasted that he had opened upward of thirty human bodies. He knows *Mona Lisa*'s head because he knows what's inside it. Not the ideas. Who cares what she's thinking? She wants eggs for her lunch? Who cares? Leonardo knows that smiling head is put together in a way even an onion would understand."

Clay's excitement was such that he trembled, as he might have were he the crowning defense witness in a case that was going his way. "God, Leonardo did not paint, because he had not managed to dissect divinity," Clay went on. "He writes—I will not recall his words correctly—*Will you seek to comprehend the mind of God, which embraces the whole universe, weighing and dissecting it as though you were making an anatomical study? Oh human stupidity. You spend your whole life with yourself and even then you don't see the most obvious thing: that you're a fool.*"

"I'm thinking I should get back to where I'm staying," Fred said. "We don't know what some of these wild cards are up to. I did wonder, about the chest...."

"I shall have to come to a decision," Clay said. "The excesses of the nineteenth century, among which I include both Walter Pater and Bernard Berenson, the critic, art dealer and charlatan, have so clouded the issues of the Italian Renaissance, even in my mind, that even when placing my own hands on the true skin of a real painting, executed by Leonardo da Vinci in 1490, in Milan, I feel I can hardly see it. I am swept away by emotion.

"Fred, Leonardo is correct. We see the world, even this work, through the glazes of our own inadequacies, not to mention the stupidities that are thrust upon us by seduction, fear, or loathing, or the stupidities of our fellows."

This was all very fine and humble, but it smacked of self-congratulation: the echo of Marie Antoinette's innocent question, when she learned that the poor were out of bread, "Can't they eat cake?"

Fred interrupted. "Yeah, well and good," he said. "You knew that was Leonardo as fast and as clearly as if you looked up the hill at a wall of falling mud and said, 'It's a mud slide.' If you want to sit in the mud afterward and play with it—I won't say play with yourself. We aren't on those terms—I can't stop you."

Clayton blushed red. "The man of action pretends impatience with the intellectual processes that inspire action. But the issue is one of speed, and not of capability."

"We're losing track of something," Fred said. "According to Mitchell, he recognized immediately the nature of the wedding chest."

"For me, the important revelation of the day is your welcome testimony, from the Atlanta lawyer, that Mr. Tilley, may he rest in peace, was a *bona fide* 'sales representative,' as he put it. In that case the sale was as legitimate as it was providential."

"Tilley could have gotten the chop because he should not have made the sale," Fred pointed out. "I had assumed that it was because he was skimming money, or cooking the books."

"We need not dwell on the unfortunate Tilley's death, except to take note that the man's demise eliminates a link in the chain that connects me to the former owner of the painting. A fool might think that the elimination of this link releases the chain's connection. But each of us, in his own way—you are impatient with mine—perceives that the missing link makes the chain just that much shorter. It brings us closer to each other. The present and the former owner."

Chapter Fifty-nine

Clay continued, "Even as we speak, the Brierstone collection and its present owner are drawing ever closer to one another." He was arranging his lengthy limbs with the intention of standing. "My researcher in London, a woman of tenacity and skill, has unearthed an inventory of the furniture and other articles of value left in the estate of Hartrack's grandfather, the last Lord Brierstone. What became of the title is another story. Never mind."

He stood, marking his place in the book with a long finger. "There is an invention called a facsimile machine," he announced. "Or fax."

"Right," Fred told him.

Clayton said, "I do not have a fax machine. It enables them to know what one is doing. However, my researcher, Margaret Dibble, offers to send to me, by fax, a copy of the inventory. What it contains I do not know. I did not wish to reveal to her what I am looking for. Not on the telephone."

"That's in character," Fred interjected.

"If I can give her the telephone number of a local fax machine, she will transmit the information. I thought to ask my attorney if I might impose, but I do not like to do that without offering to pay his hourly rate, and I do not like his hourly rate."

"Simplify this," Fred said. "Use the nearest Kinko's." Clay found the directory in the telephone table and Fred pointed out the number. "Six hours difference," he reminded Clay. "Phone her the number when she wakes up, give me a heads up. I'll collect it."

"The number you gave me, that's where you'll be?"

"If I'm not going to be there, I'll let you know. I'm thinking—what put this into my head I don't know. It's convenient: the one person who saw you, and who can associate you with the Leonardo, is dead."

"That occurred to me," Clayton said dryly. "If this is an accusation…."

"Oh, come off it. I mean it's easier to insulate you, as long as I keep our connection, yours with me, invisible. At some point, maybe our civic duty makes me tell the cops that Carl is holed up in the dead man's joint, since Carl likely blew the back of Tilley's head off and, dumb as he is, he's probably still got the gun. Then there's the Atlanta lawyer Peaslee, and the new sales rep who's supposed to be turning up tomorrow. Does your instinct tell you how to play this part of it?"

Clay looked wise and twisted his fingers together. "The judges have a phrase they like that means 'Let's put this case on the back burner, and turn the burner off.' We'll take it under advisement."

"Lend me those *Notebooks,* will you?" Fred asked. "Bernie's got nothing to read."

On the way to Bernie's Fred detoured to Pekham Street and spent a quarter hour standing back in the alley, his eye on the building where the man they had known as Franklin Tilley had set up his trap, or shop. It would not have been easy, just physically, to get that many paintings, intact, out of the U-Haul, carry them upstairs, get them hung, and tidy the wrappings away. That would have been a couple of days' work. Had Mitchell joined the effort? Or, perish the thought of his handling paintings, Carl? If they noticed, what did the neighbors think of the activity? If it were his responsibility to account for Franklin's abrupt departure from this world, Fred would have questions, and a program to follow that, in due course, might put Carl away. What further danger did he represent?

The front windows in Franklin Tilley's apartment were lighted, but there was no sign of movement there. "Another corpse," Fred said. "What's left in Franklin Tilley's apartment might as well be the contents of the estate of a man named Salai, whose ashes turned long since into the ashes of the ashes of whatever they became when Salai was through with them. Salai, his paintings, his jewels, his sisters."

If he started talking to neighbors, landlords, to Carl again, or to the lawyer Peaslee, he might have a better understanding of the moments that preceded the wrecking of Franklin's head. A dismal time, in darkness, on a wet grassy riverbank. In a way he wanted to understand it, since he had known Tilley, though briefly. In a way, it was his responsibility, some would say, to bring whoever was responsible for Tillley's death, even if Tilley himself, to justice.

But there was no justice. People who used the term meant only retribution.

Besides, Fred had taken on another responsibility, which might be antithetical to any obligation that might have been suggested under the term Clay used, his "civic duty." He had undertaken to protect Clayton Reed, and what Clayton had purchased. For the time being, if Carl was sleeping in there, let him sleep. Carl and whoever signed his pay check. There'd be time.

If he was already on the bus back to Atlanta—Atlanta wasn't very far away.

Chapter Sixty

By the time he reached Bernie's it wasn't quite eight o'clock. He'd picked up a container of spaghetti and meatballs on the way over and now, being alone again, recalled that he had other interests. Mandy, on her end of the phone line, agreed to come in an hour. "Though I should pack," she said. "The plane's at eleven."

"Pack first, then come," Fred said. "I promise, dinner will wait. I'll make sure you're up in time in the morning, whenever you say." He put the plastic container in the fridge, noted that Bernie had a bottle of expendable red wine on the shelf, which he could replace; put plates and forks on the table and settled down on the couch with Mac Curdy's edition of Leonardo's *Notebooks.*

It was different from trying to corner Suzette, or Mitchell, or Peaslee, or Clay, or the disintegrating carcass of Franklin Tilley. One could sip indifferent red wine and rifle through a book's index and quietly, innocently, follow the tracks laid down in the written record.

"What was a scudo worth in 1525?" Fred asked himself. "That's part of the story. What were Clay's figures? According to the record, when Salai died the *Leda* that has since disappeared was worth 200 scudi. The *Mona Lisa* was worth 100 some, and his little package—we assume his *Madonna* is it, for the sake of argument—was knocked down at 20 scudi? What could you buy for a scudo in 1525? A house? A container of meatballs and spaghetti?"

He began flipping through the book's index and browsing, and was quickly amazed and beguiled by the extent of the man's interests as displayed in his writing. Leonardo had something to say, just among the Ws, about water, the weasel, wedges, whirlwinds, the wheel, weights, the will, the wild boar, wineskins, wolves, women, wings, wormwood, the womb, the willow (twelve references), the wasp, walking, wagons, walnuts, washing.

Fred flipped pages and his eye fell on *ermine.* "Let's see what Leonardo thinks that woman is holding," Fred said, and found the page, "in the Krakow portrait *Lady with an Ermine.*" There on page 1080 was an entry in a Bestiary, or Book of Beasts, that Leonardo had been compiling until he lost interest. *Moderation. The ermine because of its moderation eats only once a day, and allows itself to be captured by the hunters rather than take refuge in a muddy lair, in order not to stain its purity.* In the portrait, therefore, Cecilia Gallerani was holding a symbol of her purity—odd emblem for a mistress. Interesting emblem for a mistress.

The reference showed, though, that Leonardo could think like a medieval man, tightly inside someone else's box. That was an old fable, based on no observation at all, but rather on the way a fable could persist unexamined for centuries. In the same collection, Leonardo wrote of the pelican that, if it finds its young killed by a snake in the nest, it opens its heart with its beak, showers them with blood, and so restores them to life.

"But he couldn't have believed that," Fred objected. "Is he putting fables off to one side, in their own category, apart from all scientific observation? He knows, if he's looked, that a salamander does in fact have digestive organs; that it does not live by eating and breathing fire; nor can it live in fire. He knows it can't be true, yet he writes it. His whole Bestiary is lies and old wives' tales, and the corrupt morality fables of illiterate priests. And there's not," he grumbled, "not an ape in it."

In fact the ape and monkey showed up only in the references Clay had cited earlier, which had to do with Leonardo's dissections for comparative anatomy.

"For reading the implication of those apes, we are left to our own devices," Fred complained. "If a painting can mean anything, how do we get a line on what Leonardo thought his *Madonna* meant?" Even the fig, which seemed so promising in its suggestion of nourishment, fecundity, sweetness, and incipient rot, showed nowhere in Leonardo's recorded words in a way that might signal a symbolic importance. There was only a single reference to the fig, and that came from the man's own observation, *The lowest branches of the trees which have big leaves and heavy fruits, such as cocoa palms, figs and the like, always bend toward the ground. The branches always start above the leaf.*

For as many years as he had lived in this world, and as many places as he had been, Fred had never looked to see, and could not say now five hundred years after Leonardo had made the claim, if it was true whether in trees with big leaves and heavy fruit, the branches always started above the leaf. Never mind whether it mattered.

No wonder Leonardo finished so little. He'd be in the middle of something else and ask himself, for whatever reason, if the branch of the tree always starts above the leaf? The only way to know was to find out. To look. At everything.

Nothingness has no center, Leonardo had written, *and its boundaries are nothingness.* The truth of this observation Franklin was now experiencing. But the experience was wasted on him if there was nothing left to experience it with. There might be no ham sandwich waiting for Franklin; but Fred had meatballs with spaghetti still before him.

"An important distinction," Fred remarked. "Even Leonardo would appreciate the difference between no ham sandwich and a dish of meatballs and spaghetti."

Chapter Sixty-one

Fred was still reading when Bernie's doorbell rang.

Mandy's hair sparkled with rain. She'd been longer than she intended, talking on the phone. "Cold feet," she explained. "On the part of the bride. She's out there already, doing the cocktail parties with the friends of Mummy's, and trying to pacify the priest and all, and she's about ready to chuck it."

Fred hung her transparent raincoat in the garage and motioned her upstairs. She was in jeans and a yellow sweatshirt spotted with green paint, oddly festive.

"Where *do* you live," she asked.

"Cross between a house in Charlestown and 'no fixed abode,' Fred confessed. "Until something makes me settle down."

She looked doubtfully around Bernie's space, prowling the walls while Fred dumped their dinner into a saucepan and started it warming.

"Slowly," she called from the wall where Bernie kept the sound system. "Put the burner on warm or you'll burn it. Your friend has enough Dvořák to just about sink that subject."

"You aren't vegetarian are you?" Fred asked, pouring wine for her.

"It depends what I'm passing up," she said. "Don't worry about it. On meatballs I take a pass. More for you."

Fred raised his glass and let it clink against hers. "You and Leonardo da Vinci," he said.

"He's vegetarian?"

"Was," Fred said. "I'm reading his notebooks almost as we speak. I quote, not accurately. *If you are, as you claim, the king of the beasts*—[he's talking to us humans] *you are the greatest beast of all of them—why don't you help them? Then they can give you their young so that you can gratify your palate. For the sake of your palate, after all, you have undertaken to make of yourself a tomb for all of the animals.* It makes you think twice about the genus *meatball.*"

"Filthy day. Filthy night," Mandy said, gesturing toward the window as they sat to the meal Fred had dumped from the saucepan, sorting all the meatballs onto his plate and giving Mandy the bulk of the pasta.

"After we eat, if you want to, I thought we might make love, as long as it's raining," Fred said.

"That's where he sleeps, your friend?" Mandy asked. "On the couch? Does it pull out?"

"I'll have to check," Fred said.

When the time came, it turned out that Bernie's couch was no more than a couch, though Fred found sheets to arrange on it as best he could.

"Never mind," Mandy said. "I should go home anyway, after. Seduce me. Undress me. Talk to me of Leonardo."

Fred put a hand through her hair and embraced her before he started working at her clothes. "Leonardo knew about anticipation also," he said. *"It is easier to resist at the beginning than at the end,* he wrote." Fred maneuvered the sweatshirt over her head. This exposed the snake tattoo, old friend now, and a necklace she wore, surprise, made of red beads that glowed like glass. She was wearing a sheer garment for which women must have a name. It covered the torso and tucked in at her waist.

"Tell me more," she invited.

"Bad habit of mine, I know," Fred said. "I happen to remember things I read."

The skirt of the sheer garment did the job of a very short skirt below, as appeared when the jeans were lowered. It was as white as it was transparent, showing the narrow pants underneath, and the bra Fred would still have to figure out. With his large hands he stroked Mandy's body through the garment until he found a way to peel it down and let it fall to her feet. Mandy helped no more than politeness required. "Yes?" she demanded.

Fred studied her naked back next, looking for the secret of the bra's engineering. Easy for Leonardo! "Here's one of Leonardo's maxims," Fred said, "He's a genius. Everyone knows it. Do a survey among all people living in the known world, more of them know Leonardo than Julius Caesar. *Dust makes damage.* How can you argue with that? We should carve it over the post office door."

Mandy chuckled absently. The movement of her rib cage helped Fred find and unhitch the mechanism that held the bra's ends together in back, and he relieved her of the garment, dropping it on the table behind her, but at a distance from their plates. The breasts were firm and round and soft, their nipples pinker than they might be because the red glass of the beads around her neck was near them.

"The necklace?" Fred asked.

Mandy shook her head and leaned into him. "It's not in the way."

Fred slid his hands down her smooth back again, under the pants, and snaked them downward. "*Movement tends toward the center of gravity,*" he said. "If you don't mind, I'll lift you out of the rest of this."

"I don't mind if you'll stop quoting Leonardo," she said. "Three's a crowd." She'd gone quite serious. Fred lifted her out of the puddle of clothing and held her while she pried her shoes off, one foot at a time. He held her as if he were rescuing her from the burning building.

She whispered, "Isn't it nice that it takes a long time? Put me down now. Take your things off. No, I will."

Fred had laid her elegant body down on the couch and, his hands free for the first time, had begun with his shirt buttons. Blue Oxford cloth. Get it done. Mandy swung around, sat up, and her hands went straight to his belt.

"What was that line about the center of gravity?" she asked, finding his.

"You told me to stop quoting."

"Just the one line again. I liked it."

"*Movement tends toward the center of gravity,*" Fred repeated.

"It's true," Mandy said. "Take your own shirt off. I'm busy."

Fred let the shirt fall behind him and stepped out of his shoes.

Chapter Sixty-two

"Some of Leonardo's maxims," Fred said, after several minutes had elapsed, "if I may?"

"There's no turning back now," Mandy said. "Not for me. It's nice what you're doing. If you want to talk, talk. Just keep…good."

"Some of his maxims are easy enough to follow," Fred said. "Even self-serving. Such as this one: *I never weary of being useful.*"

"No fear," Mandy encouraged him. "You're being useful."

"So I didn't give it much thought," Fred continued. "Other sayings he seemed not to finish, like most of the rest of what he started. Until now I thought they didn't pertain to anything."

"Example?"

"*Not to leave the furrow,*" Fred quoted.

Her laughter was eclipsed by a gasp.

"More?" Fred asked.

"The fucking couch is too small," she said. "There's a crick—yikes!—We've gotta try something else or I'll break a hip."

"*Every obstacle yields to effort,*" Fred said, rising from her.

Mandy stood, her hands on her hips. "There's the table or the floor," she said. "I vote for the floor."

The telephone rang.

Fred stripped the bedclothes from the couch and picked up its three generous pillows. "Compromise," he offered.

"Who cares about sheets?" Mandy demanded.

Laid on the floor, the pillows gave generous room for Fred to lie beside her.

The telephone stopped ringing. "You don't have to get that?" she asked.

"They'll call back if it's important."

Fred stroked her torso as she snuggled against him, one arm under her head and neck, the two of them getting past the interruption. The earrings she wore matched, with their beads, the red necklace. Her dark hair streamed across the sheets. She was alive in Fred's hands and arms until she cried out, and cried out again, and began crying with surprisingly hot and copious tears. "I'm so sorry."

"Do I dare use your friend's bathroom?" Mandy asked after a while, tracing an idle finger above Fred's breastbone and letting it wander toward his groin. Her fingernails were pink, not with paint, but on their own, but less pink than her nipples. "It's great not to answer the phone," Mandy said. "I love sometimes on a Sunday morning to just lie in bed and not answer the phone."

"It's a luxury," Fred said. "Maybe a bit anti-social. My guy, who I'm working for now, doesn't have an answering machine. Why did you say 'I'm sorry'? What's the trouble? You have nothing to be—what you're doing right now could get us in trouble again. To quote—may I quote?"

"Good God. Do you remember everything you read?"

"For a while. Then it goes away. Otherwise I'd have a head like a junk shop. You'll hate me, since I forgot your name, and that's important to me. It's trivial, this other stuff, what I remember. Leonardo tended to think in fables, but he could also be an acute observer. Yes, I foresee trouble on its way."

"While we're waiting for trouble," Mandy said, beginning to concentrate, "you might as well tell me your fable."

"More an observation Leonardo made," Fred said. "About the anatomical specimen currently under observation. *Sometimes it confers with the human intelligence but it also sometimes has an intelligence of its own. In spite of what a man wants, it can be obstinate and go its own way. Sometimes it moves by itself, whether the man wants that or not. The man can be asleep, it's awake, and vice versa.* He goes on and concludes that this creature has a life and intelligence of its own, separate from the man. An independent beast."

"A pet," Mandy said. "I know, a pet monkey, with fur."

"Now you mention it," Fred said. "Then Leonardo goes on that therefore men shouldn't hide them under their clothes, but instead...."

"Not that easy to hide anyway," Mandy said. "I can try. Stay where you are. Pay no attention. I'll...."

Deftly, she straddled him.

Chapter Sixty-three

"I'll walk you back," Fred said while Mandy began to get herself together. It was after eleven. He unleashed Bernie's phone and dialed Clayton's number.

"Heard the phone ring," he said. "Couldn't get to it. You called?"

"I am sleeping," Clay scolded. "Time enough in the morning."

"Was it you?"

"I am sleeping," Clay repeated, and the connection went.

"Give me the number here," Mandy demanded. "In case I notice I've lost an earring."

She was oddly subdued when Fred left her at her street door, and would not invite him up. "Gotta shift gears," she said. "Get ready for the next thing."

"The airplane trip. The wedding. Cleveland," Fred said. "Sunday night."

"All the above."

"Anticipation," Fred agreed.

The rain had slowed. No one would claim that it had stopped. It was poised, more or less, waiting to increase to a flow you could call rain again.

The telephone was ringing when he let himself into Bernie's garage. Still ringing when he got upstairs.

"I'm afraid." Suzette Shaughnessy's voice, husky, subdued and tense.

Fred said, "Can you talk? Where are you?"

Silence. "He'll hear me."

"Who?"

"The man who was there before. Carl. He's...."

"Where?"

"Same place. I made a mistake, came back."

"You're there now? I'll be...."

"I can't," she whispered hoarsely. The connection was gone.

Fred eased into the windbreaker again, flexing his arms. He should run, or telephone to get her anonymous help, but all his instincts told him to take it slow. So far, Suzette at her most obvious had invariably been Suzette at her most devious.

What was going on?

Bernie's number was printed on the face of the phone. She'd picked it off while she was here, while he was talking with Mitchell. Yes. And since he told her it was out of service, she had taken it for granted—being used to the art business—that couldn't be true.

How long since the first call? Assume it had been Suzette an hour before, after his and Mandy's late supper, attempting to interrupt the other diversion, and before he walked her home.

He reached the wet sidewalk and started downhill.

That was a long time for one sustained emergency. Or had the first call been to invite him to come with her, hang around, maybe in the background, while she tried her own methods on Carl?

Then failing to raise Fred, she'd set off to try her luck by herself?

If so, by this time she and Carl had undoubtedly concluded that they had a common interest. Just the one project they could work together. She wanted Clayton's chest. His Leonardo. Which everyone, half-paralyzed with the desire to protect self-interest by prevarication, had agreed, by common consent, simply to call *the chest.* Fred was all she could work on. Also, Fred had seen to it that she be convinced he owned it now. She wouldn't say so, but she knew it was worth the gross national product of Slobovia. Otherwise none of this made sense. She'd do what she had to.

Half his instincts, stirred by the agonized worry in her voice, told him to run. It was what she wanted him to do. If it was also what she needed him to do, too bad. The winning half of his instincts, almost smugly, counseled a brisk and watchful midnight stroll instead: citizen responding to the Surgeon General's advice to walk off unnecessary flab after dessert rather than climb into that extra beer. Fred wasn't far from Pekham Street. He'd get there.

Suppose that by now Suzette and Carl had formed an alliance. Or Suzette and Peaslee, if he was still around. In that case, since she was convinced Fred had the Leonardo, Carl should be waiting in the alley with some persuasion. It must be another honey trap. It was how the opposition thought. The only difference was that, since they'd already tried Fred once, and failed, with sex, this time the trap was baited with the pheromones not of sex, but fear. The damsel in distress. "Which boils down to sex anyway," Fred grumbled. "She's not an old man."

The streets were not without occasional traffic, even of the odd pedestrian dodging rain that had begun to blow in sheets, shaking the dark new leaves on the bristling trees of Beacon Hill and denting new blossoms that seemed to clang with it until Fred shook his head and put the noise where it belonged, into the charged gutters and on the metal tops of trash containers waiting in the side yards.

When he turned onto Pekham Street, maintaining his quick saunter, it was clear that whatever the trap might be, it was already sprung. Five blocks away, downhill, a knot of activity churned there, almost facing Franklin Tilley's building: the swirling blue lights, the sirens, the officious uniforms in orange slickers, the excess of municipal squad cars, fire trucks, ambulances.

Fred let his pace pick up, as anyone's would. Suzette's blonde hair rose in a cloud before him, matted with blood and brains, the back of her skull blown off. Rain pounded onto the black raincoat, bunched under her...no. Carl had been waiting in the alley all right, but in a horizontal posture. That was Carl. Under the streetlights the large hole in his T-shirt leaked diluted blood into the tilted puddles of Pekham Street.

No, that was still wrong. Fred kept walking. Pekham Street was tilted. Puddles don't tilt. Trick of the eye, that was. Carl, on the folding stretcher, the baggy shorts wet with rain, and without the Nikes, was being loaded into a gaping vehicle. Fred kept walking. No worried Suzette huddled in the shadows, or stood hobnobbing with emergency personnel.

The windows of Franklin Tilley's apartment were dark. In the other windows of the building, and of the surrounding buildings, dark shapes moved inquisitively in front of dim light. The inhabitants of Beacon Hill would keep their windows modestly lit during what must become an unpleasant tragedy. Nobody who lived in such surroundings would wish to be seen to have a prurient interest.

Fred walked on to Charles Street, swung right toward the subway and was almost there before he remembered, "It won't be running now. Too late." He walked on as far as the Ritz, a good half hour, and stood across from it, thinking. Three in the morning. Without causing a commotion from which he and Clayton might never recover, there was no way to learn if Suzette was in her room. The desk wouldn't ring, they wouldn't tell him if she was there. Pay that much for a room, they're not going to let on to a dismal stranger whether you are at home or not. No way was he going to get through the lobby at this time of night, and let himself up to her floor either by elevator or the fire stairs.

She was here; or somewhere else, and healthy, Fred had no doubt. Hell, she could be holed up with Peaslee, in Franklin's pad.

The very few things Fred knew for certain could be arranged and rearranged a hundred ways.

He started walking again. What stood out was the likelihood that, for whatever reason might be percolating in that elusive brain, Suzette had expected and wanted Fred to find himself involved in the consequences of Carl's abrupt departure from this vale of tears.

Unless she'd been on the up and up. Even if that was true, Carl was no threat now, was he?

Look Suzette in the eye and ask. That was the only way to learn what lie she'd tell. Find her tomorrow. She wouldn't go far. She wanted Clay's *Madonna.* She'd come looking for him. He could rely on that.

Find her tomorrow. Not tonight.

He'd stay by the *Madonna.*

Fred let himself quietly into his office on Mountjoy Street, and stretched out on the couch. "They're getting serious," he muttered, before he slept.

Chapter Sixty-four

Fred woke, bathed in a sudden sweat, at the sound of Clayton's foot on the spiral staircase. "It's noon," Clayton was saying. Six A.M. by Fred's watch. He'd gotten onto his feet before Clay reached the room. "London time," Clay explained. "Being a light sleeper, I heard you come in."

"Carl's been killed," Fred said. "I have to move. Don't know...."

"I telephoned Miss Dibble at two this morning," Clay went on. "And gave her...Carl?"

"I mentioned Carl to you," Fred said. "Played the part of a bodyguard or enforcer over on Pekham Street."

"Of course I remember. I never had the pleasure," Clay said. "Killed?"

"Hole in the chest. Gunshot. Suzette's involved, Shaughnessy."

"The dealer," Clay dismissed her.

"Yes. Since I don't understand where we are, I grabbed a couple hours shuteye. Didn't want to wake you again. Figured it would wait."

"She promised to fax me the inventory," Clay said. "While we're waiting...? I regret I have no coffee, Fred. It is a stimulant. I shall go for the fax. I shall be glad to bring coffee back for you, if I pass a suitable establishment that is open at this time of day."

"I'll go," Fred said. "You start adjusting your mind. I am going to have to do some version of what you call my civic duty before many more hours have passed. Prepare your mind. Before the day's out, your house could be filled with cops."

"I have done nothing...." Clay started.

"They'll be glad to hear it," Fred promised him. "Do we hide the *Madonna* or what? If we hide her, it has to be outside the house, and it has to be quick. You be thinking. I'll go for the fax."

~ ~ ~

There was no rain. It had so absolutely departed from the dawning sky that there seemed no possible explanation for the wetness of the streets. Fred's watch read six-fifteen.

Boston is not a large city. Nothing like the City That Never Sleeps—New York. But there are island oases of wakefulness. Fred stopped for coffee at a Dunkin' Donuts and carried it with him to the Kinko's on Beacon Hill.

"If I'm going to work with this joker," he remarked, "he has to learn new tricks. Putting in his own fax machine would be a start."

"Tell me about it," the girl back of the counter agreed. She was rummaging under the counter for Fred's order. "Tell him to put in a copy machine while he's at it. I'll go home."

"Let me ask you this," Fred started. The girl was sullen, tired, bored, and bedraggled. She could use some cheering up. But nothing occurred to Fred to say that might accomplish that mission.

"Yeah?" she said.

"Just a dumb observation I was going to make," Fred said. "But it's too dumb to make. And dumb as it is, I can't even think of it. Six o'clock in the morning, everything's pretty dumb."

"Tell me about it," she said. "I've been on since eleven."

"I'll tell him not to buy the machine," Fred promised. "This way I get out, see people."

"Tell me about it," she said. "Also this way I keep my job."

The city was waking slowly. The air, drowsy with moisture, was clean and fresh and promised all kinds of good things. Lights in the buildings flickered on here and there as early risers found the bathroom switches and reached for the taps. Taxis prowled through the streets, looking for fares on their way to stand in long lines at the airport for early flights.

Fred avoided Pekham Street, but stopped again at the Dunkin' Donuts to buy breakfast. Coffee and doughnuts. He bought extra doughnuts. Clayton might want an early morning doughnut along with his herbal tea, his Hint o' Mint or Cinnamon Scam. Possibly nobody had told him that sugar was a stimulant; like anything else that helps you stay alive.

"I am all a-tremble," Clay said, reaching out for the Kinko's bag and resisting, with a shuddering smirk of righteousness, the doughnuts' siren song. "You didn't look?"

Fred shook his head. "What do we do with the *Madonna?* Hide her?"

"Put her in the racks with the other paintings," Clay instructed. "Out of the limelight. Move the love seat back where it was. Let the house not proclaim that anything unusual is resident here. I shall be reading the document."

Fred climbed to Clay's parlor, wrapped the *Madonna* in the Kashmir shawl from the piano's top, and carried her down the stairs. What did she weigh, ten pounds? In his arms she was ten pounds of coiled lightning.

"Unwrap it," Clay instructed, looking up, "so it looks like the others. Be careful, sliding it in. Don't scratch it. And don't allow those hinges to scratch anything else."

"Right," Fred said. He'd been in and out for three days and, despite Clayton's invitation, had not had time to survey, much less study, the paintings Clay kept in the racks; not even what must be elsewhere in the house, on the second and third floors. If he stuck around, there'd be a lot to see. He took her shawl off and slid the *Madonna* into a space next to a painting on wood of similar size, a man in evening dress, 1930s, signed Beckman. He put cardboard between them. "Don't want those two getting up to mischief," he said.

"Interesting," Clay was saying to himself at the desk, studying the inventory. "It's dry as it should be. Facts only. No enthusiasms. Yes, here's the Bronzino I mentioned, the *Sebastian Transfixed* that sold last year in London, to Agnelli. With a suitable low appraisal. The appraisal for an estate is always low. And here is the Mantegna, so-called. Hah! *Item: A Penitent Magdalene*, it reads, with the measurements. *Italian School, fifteenth century, wood, dirty,* is how it is described. No mention of Mantegna at all. No attribution. Not even a suggestion. That attribution was foisted onto the painting after this appraisal, some time during the last seventy years. We see now what we are dealing with. Yes, here also is the Titian." He did not look up, continuing his eye and finger's track down the list Miss Dibble had sent him. "Its condition is noted: *poor*. Thank you, yes, Fred, if you would, put the shawl back as it was. My wife's photograph on it. And the love seat where it was.

"If we do have the visitors you threaten, let them see no more than what they already expect to see: a quiet home in which are concerned and upright citizens. That is what will be seen unless something is out of place."

Upstairs in the parlor again Fred replaced the shawl, and the photograph; moved the love seat and the chairs from which he and Clayton had surveyed the *Madonna;* and finally smoothed out the indentation on the love seat's seat's pink plush, where the *Madonna* had rested, eliminating all trace of her from the parlor. Then, acting on an impulse he did not know had been growing since the night before, he commandeered the telephone and made it divulge the number for that library in Cambridge in whose outlying park he had been known to camp in the days before the Charlestown place.

"Let me have reference," he demanded.

"Reference," a female voice told him, after a wait. "Ms. Riley."

"Just a minute. No," the voice said, "for that I'd look in one of those small French literary periodicals from the 1920's. Try *Le Navire d'Argent*, something like that. That's where Joyce published the opening of *Finnegans Wake*. We wouldn't have it here. Try down the road, at Widener. Or the BPL. Sorry, yes?"

"My question," Fred said, "I want to know, how much was a scudo worth, in Milan, in 1525?"

"Milan, 1525?" Ms. Riley said.

"Yes. Part of the larger question, was twenty scudi, in 1525, worth more or less than the gross national product of Paraguay? No, that's more than I want to know. Just—how much was a scudo worth, in today's money, in 1525 in Milan. Okay? I'll take it from there. Can you do that, Ms. Riley?"

"I don't know the answer, but I can find out," Ms. Riley said. "Can you call back?"

"I'll probably stop over," Fred said.

"If it takes more than an hour, we have to charge you," Ms. Riley said.

"That's Okay."

"But it won't take an hour," she said. "I'm on until five. After that, I'll leave the information, and the bill if there is one but there won't be. Your name?"

Clay's exclamation, below, sounded almost like mortal agony.

"Fred," Fred said. "I'll come by this afternoon, maybe tomorrow."

When Fred reached Clay he was on his feet, aghast, his mouth hanging open, the sheaf of Kinko's fax paper rustling in his grip.

"Listen to this," he said, when he could make his mouth work.

"You have my attention. You sounded like the aunt in the third act finding the corpse in the window seat."

"Listen," Clay said. He raised the papers and read in a trembling voice, "*Item: One ornamental wooden coffer, The Annunciation, School of Leonardo….*"

"Holy mackerel!" Fred said. "There's two?"

"*Da Vinci,*" Clayton finished. He let the papers drop to his side and stared. "Fifty thousand pounds, in the appraisal. More than the value they gave the Bronzino, I might add," he said lamely.

"Cripes," Fred said. "Brierstone had another Leonardo?"

Clay shook his head, stunned. "It all comes clear," he said. "I see now. The angels, the gilding. Of course. The top of the box was—*is*—has to be a da Vinci *Annunciation.* An early painting it must be, as we know from the manner of the painting on the corpus of the chest. An early work, done in Florence, before Leonardo departed for Milan in 1489, while he was still apprenticed to Verrocchio's shop.

"Fred, I've been blind. Seeing only what I expected to see, I dismissed what I saw, because the body of the chest did not fit with my *Madonna.* But that is only because my *Madonna* was done a decade later.

"I am in a fever. There is another Leonardo in this city. There are two, and I am in a position to own them both."

Chapter Sixty-five

"No wonder the opposition is in such a commotion," Fred said. "Running around seducing people. Lying out of every orifice. Killing people. They want the rest of the package. They took it apart to ship it; made a mongrel out of the chest so nobody would care about it in the container. With the plan, when they got here…but hold on. That's not much, that appraisal, fifty thousand pounds. For Leonardo?"

"At the time the world was very different," Clay said. "These things were not regarded as they are today. A lot has happened since thieves walked off with the Louvre's *Mona Lisa* in 1911. Which they could do because nobody valued her enough at the time even to keep an eye on her."

"A Leonardo *Annunciation.* So that's the big thing Franklin was waiting for," Fred said. "Waiting for, possibly dying for."

Clay said, "Listen to me. I know it's in my notes. On your desk. Blinded, I paid no attention to anything prior to 1490. I'll find it again. Among the paintings from Leonardo's hand, lost paintings, known but unaccounted for, but in the record: there were several *Madonnas* he had completed *before* he left Florence.

"An *Annunciation*! Because of the angels on the chest, I see it now. You know the one in the Uffizi. The angel on the left. An early work attributed to Ghirlandaio until the late 1800s. Nobody knew. Nothing was ever signed. In that painting, Leonardo included a background of the Florence landscape. In this one, there may be no more than a hint of architecture, since the function of the image is different. From the remainder of the chest's decoration I can see it. Angels and lilies, the symbol the Virgin holds when the angel speaks to her. Gabriel. Or does the angel hold it? I am in such a tizzy. 'Hail, full of grace.' The angel kneels. Yes. There are two arches, in gold. In one, the left side, the angel bearing the lily. The virgin is in the other. Where is it? It's the top of my chest. Has to be."

"*School of Leonardo* it says, remember? On the appraisal," Fred pointed out.

"Of course that's what the *appraisal* says. An estate appraisal gives every advantage it can to the estate. I was blind. I must study the chest again," Clay demanded. "I will not rest until I do. Find the *Annunciation*. I repeat, where is it?"

"We should probably ask Mitchell," Fred said. "But given that nothing is what meets the eye, take it slow. I admit you've got me curious. Even if we can find it, and get past the intervening complications that multiply by the day, how many millions do they want for it? You ready to bid against Agnelli? Take it easy, stay out of sight. I'll take another look at the chest."

He left Clay scrambling like a terrier through the notes on his desk.

While Fred tapped Bernie's secret code onto the buttons of his alarm pad, Suzette Shaughnessy stepped out of the shadows of a neighboring doorway. It had started to rain again. Dr. Mitchell, slightly behind her, held a blue umbrella over the pair of them. The umbrella Mitchell held in his left hand. It was with his right that he pressed the gun's muzzle against the small of Suzette Shaughnessy's back. He was still dressed as he had been on their first meeting, in the tired blue suit, the vintage fedora, the trench coat from a movie nobody had seen, not even on late night television, for thirty years.

Suzette, bareheaded, pouted apologies. Mitchell, nudging her from behind, told Fred, "We're coming in."

"Good," Fred said. "I didn't know where to find you." He opened the entrance next to the big overhead door, then stepped back and let the two shove in, Suzette stumbling, Mitchell propelling her in front of him. Mitchell dropped the umbrella to the garage floor, keeping a wary eye on Fred until Fred closed them in.

"Sorry," Suzette said. "He just suddenly got like this."

"Upstairs," Mitchell ordered.

"We're working together," Suzette protested, more or less to the space around them, as Fred, following Mitchell's gestures, led the way upstairs into Bernie's living space.

Suzette followed, Mitchell behind her, keeping the gun's muzzle firmly in the small of Suzette's back. She shivered in the black raincoat. Her face wavered with banners of pink and white, the fear taking her that way.

"What is it with you people?" Fred asked, letting his eyes flick back and forth from Mitchell to Suzette.

"On the couch," Mitchell demanded. "Not you, Suzette. Him. Fred. Keep your hands where I can see them."

"She'll faint if she doesn't sit down." Fred advised. "She'll flop down like a turd."

Mitchell's eyes darted around the room. "You," he told Fred again. "On the couch."

"We assume I care if the lady lives or dies," Fred said, standing his ground.

"The chest," Mitchell said.

"Downstairs."

"I knew it," Suzette said.

"She'll faint," Fred repeated.

Suzette winked, moaned, and dropped like a turd. Fred, lurching sideways to avoid getting tangled in her limbs, twisted and managed a decisive swipe at the side of Mitchell's head. The gun's report was almost absorbed by the room's rugs, drapes, and Bernie's couch and sound system.

"I'm all right," Suzette called. Fred, standing over the twisting professor, kicked the gun out of his hand and then kicked him again, with precision, back of the ear, on the other side of the head.

"He won't be out long," Fred warned. "Find something to tie him with." He flipped Mitchell onto his back while Suzette went prospecting in Bernie's kitchen cupboards. "Quick," Fred urged. Suzette came back with twine and a pair of kitchen scissors. "Get his shoes off," he ordered. While Suzette worked at the black wingtips, he tied Mitchell's thumbs together, and then his wrists, behind his back. "Socks too," he said. The professor's naked feet were nothing you'd want to find under your Christmas tree. Fred took more twine and tied the big toes together, then the ankles. Suzette had watched the procedure carefully, absorbing information in case she could use it later in her new life as an art dealer. She stood up then, twisting herself out of her wet coat and throwing it on the linoleum floor of Bernie's kitchen area. She was wearing a blue dress under the coat. Blue linen, cotton, something like that. It didn't look warm enough. Locating a mirror, she checked herself in that.

"It hit the couch," Fred said. The bullet had disappeared into the Hurculon upholstery of the couch's plaid back.

"What do you, sleep on the floor?" Suzette demanded. The sheets were still spread out there, as he and Mandy had left them.

"Don't touch the gun," Fred cautioned. Suzette was starting to wander. "Mitchell's prints are on it. Leave it where it is." Mitchell's gun, formerly Franklin Tilley's, was lying on the sheets where he'd kicked it.

Suzette said, "Downstairs. You had it the whole time. I knew it, Mitchell," she said. "I told you...." She swerved away abruptly from the direction in which her words were heading, and gave Fred a tentative smile that, in a moment, lit the room before it was replaced by a look of dawning alarm. "It's like I'm on fire," she said. "God, Fred. That was close. Thanks for the graphic image. Me doing my famous impersonation of a flopping turd."

Mitchell stirred.

Suzette stroked the bodice of the summery blue dress and straightened its sides. "I thought I was going to have to buy another dress," she said. "That's all I thought. Can you imagine?" She took a hesitant step in Fred's direction.

Chapter Sixty-six

"The neighbors don't care when someone fires a gun?" Suzette asked.

Fred shrugged. "It's Beacon Hill. It wasn't loud. If the neighbors hear it, and if they know what it is, they don't want to make waves."

"Maybe life sucks," she said, taking another hesitant step in Fred's direction. "But it's better than the alternative. I'm going to sit down before I really do fall." She sank into the couch.

"Now we talk," Fred said.

"He would have killed me," Suzette said. The observation sounded like an explanation more than an apology.

"Yes, but he didn't," Fred countered. "The way I took him, you were never in danger. He doesn't know what he's doing. Gets lucky sometimes, but he's an amateur. Meanwhile, your delayed reaction is only fear. Leftover fear. Don't worry about it. Fear's a good thing. *Fear is the prolongation of life.* Also, as the man said, *Fear springs to life more quickly than anything else.*"

Suzette heaved a long sigh and her face softened unmistakably. "Fred, have you noticed," she reached a trembling hand out to touch his arm, "could maybe we put Mitchell out of sight? How, when you are almost killed, the only thing you can think about next is to make love with someone?"

"Sure," Fred told her. "I have to tell you, mostly, in my experience, there isn't a sensible way to act on those feelings. Mitchell didn't walk you over at gunpoint."

Suzette started to tremble. She did it well. "I'm still afraid," she said.

Fred shifted Mitchell to one side and put a straight chair where he could sit and see her.

"Right," he said. "Last night, about midnight, you were afraid of Carl. Any new word on Carl?"

"We do this together," Suzette said. "It's downstairs. Show me. We share, fifty-fifty."

"We're talking about Carl."

"It would be awful if something had happened to Mitchell," Suzette suggested. "Like in self-defense."

"Too late," Fred said. "The gun stays where it is. Nothing happens to Mitchell. Forensics would wonder about the marks on his hands and feet, where he was tied. We're talking about Carl."

"Mitchell killed him. It was awful," she said. "Fifty-fifty."

"That marble top, we took that off," Fred said. "To be totally honest with you, that's already on its way out of the country. Client who wants—you know how some people collect everything they can find with pigs? Calendars, dish towels, letter openers, soup tureens, cookie jars? This guy likes monkeys, and he's got a weird streak. Saudi Arabian. Money to roll in? He doesn't care. So I can't sell the chest is the problem. It's not all there."

"Who gives a shit?" Suzette said. "You sold the top? We don't need it. Forget it. As long as you have the rest. You have the box, I have the top. Well, Mitchell has it, but I know.... The owner gets in today. Who in my opinion should have been here the whole time and we'd never have gotten into this trouble with Franklin and Mitchell and the rest of it. So. But Franklin's out of it now."

"Dead," Fred said.

"Yikes! And Mitchell's out obviously, since he killed Carl. I don't care if he says it was self-defense. How did he have the gun, then? Like you say, his prints are on the gun. And I can provide Agnelli. I meet him tonight at the Ritz bar. We both do, I mean. Fifty-fifty. So we're still Okay."

"Right," Fred said. "On the subject of Carl, between twelve o'clock last night and now, what are we, eight in the morning? Where were you? You and Mitchell?"

Mitchell groaned.

"Mitchell, you have something to say?" Fred suggested.

Suzette, not breaking stride, continued, "Mitchell's still my partner, just in this one project. Don't worry, Mitchell. I'm going to take care of you, make sure you get your share. Even for self defense, those lawyers are going to want thousands."

"I want a lawyer," Mitchell said, his voice deflated almost to non-existence.

"Right," Suzette agreed. "Don't say anything to anyone about anything. Stand mute, it's called. Until you get a lawyer. He'll say the same thing."

Fred said, "Carl went out into the rain last night, no shoes. An observation I'm making."

"The chest's downstairs, Mitchell," Suzette said. "Like I said. Fred, I haven't exactly leveled with you up to now. Let's have coffee."

"No. A: You called me. D: Carl was killed. L: Mitchell turned up this morning, here, with a gun in your back. Fill me in. The missing letters. Unless Mitchell wants to." He glanced in the direction of Mitchell, whose jaws remained clamped shut defiantly.

"He's going to deny everything," Suzette started. "His lawyer will make him. Since he can't lie like everyone else in the art business. Anyway. You're sure there's no coffee? For your partner? Okay. The fast version. I decide to try Carl again. Put something together. I go over. The other guy, the lawyer, is already gone. You saw him. Big shot. Useless. Back to Atlanta. Carl invites me up, I go up. He's alone. I take off my shoes, one thing leads to another.

"The funny thing," Suzette said, "Carl's big. And he scares the wee wee out of you, talking tough. And all. But Franklin Tilley had something I never saw, because he had Carl buffaloed. Walked around in the apartment in his socks. Plus, and two, he was done in three minutes. Guys that work out and act tough, I've noticed, it frequently goes like that. The whole thing, whereas the wimps and weaklings, like the academics, oftentimes it's…what it comes down to, all that muscle doesn't have anything to do with it at all. Exercise all you want, there isn't a muscle in there. Then he pulled that gun….

"Listen, if I can't get Agnelli in there tonight, it's the last time I even get close to him. I didn't level with you before, now I will. It's worth as much as an aircraft carrier."

"You've lost me."

"I was running away," Suzette said, panting, her eyes bright. "With him coming after, Carl, getting out of that place. How is he going to have time to put those sneakers on? Ten million at least. My commission's ten percent. A million dollars."

Mitchell glared.

"Which I divide fifty-fifty with Mitchell. But, here's where you come in. We put the box back with the top, we sell it for more. Ask what you want, I get half."

"Everyone lies," Mitchell intoned from the floor. "Make him show you the chest. Don't be a fool, Suzette."

Fred looked over the situation: Mitchell laid out on the floor, well bound; Suzette unable to keep her eyes from flickering toward the gun. "I need a hand with it on these stairs," he said. "Suzette?"

"Don't play games," Suzette said. "There's no time. We have to suck up to the owner. That could take most of the day. If we don't land Agnelli tonight, he's gone. I promise we don't have time to fool around. You're in the big leagues now, Fred. We are talking Leonardo da Vinci."

"Make him show it to us," Mitchell demanded.

Chapter Sixty-seven

"You were together all night," Fred said to Suzette, behind her on the stairs. "You and Mitchell."

"Scared to death," Suzette explained. "After what happened to Carl? I called you, but you didn't come in time, so I called Mitchell."

"Ah," Fred said.

He pulled the tarp back from Bernie's Lagonda and exposed the chest where he had stashed it, still in its green plastic trash bags, its bottom resting on newspapers to protect it from the possibility of oil.

"He's got it," Suzette called up the stairs. "It's here, Mitchell." She dropped her voice. "No offense. We couldn't figure out how to get past the alarm. It's all we were going to do, wait for you inside, Fred. Out of the rain. You didn't damage it, did you? Getting that crazy top off. Fred, I don't understand you. You don't care that you own a chest painted by Leonardo?"

"Doesn't balance favorably against a couple of dead men," Fred said. "Neither one of them worth much. Let's get it upstairs. Take the front."

"For God's sake don't harm it," Mitchell called.

Suzette whispered, stooping to grab one handle, "I spent the night with him. Had to, since we're working together. He's holed up in a stinking rat's nest belongs to a friend of his, near the museum, with the paintings. I'll level with you now. It is an *Annunciation* by da Vinci. Gorgeous. Pristine. Never been seen.

Perfect. Like I say, Mitchell has it, but it's not his. He got in a snit with Franklin and ran off with it. Lover's quarrel.

"What we do, we leave Mitchell where he is, pick up the painting, carry it back to Pekham Street, deliver it to the owner—I have the guy's name now, finally, from Carl—and promise to come back tonight with Agnelli. And with the chest. Or we carry it with us."

"Upstairs," Fred directed. The phone was ringing.

Mitchell's eyes bugged when the chest was placed on the rug beside him. "I thought I would never see it again," he said.

Fred picked up the phone.

"Say nothing more than you must on the telephone." Clay's voice. "Pitchers have ears."

"Visitors?" Fred asked.

"I have heard nothing. I should have come to look at it with you. What do you…?"

"Not a good time," Fred said. "He's out of the country, as a matter of fact. I'm keeping an eye on the place."

"Ah," Clay understood. "Visitors. Understood. Excellent. Excellent, Fred. I shall await…I leave it in your good hands," Clay said. He hung up, saying, probably to himself, "My instincts are never wrong."

Mitchell had managed to sit up and he was doing what he could to examine the topless chest's surfaces, inside and out. "It's no worse than it was," he announced, his eyes following the scrolling designs, doing an inventory of the angels' wing feathers.

"Fifty-fifty," Suzette whispered.

"It's intact," Mitchell said. "God have mercy."

Fred said, "Maybe you have the patience to wait."

Rain stroked the windows of Bernie's living space.

Mitchell said, "I don't care what happens to me."

"That's wise," Fred counseled. "Except for the top, it's as you first saw it. In England. In the Brierstone…."

"It was sitting there in the hall," Mitchell snarled. "English people! Aristocrats! They kept boots in it. A wedding chest. Perfect subject for the occasion. The *Annunciation* on it that you'd think would break their backs with its beauty. English gentry. They lived with it all this time and couldn't see it under their noses, because they knew it only for how they used it, a box for their boots. It was a masterpiece. I knew it immediately. Leonardo's *Annunciation* that hangs in the Uffizi, in Florence. You know the painting. Everyone knows it. It is on a thousand Christmas cards.

"My heart stopped and stood still, and then flooded with suspicion and delight. Then with alarm."

"Go easy, Mitchell," Suzette cautioned.

"My client required the shipment to move without attracting attention. The customs officers on both sides of the Atlantic would recognize the superb quality of the chest, I told myself, even though the Brierstone family clearly did not. Suppose one of them said to another, 'Don't I know this painting?' Suspicions would be aroused. Was the chest stolen? The whole shipment would be subject to scrutiny, despite the reputation of the diplomat in question, into whose container the shipment was to be placed.

"It had to be hidden somehow, and as you know, the chest was of considerable size."

Mitchell paused and attempted to make himself comfortable. It was difficult, delivering a lecture in art history with his hands tied behind him. "Now, at this stage in my presentation, I beg for your understanding. I must confess an indiscretion, though I am an honest man. We won't argue about what might be due to customs officers. Some things take precedence.

"I confess it. I did both imagine and execute a ruse."

"Okay," Suzette said. She'd been perched nervously on the edge of the couch, listening to Mitchell's account.

"Fortunately, my researches have included more than a little practical experience in the methods used by the craftsmen I have studied, that group of Sienese masters of whom I told you, it seems now, so long ago. I removed the top from the chest, the *Annunciation.* Without it the chest might attract no notice, I thought. The top I determined to carry myself, with my luggage. How I disguised it I will not tell you. It was a risk. I took it. If it was questioned I would respond as I was guided. It was not questioned. I am as poor as I look.

"Even without its top, the chest was handsome. I worried that being incomplete, it would stand out. In the garret where much of the collection was stored, I had noticed a wooden panel large enough to be substituted for the top I had removed. It was almost old enough to pass muster to a dull eye—early sixteenth century. Painted on it was a scene so blasphemous I could hardly bring myself to handle it. The mother of God and her child, in converse with an obscenity of monkeys. It was grotesque and embarrassing. Perfect. Only because the cause was good, I steeled myself, cut it to fit, and attached it to the chest, using the methods suitable to its age.

"And now I did the only thing I am ashamed of." Mitchell stopped, trembled, and blushed like a fat boy of fourteen.

The phone rang.

"*Item.*" Clay's voice.

"No," Fred said. "This is Fred. Bernie's traveling. Is there a message?"

Clay paused for effect. "I should not say this on the telephone. Amongst the inventory, listed with the candlesticks, glass and silver, number 437, *item: a mother and child with monkeys. Continental school. Wood. Dirty. £2.*"

"I can leave a note for him," Fred said. "*Continental,* eh? Don't know when he'll be back. On the other matter, don't hold your breath."

Clay was almost chortling with pleasure. "The provenance is confirmed. Alas, it was slightly larger."

"I'll leave him a note," Fred promised.

"Now," Mitchell repeated, taking up his story again, "I did the only thing I am ashamed of."

Fred held his peace. Mitchell, blinded by its apparent blasphemy, hadn't seen the *Madonna* at all! He couldn't see the Leonardo for the apes!

"What I did next, I admit, was fraud," Mitchell stammered on. "However harmless. The intent was to mislead. I was carried away, swept up in the stream of events. Examining my conscience now, I must confess to arrogance. I wanted to prove to myself that I could do it.

"Because the cuts I had made exposed new wood that had not darkened as the other edges had, I was obliged to act dishonestly. Not only did I sand down and smooth and give a fraudulent patina to those edges: I darkened them!"

"So what?" Suzette demanded.

"That makes me a forger. I will regret it until my dying day."

Chapter Sixty-eight

"So," Suzette said. "Let's get this show on the road."

The phone rang.

"Just—Fred? Before I head for the airport." Mandy's voice.

"Hey," Fred said. "Can I call you back?"

"No. Let me talk. I'll be fast. I woke up, I was dreaming of a new course called *Parliamentary Math,"* she said. "My dreams are useless. You dream?"

"I'll call back," Fred said.

"No, wait." Were those tears? "The thing is, Fred, I should tell you, when this semester's over, I'm going to Portland. That's two weeks."

"Maine? That's not so...."

"Oregon. My big break. I'm going to teach math in a community college there, and while I get settled I have a job doing summer school classes for kids who flunked high school courses."

"Oregon," Fred said.

"I like the West Coast. I like the way people think."

Fred couldn't compete with the way people thought on the West Coast. He looked across the room at Suzette. At Mitchell, who stared at the chest. At the gun in its nest of used bed sheets.

"Come on, Fred. We had such a nice time," Mandy said.

"I guess...I don't much care where I live," Fred began.

"No. For me it has to be a fresh start all the way. I wanted to tell you last night, Fred, but I couldn't. And now there's this wedding...Fred?"

"What do you look forward to in Oregon?" Fred asked, making his voice as friendly as he could.

Mandy had a paragraph of things she looked forward to but before she was well into it Fred had to tell her, "Good luck with the new job and the new place."

"So," Suzette said. "How do we play this? Here's what I suggest. Mitchell we keep out of sight. We go pick up the *Annunciation*, get the package together again. We can convince the owner to do it since you have the chest here, and he'll be so happy to have his Leonardo again,"

"Not Leonardo," Mitchell said.

Suzette lunged toward the gun. Fred scooped her out of the air and dropped her onto the couch again. "Let the man talk," he demanded.

"Don't listen to him," Suzette said. "He's crazy."

Mitchell droned on, as if there had been no interruption, "I had in my care, I was convinced, not a Leonardo at all, but what must be the greatest work ever created by that master, the subject of my long study, Icilio Federico Joni. It is a spectacular Joni," Mitchell announced. "The best, perhaps, that has appeared. Of museum quality. That he is the painter I now have no doubt. I have had ample time, here in Boston, to study the top. I know Joni's hand. Even concealed in the best of his imitations, I know it. The chest...."

"Bastard," Suzette shrieked.

"The chest, aside from the painting, which is Joni's, I suspect to be the work of a collaborator, most likely Igino Gottardi. He was not careful with his glue, which tests modern. The wood is old, from furniture of the period. No question. But the joints? No, they will not pass muster, as I told my client. Of course my conclusion will require corroboration from a colleague in Milan."

"So it's a fake," Fred said, moving toward the phone. "The whole thing. The top. The *Annunciation*."

"Not fake. You lie! An imitation. An *hommage*. An *original* Joni," Mitchell shrieked, then whispered his conclusion, "made,

I would say, between 1900 and 1910, at the high point of his career."

"An *original* forgery. Who cares?" Fred said, "since it's a forgery?"

"I will ask you not to use that word again," Mitchell said. "Not in my hearing. The *work* is not forgery."

"I've gotta call that girl back," Fred said. "Give me a minute."

"Yes?" Clay's voice.

"That thing," Fred said. "Not what we wanted. Sorry."

Clay's silence stretched while Fred noticed the rain trickling down the windows, and Suzette's eyes fixed on the chest now, with money struggling to surface in them.

"You have this on good authority?" Clay demanded.

"The best."

"Unfortunate," Clay said. "Still...." He rang off.

Mitchell said eagerly, "I will publish the work. Just by itself it is worthy of a book. At least of a learned article. I am grateful to you. The top will be reunited to the chest. Hinges will be a problem," he noticed, thinking ahead. "Half the hinges are gone. We'll make more. I know how to rust them appropriately. There's a man...."

"You're going to be busy," Fred said.

"Yes. With my book. The *Annunciation Wedding Chest* will be first published as a Joni, by its discoverer. Not as Tilley wanted."

"I was wondering when we'd get to Franklin Tilley."

"I regret to say, a dishonest man," Mitchell announced. "May I sit on a chair?"

Suzette pulled a pack of cigarettes from a raincoat pocket, tapped it against the arm of the couch, and lit one. She blew a deliberative plume of smoke. "We're wasting time with this fool," she announced. "Wanting to find a masterpiece by this forger he's in love with, of course he pretends to find one."

"At first I misjudged him," Mitchell said. Fred was hoisting him off the floor, getting his buttocks onto one of the straight chairs. "I believed the respect was mutual. When I finally understood that, despite my protests, he was determined to sell the work as from the hand of Leonardo…."

"He shot him," Suzette helped.

"On that subject I rest mute," Mitchell said.

Chapter Sixty-nine

"He was adamant. The work must be sold as a Leonardo. He was prepared, on behalf of my client, and with his commissions in mind, to perpetrate fraud. The *Magdalene* must be offered as a Mantegna. Well and good. I held no brief for the *Magdalene. Caveat emptor.* It was his crime, not mine. But at the misrepresentation of the Icilio Joni I would not connive. I was the Joni expert. If I represented myself as having been hoodwinked by my subject, I could never hold up my head again."

"Here's what the jury will think," Suzette said, blowing smoke. "The old man shot his lover. Then shot Carl. Lover's quarrel. Because Carl…Franklin was cheating on him with Carl."

Mitchell shook his head mournfully. "It made no difference to Franklin Tilley that, as a Joni, the work has true value, both financial and historic," he announced. "Were it offered as Leonardo, and the seller were then exposed as a fraud—notice I say the seller, not the work—the value of the work would become anomalous.

"It is a mark of the market's perversity," Mitchell said. "A little Madonna and Child in tempera and gold on wood, that might have entered the market in 1920 attributed to, for example, Duccio di Buoninsegna, of modest value in 1920 even as Duccio, but later unmasked as one of Joni's masterly imitations, might command a truly serious price on today's market, once proved to be a genuine work from Joni's hand. Incidentally, since it is I who am the expert, I alone can present an opinion that qualifies the work as being from Joni's hand.

"There are collectors—I know them, I told Franklin—who, once we put it together again…so intent was he on selling the *Annunciation* as a Leonardo that he burned his bridges. Because I had already told him that the body of the chest was of recent origin, he disposed of it. Couldn't have it around, he said, to cast doubt on the *Annunciation.* He told me first that he had burned it. He would not listen when I explained that once we put the chest together again, it would have a value of as much as a hundred fifty thousand dollars," Marshall said. "On the open market. Perhaps more."

He paused and looked at Fred with a vacant speculation that seemed to demand response.

"You didn't want the chest," Fred told Suzette. "Neither of you. Not you. Not Franklin. You knew it would never pass."

"Mitchell wanted it," Suzette said. Her eyes flickered toward the gun, which Fred might do well now to put out of harm's way. It was clear now; at least the probability made sense. She'd wanted to get next to the chest again, destroy it if she could; and anyone associated with it, if need be. Fred next, then Mitchell? Having used herself to smuggle Mitchell in here, with the gun. What ruse had tempted Carl into the alley, in the rain, without his shoes? Whose hand had held the gun? By what means had Suzette, or Mitchell, or both of them together, led Franklin Tilley out to the river's edge? She'd been part of this trail of death. Good luck to the jury who tried to figure it out.

Suzette lit the room with a dazzling smile. Fred kicked the gun, sheets and all, under the couch.

"If there's a reward," Suzette said, "we split fifty-fifty. I brought Mitchell here after all. Shit," she added. "What's the odds? It's up to you, Fred, I guess, if this old man gets to tell his story. Maybe it doesn't matter. We can still sell the *Annunciation.* Cripes, you tell me. Who cares what Mitchell says? Who's going to believe a murderer?"

Chapter Seventy

It was a good three hours before Fred was able to close the door on his guests, with their armed and uniformed escort, Suzette expressing brilliant surprise at the suggestion that she might be anything more than a hapless victim in this tragedy. Fred had had to accept the obligation to keep himself available here, at Bernie's, where there was still nothing to read but Leonardo's *Notebooks*. Then it took twenty minutes to try to explain the situation to Clayton on the telephone, honoring his paranoid version of secure communication by speaking as far as possible without using nouns.

"What chance is there that the villain saved the edges he sawed off? What chance that we can get them?"

"None," Fred said. "What's more, we can't show any interest in doing it. We just breathe easy that nobody seems to miss the thing. It was a fair purchase. Don't monkey with it."

"What of the owner? The man—I mention no names, not on the telephone—from whose collection the item in question originates?"

"Before I telephoned you I made another call. On Bernie's bill, if he tries the number, it will answer as *not in service*. The owner made a mistake risking a trip to Pekham Street. As soon as he arrives, he'll be picked up. Among other things, people will wonder what he wants to buy, and where, for so much money. If he ever leaves this country at all, after our people are happy with his answers, he's due for about twenty years of true discomfort in England."

"And you. You are comfortable where you are?"

Fred looked around. Maybe he'd figure out how to make Bernie's system play music. Maybe he'd clean up some, see if Mandy, when she came back Sunday night...no. That was done.

"I reckon," he said. "If I get restless, I might make a library run. Got a piece of research pending."

"I still can't believe it," Clay said cautiously. "Nobody, not even the professor, the expert, who should know his field, could see the *Madonna* for what it was, without the big frame, the dim lights, the trumpet music and the fawning tourists. Not even the expert. As we look further into its history, we will undoubtedly find that he is not the first man who read it wrong.

"What we ultimately do with the object you have in keeping there, I don't know," Clay continued, after he appeared to understand enough to keep him where he was. "You believe the man, I take it? I must resign myself to my loss?"

He was talking about the *Annunciation:* a passing figment.

"That's my conclusion. It has to be a fraud. According to Dr. Mitchell. Of course, everyone in the art business lies. But in my opinion, Mitchell is the genuine exception."

To receive a free catalog of Poisoned Pen Press titles, please contact us in one of the following ways:

Phone: 1-800-421-3976
Facsimile: 1-480-949-1707
E-mail: info@poisonedpenpress.com
Website: www.poisonedpenpress.com

Poisoned Pen Press
6962 E. First Ave. Ste. 103
Scottsdale, AZ 85251